THE MANY LIVES OF SAM WELLS

A TIME TRAVEL THRILLER

IVY MYSTERY SERIES
BOOK TWO

MICHELLE FILES

Edited by
CECILY BROOKES

MICHELLEFILES.COM

INTRODUCTION

A serial killer. A family torn. Time travel with a twist.

The continuing saga of the Wells family.

This time, Ivy's grandfather, Sam, is finding himself reliving his lives over and over. Sam Wells dies at 79 years old. Then things get worse.

When he opens his eyes as a young college student, he remembers everything from his past life, including the identity of the serial killer who is terrorizing their small town. Many young women are murdered, and Sam knows who did it.

Over several lives, Sam struggles in a desperate race through time to stop the serial killer. All the while, he pines for the woman who got away.

It's never too late to die and try again.

Teens and adults alike will love this time travel thriller. Get your copy of this gripping time travel series.

Ivy Mystery Series:

The Many Lives of Ivy Wells - Book 1
The Many Lives of Sam Wells - Book 2
The Many Lives of Jack Wells - Book 3
The Many Lives of Georgie Wells - Book 4

Novels by Michelle Files:

TYLER MYSTERY SERIES
Girl Lost
A Reckless Life

WILDFLOWER MYSTERY SERIES
Secrets of Wildflower Island
Desperation on Wildflower Island
Storm on Wildflower Island
Thorns on Wildflower Island

IVY WELLS MYSTERY SERIES
The Many Lives of Ivy Wells
The Many Lives of Sam Wells
The Many Lives of Jack Wells

STONE MOUNTAIN FAMILY SAGA
Winters Legend on Stone Mountain
A Dangerous Game on Stone Mountain
Deceit on Stone Mountain

DARKNESS MYSTERY SERIES
Escape the Dark
The Dark Years
The Children

For information on any of Michelle's books:
www.MichelleFiles.com

PART 1

CHAPTER 1

"Why are you...doing this? Please...stop." The words came out in shuddering gasps.

The young woman, not much more than a teenager really, was begging for her life. I barely heard her. The only thing I was concentrating on was squeezing the life out of her. My hands were wrapped tightly around her neck. I could smell the acrid scent of fear. Many may tell you that fear doesn't really have an odor. They are wrong.

I could feel her neck pulsing under my hands. Thump thump. Thump thump. Thump thump. It made my entire body tingle as her body was struggling to survive. It was trying to get oxygen and blood to her brain. It was all futile.

She struggled, to no avail. Her face had turned into a bright shade of crimson. Then it seemed to meld into an almost violet color, as she began to lose consciousness, and her ability to fight waned. She dropped her arms to her side in defeat. It made me smile.

Still...I held on. It took a while to strangle someone. It wasn't like in the movies, where they passed out within the loose, rough skin, peppered with age spots. Her face was so sad. She knew I was dying. All of them did. And most of all, I did.

"Ivy, you hang in there. Okay Sweetheart?" I wheezed out between ragged breaths.

She nodded and gave me a half smile. I didn't need to elaborate. She knew exactly what I was talking about. We had a pretty close relationship and she had told me a lot about her husband, Simon. He was a bad seed.

Leaning in, Ivy whispered in my ear. "Grandpa, I'm taking your advice. The kids and I are leaving town for a while."

When she stood back up, I gave her a sad sort of smile and a reassuring squeeze of her hand. Yes, she needed to get away from Simon, and yes, the kids did too. But I felt badly for Walter. He might never see his daughter and grandchildren again. As for me? Well, I wouldn't be around to find out how that story ended. I just prayed that it would all work out for my beloved granddaughter and great grandchildren. I loved them all so dearly.

With my body failing me, I drew in short, jagged breaths, struggling to breathe. Lung cancer was a horrible, painful way to die. I had lost a lot of weight over the last few months, and was all skin and bones. Previously, I had been a bit plump, which was not a bad thing for an old man.

I coughed roughly as I tried to speak. I barely had the strength to breathe or speak, much less to try to cough.

"Dad, are you all right?" The pained face of my son, Walter, looked into my eyes.

Wheezing, I responded. "Well…not really. I'm about… to…die."

No one in the room argued with me. They all knew it was inevitable. And would be soon. Very soon.

I looked over at my wife, Elizabeth. She didn't speak. She didn't even look my way. No tears graced her face. There was no emotion either. That was all my fault. Every single bit of it. Because I was in an unhappy marriage, so was Elizabeth.

Then it happened. I could no longer breathe. As I struggled to get any air at all, the machines in the room all went wild. I could hear them, but paid them no attention. Over my struggle, I could hear the gasps and cries of my family. It broke my heart that they would all watch me die.

The small hospital room began filling with nurses, who gently pushed my family aside, so that they could attend to me. All they could do was make me more comfortable though. I had given them previous instructions to not resuscitate me. What was the point? I would die shortly anyway, no matter what they did. No need to prolong my suffering.

I felt the medication working its way into my arm and head straight for my brain, causing my pain to disappear, and putting me in a bit of a euphoric state. But the struggle to breathe didn't change. This was it. My time. Right now.

When I felt the bed I was in beginning to shake, I barely paid it any attention. I heard someone shout the word 'earthquake.' Just then, the room went dark. A power outage? What else would it be?

Then my life went dark. I could hear the frantic voices of my family fading, as I drifted away. My time on earth was done.

CHAPTER 2

Suddenly, I could breathe again. It was a wonderful feeling.

I opened my eyes, expecting to see my family standing by. But they weren't there. I actually found myself walking in the bright sunshine and slammed my eyes shut almost immediately. Going from the florescent lighting of a hospital room, to the bright sunlight was a shock to the senses.

Before I could stop them, my legs collapsed out from under me and I hit the pavement hard. I was still conscious though and heard excited shouting all around me.

"Are you okay?" I heard an unfamiliar voice say.

My eyes were still shut when I felt someone gently shake my left shoulder.

"Can you hear me?" It was the same young man's voice.

"I'll go get the nurse." I heard a girl's voice that time.

"Um, yeah...I'm...fine," I said, slowly opening my eyes.

There were at least a dozen unfamiliar faces standing over me on the sidewalk, all looking down at me.

"What's...going on?" I tried sitting up. Someone grabbed me under an arm and helped me to a sitting position.

"You passed out," another voice explained.

I tried to stand up.

"You should take a minute before you stand up. If you pass out again, you might get hurt," someone said.

I ignored her. Several hands reached out to help me to my feet.

"Give him some air."

I looked up at the speaker. It was a cute, blonde girl. She couldn't have been more than 18 or 19 years old.

"Thank you, sweetheart," I muttered her way.

The crowd stepped back. That gave me a better view of my surroundings. I definitely was not in a hospital room. Or at a hospital at all. It looked like a school campus. How did I get here? I wondered.

"Sam, are you all right?"

I didn't recognize the voice immediately. I turned in the direction that the voice had come from. It was a young man, about 18 or 19 years old. He looked vaguely familiar, but I couldn't quite place him.

"What is going…" I started to say.

"Everybody, move out of the way and let me see the boy."

The middle aged woman, maybe 20 or 25 years younger than I was, was wearing an old starched, white nurse's uniform. It came down just below her knees and she was adorned with the old fashioned nurse's cap. Even her choice of shoes was old fashioned. She wore white pumps. For the oddest reason, I was mesmerized with her look. I hadn't seen anyone dressed like that for decades. At least not apart from Halloween anyway.

"Young man, can you tell me what happened?" she asked me, taking my arm to steady me.

Young man? Was she talking to me? It seemed as if she was.

"I…uh…I was in the hospital, about to…and then I was

9

standing here. Then I fell, I guess. I don't know how I got here," I did my best to answer her.

"You may have a concussion. Come with me."

She didn't wait for an answer, as she was still holding my arm. The nurse led me up the sidewalk, toward the large brick building looming in front of us. I seemed to have no choice but to comply. She had a death grip on my arm.

The building in front of me seemed oddly familiar, with its red brick front and contrasting bright white shutters adorning them. My eyes followed the long sweeping strands of ivy making their way up the building. Some had even managed to reach the roofline and disappear somewhere over the top. I imagined it creeping across the roof and down the other side, like some sort of thief in the night.

Though I seemed to have noticed everything around me, what I hadn't yet realized, until that very moment, was that I was breathing normally. The ragged gasps for breath that had been part of my every day life for so long, were gone. I sucked in a lungful of fresh fall air. It was crisp and clear and my lungs felt so wonderful that I almost didn't want to release it.

"What are you doing?"

Her sharp voice brought me back to reality and I let the air in my lungs escape in one quick exhale.

"You are going to pass out again if you keep holding your breath like that. Just try to breathe normally," she ordered.

We walked up the brick steps and into the building. She led me down a long corridor and into the nurses office. The smell of alcohol and other disinfectants assaulted my senses and took me right back to that hospital room I had just left. At least I think I had just left it. The whole thing was starting to feel very strange. Had I been imagining dying only minutes prior? Where was my family?

The nurse sat me down roughly in a chair in the exam

room, and promptly turned and walked out the door. Looking up, I caught a glimpse of myself in the wall mirror. I gasped.

"What?!" I said louder than I had meant to.

I jumped up and covered the distance between the chair and the mirror in a fraction of a second. I leaned in, so that my face was only inches from the mirror. Oh my god, I looked like I was 18 years old again.

Reaching up to touch my face, just to make sure what I saw was really happening, I felt a smooth, young face. No wrinkles, no age spots. No sad, regretful eyes. Wow.

And my hair! It was back. I no longer had a bald head with just a bit of gray hair hanging on for dear life. My red hair was back. The red hair was a family trait. Not everyone in the family had it, but a good number of us did.

I ran my fingers through my short red hair. The feeling was fantastic. I hadn't been able to do that for a very long time.

I began to wonder again if I had imagined the entire thing. My whole life. My 60 year marriage to Elizabeth. My son, Walter. My grandchildren, Ivy and Parker. Even my great grandchildren, Hunter and Courtney.

I couldn't possibly have made up all those people, and lived an entire life inside my head. Could I?

While I continued to peruse my face and young body in the mirror, the nurse walked into the room.

"Please have a seat on the exam table." She pointed. I obliged.

"Where am I?" I asked her.

"You are in the nurse's office."

"Yes, I can see that. But where is that?" I persisted.

"At the university. Are you not a student here? If you aren't, then I have to send you on your way. This facility is only for students," she explained.

"What? I'm at the university?"

That's when I realized that I really was a young man again, and I was in college again. What the hell was happening to me?

Before she answered my question, a churning began deep within me. I couldn't place it at first. It started somewhere deep in my core and slowly made its way through my body. Then the urge hit. Oh no, I thought to myself. I looked up at the nurse. At that moment, all I wanted to do was wrap my hands around her throat. And squeeze. It was a feeling I hadn't had in decades. But it was back. I couldn't let that happen again. I would do whatever it took to not let the compulsions take control over my body. I couldn't go through a lifetime again like that.

"I gotta go."

Jumping off of the table, I ran out the door of the exam room, down the long hall that we had just covered a few minutes prior, and burst out of the front glass door of the administration building.

I ran down the steps and out onto the grass. I stopped for a moment to catch my breath, before I realized that I didn't need to. There was no gasping for air, due to the lung cancer that had ravaged my body. There was only youthfulness in my lungs and legs.

I had no idea how it had happened, but was thrilled that it had. I was 18 years old again. Was this my chance to live my life again and change the outcome?

The urge to kill was gone. For the time being at least. I breathed a sigh of relief.

I looked up and around at my surroundings. The cars parked along the curb were straight out of the 1950s and 1960s. The clothing that the meandering students wore were 1960s. There was no mistaking that.

Most of the girls were wearing dresses and heels. That

was something that had certainly changed over the years. A few wore slim fitting pants. Many of the girls had headbands in their hair, and a flipped up at the ends hairstyle. It reminded me of Samantha on the TV show, Bewitched. I'm pretty sure that was on in the 60s.

The boys all had on some sort of slacks and button up dress shirts. Their hair was short and neat.

Wow, had things changed over the years.

Another thing I noticed was that everyone seemed to be smoking. Nope. I would absolutely not be making that mistake again. Lung cancer was a slow, horrible, painful way to die. I wished that I could explain that to all the young people smoking in front of me, but I knew that they would never listen to me. They all thought it was healthy. That's what the TV commercials used to tell them. I was nobody to them. No, they would never take my word for it.

I suddenly felt like I was starving, and realized that my appetite was back. I hadn't eaten much at all over the last few months. I just couldn't stomach the thought of food. Now I wanted nothing more than a big juicy burger and fries.

I stood there in the middle of the grass trying to remember where the cafeteria was, and whether I had any money. I dug into my pants pockets and pulled out a handful of dollar bills. This would have to do, I guess. I had no recollection of what a meal at a college cafeteria cost in the 1960s.

I stopped a pretty young woman in a pink sweater. She looked vaguely familiar, yet I couldn't place her. Her short blonde hair danced in the breeze. "Excuse me. Can you tell me where the cafeteria is?"

She gave me directions. I thanked her, and was on my way.

After stuffing myself with two cheeseburgers, fries, and soda, to the point of almost vomiting it all up, I leaned back in my chair in the cafeteria and pondered what to do now.

School was out of the question. That was something I was absolutely sure of. I hated it the first time and would never, ever, do it again.

If not school, then what would I do? Get a job, I guess. Or maybe go see my parents. My parents. They had both been gone so long in my world, that seeing them again seemed very odd. They would be like strangers to me. Wouldn't they? Both of them passed more than 25 years ago. But, if I'm 18 now, then they are both still alive. The thought thrilled and terrified me at the same time. Yes, I have to go see them. Who else ever gets a chance to see their deceased parents again? No one. Not until now anyway.

But first, I should go find my dorm room. Maybe I had money stashed there. Besides, I guess if I was going to leave school, I should pack my stuff up. Dang, where is my dorm? Sixty years is a really long time to remember where a dorm is. Once I graduated the first time, all of that left my brain immediately. No need to clog it up with inconsequential things like that.

I spent the next 30 minutes or so wandering around campus, trying to find something familiar. Something that would remind me where my dorm was.

"Wells! Where the hell have you been?"

I spun around to see Henry, my college roommate. I recognized him immediately, even though we hadn't seen each other since the day we graduated. That was mostly my fault. He had reached out a few times, but I was busy, and he eventually gave up.

"Henry. It's so good to see you. I've missed you," I told him, with sincerity in my voice.

Henry stopped dead in his tracks. "You've missed me? Didn't you just see me this morning? Too much to drink last night?" he laughed.

I laughed with him. I would need to be careful about the

things I said. I could come across as a bit crazy by making statements like that.

I watched as Henry pulled out a cigarette and lit it up. He held the pack toward me.

I held up my hand. "Um, no thanks. I quit."

"Since when?" Henry asked, with an incredulous stare.

"Since now," I told him.

"Why?" That look was still on his face.

I could understand his surprise at my declaration. We were currently living in a time of history where most adults, and probably most teenagers, smoked. It was just what people did.

I shrugged. "I just don't want to."

There was no way that I was going down that road again. The cigarette did look tempting though. But it didn't matter. I was through with smoking for good.

"Hey, walk back to the dorm with me. I need to get something." I hoped it would be a way to get Henry to lead me there, so I wouldn't have to ask him where it was. That would definitely look strange.

"Yeah, okay. I don't have another class for about an hour anyway. When is your next one?" Henry asked as we walked.

"Oh, I don't know. Doesn't matter anyway. I'm quitting school."

Henry stopped short. I turned to look back at him and he was staring at me with that look on his face again.

"You're what?!" he almost yelled.

I looked around, hoping no one had heard us. Gesturing for him to continue walking, he jogged a few steps and caught up with me.

"I'm quitting school," I said in almost a whisper.

"Your dad is gonna kill you, ya know," he announced.

"Yeah, I know."

CHAPTER 3

I spent the night in my old dorm room. It was such an odd feeling. It was as if 60 years had just vanished. I guess in a way, they had.

I didn't get much sleep that night. All of the crazy things that had just happened to me were bouncing around in my mind all night. It still all seemed like a dream. How could any of this be happening for real?

The first thing I did the next morning was to pack the few things I wanted to keep, and left the rest for Henry. There were very few things that I needed.

Walking to the administration office, I passed that same girl from the day before, the one in the pink sweater. She was dressed in sea foam green this time. It suited her.

Just as we passed each other on the sidewalk, my heart rate quickened. It wasn't lust, which was usual for a man my age. It was something different. Something I recognized immediately.

It was that urge again. It was all I could do to keep walking and not go after her. Even if I had wanted to give in, we were in broad daylight, in the middle of a college campus.

Taking deep, purposeful breaths, I pushed back that urge and kept walking. I didn't dare turn around.

After I officially quit school, I walked to the bus station. Thankfully I had some cash stashed away in my dorm room desk. I didn't think I had the nerve to call my folks for bus money.

I had a lot of time to think during the long bus ride home. I hadn't called my parents to tell them I was coming. What would I have said? I figured I might as well get it all over with in one fell swoop when I arrived. They would be angry with me for quitting school, and a bit disappointed, I'm sure. But they would get over it. It was my life and I was going to live it the way I wanted to, whether they liked it or not.

I wondered about Elizabeth, and what she was doing now. We had previously spent 60 years together. Though she was a nice person, she just wasn't the love of my life. She wasn't the one I wanted to do things all over with.

No, I wouldn't have my son, Walter, in this life, and that saddened me. But, I was desperately unhappy last time, and couldn't put myself through that again, no matter the cost. I knew that I might very well regret that decision later, and then it would be too late. But I had made up my mind. I wanted a different life this time. I wouldn't settle for a life of regrets.

Elizabeth would be better off without me also. She deserved someone that thought she had hung the moon. Someone who would cherish her every moment of their lives. That man was not me. I knew in my heart that I was doing her a favor, whether she ever knew it or not.

I was still a bit freaked out by the idea of living my life over. Did everybody get to do that? Or was I just the lucky one?

I know I remember dying. I believe there was an earthquake and power outage just as it happened. I think so anyway. Or maybe that's just what it felt like to die. Maybe everyone felt a shaking sensation and then it all goes black. Maybe I wasn't unique. There was no way of knowing though, unless I found someone that it had also happened to.

Doubtful that would ever happen though. I couldn't really go around asking people about it. I think here's how that might go:

"Hi, I'm Sam. I'm reliving my life over. And you?"

No, that wouldn't go over well at all. I laughed out loud in the bus and noticed a few odd glances my way. I shrugged and ignored them.

If I was living my life again, then I guess that technically, everyone around me was living theirs again. But it didn't seem like any of them remembered that fact. If they did, I think life would be very different this time. But that wasn't the case. Everything seemed exactly as it was last time.

People dressed the same, talked the same, had the same cars. When I talked to Henry, he seemed to have no recollection of a previous life. He probably would have told me if he had. But then again, I didn't tell him.

Ugh, it was very confusing. I decided that I was not going to lament over it. I was here, and that was wonderful, and I hoped that I was going to get to live it all again. There was no way of knowing if that would happen though.

The only thing that gave me pause about my new life was that it was beginning at around the same time that I began killing in my first life. My first kill back then was at 18 years old, which is where I currently found myself. I spent several years killing young women. I knew it was wrong, even then. But that didn't stop me. I couldn't help it. Something deep within controlled me.

It must be in my DNA to kill. I couldn't help it. Try as I did, I couldn't stop it. Something would come over me and I was drawn to kill. If I could change this about myself, I would. Lord knows I would. I always felt regret once it was over, but that doesn't change the fact that the deed had already been done by that point.

While I was killing, there was no regret. There was no remorse. There was not even hatred for the victim. It was just me doing what I had to do. It was just another biological system within me, that happened automatically. Like breathing, or my heart beating. I had no control over the process.

I knew that I was a handsome man. That's not bragging. It's just a fact. Many women had told me so. Women were drawn to me. They always had been, and that was their downfall. Even as a young child, it seemed that the little girls wanted to be around me. It got even more so as I grew into a tall, handsome teenager, with a square jaw and dimples that the girls always wanted to touch.

One night, at around 16 years old, something new came over me. I began feeling a need to hurt something. Hurt someone. I didn't know what to make of it at the time, and managed to suppress those feelings for two years. I couldn't talk to anyone. I knew that if I did, it would come back at me somehow. The looney bin, jail, something else? I didn't know what, and didn't want to find out.

Once I turned 18 though, I couldn't suppress the urges any longer. I thought about the pretty young thing that I had made out with at the lake. Then snapped her neck, like it was nothing. It was quick and it was painless. But it caused a release in me that had been building up for years. I carefully placed her body in the bushes next to the lake and drove away. I never thought about her again.

Sitting there in the bus that day, her face came back to me. I gasped as I recalled the girl. It was the very same one in the pink sweater that had given me directions to the cafeteria the day before. I began shaking at the thought. The only thing that gave me solace was the fact that I hadn't killed her in this lifetime. Perhaps she would live to be an old woman, with grandchildren of her own. Grandchildren that never existed in my first lifetime. That thought made me happy.

At around 30 years old, in my first life, I had stopped the killing. It was as if something just switched off in me. One night, I strangled a young woman in an alley, and never looked back. The next day, the urge to kill was gone. Completely gone. And it never returned. I was baffled by the whole thing and wondered if that were the case with other serial killers. Yes, that's exactly what I was. A serial killer. I couldn't admit that back then. But I can now.

This time, I would do everything that I could to not be that person again. The problem was that I could already feel those urges. It was what I imagined being hooked on something like heroine would feel like. My body had an actual physical craving to kill. I don't know how else to explain it.

On the bus ride home, I attributed what I felt to withdrawals. My body shook uncontrollably. My eyes wandered over the passengers, looking for just the perfect one. I forced myself to shut my eyes. It helped, for a time anyway. I was captive on that bus for many hours. The other passengers would be safe.

I couldn't predict what might happen when I arrived back home.

Now that I had quit college, I needed to figure out what to do. I knew that I would have to get a job as soon as I arrived home. Me lying around the house, a college dropout, would not go over well with my father. He would kick my butt to the curb before he let that happen.

It was late afternoon when I walked in the front door of my house. My father hadn't yet come home from work. Before I saw or even heard my mother, I knew exactly where she was. The kitchen. The aromatic, salty air made my salivary glands begin working overtime. Mom was making ham for dinner. I was sure of it. And the unmistakable scent of fresh baked bread wafted through the house. I was suddenly ravenous.

I could hear my mother in the kitchen preparing dinner. She didn't have an outside job. She was a housewife. That's what a lot of women did back in the sixties. My mother was no different.

Though I knew it might happen, I tried not to let it. But it didn't matter, I burst out crying the moment I saw my mother. Dropping my backpack, I crossed the kitchen floor in a second and wrapped my arms around her.

"Sam, what on earth?" my mother responded, as she wrapped her arms around her sobbing son.

It had been about 25 years since I had last seen her. And even then, she was old and tired, and dying. This 1960s version of her was 40 years old and beautiful. I had forgotten how beautiful she had been. I couldn't let go, and just let the tears flow freely.

"Mom, I've missed you," I wailed.

"Sam, it's only been a few weeks since you went off to school. And why are you here, and not there?" She pulled back out of my embrace and wiped my tears with a cloth as she spoke.

"Oh, um, well, I kind of quit school," I told her sheepishly.

"Is that right?" My mother wasn't the type that shocked easily. She took almost everything in stride. "You are probably hungry. Sit down and I'll make you a sandwich."

I sat down at the kitchen table. "Aren't you making dinner? I can wait," I told her.

"It'll be a while. You need to eat now. I can see it in your face." She pulled a fresh loaf of bread from the oven and began making me a sandwich.

"And why did you quit school?" she asked me while she worked.

"It's just not for me, Mom," I told her honestly. "I want to get a job now and start saving my money for the future. I have big plans."

"What are these big plans of yours?" she asked me, handing me a plate with the sandwich and chips on it. "Want a soda?"

I nodded. "Well, I haven't figured everything out quite yet, but I'll let you know as soon as I do." I took a huge bite. It was just a simple sandwich, but I had never tasted anything so wonderful in my entire life.

My mother smiled at me. I saw no judgment in her face. Only love. I had known my entire life that my mother loved me unconditionally. Did she always like my decisions? Probably not. She usually kept her opinions to herself. That was just the way she was.

When I had gotten Elizabeth pregnant, in that lifetime so long ago, and then married her, my mother never said a word about it. She just welcomed Elizabeth, and then baby Walter, into the family, as if it was all completely normal. Which, in the early 1960's, it certainly was not. That was a time in history when girls still went off to 'visit an aunt' for the summer. They would have their baby and return back to school as if nothing had happened. Very often, the father of the child never had a clue. I was glad that repressive time in history was over. At least I thought it was. But I was 79 years old, and very much out of the loop with the way the world was.

I sat there, at the kitchen table, and just watched my mother work on dinner. I couldn't take my eyes off of her. She was so young, and so beautiful. I had missed her terribly.

I offered to help, but she declined. "You'll only be in the way," she told me.

"You know, why don't you go visit Elizabeth. I'm sure she'll be thrilled to see you."

"Elizabeth?" It was the only response I could think of.

"Yes, Elizabeth. Your girlfriend. Did you forget her already, Mr. College Man?" My mother laughed at her own joke.

"Oh, no, of course not. But I don't think we are seeing each other anymore," I told her.

My mother turned around and narrowed her eyes at me. "Does she know that? Because I just saw her walking her dog yesterday and she asked about you. She said she can't wait until you come home for Thanksgiving. To me, that sounds like someone who thinks you are still her boyfriend."

"Oh." I smiled sheepishly. "I guess I should go see her."

"That would be a good idea, young man. It is not gentlemanly to leave your girlfriend waiting at home, if you have no intention of continuing the relationship."

"Yeah, I know," I agreed.

I was genuinely surprised at my mother. She didn't usually give such strong opinions on things. At least she didn't used to. Perhaps she was different in this lifetime.

I promptly headed up the street to Elizabeth's house.

CHAPTER 4

Though some things were fuzzy, I had crystal clear recollection of where Elizabeth lived. When her parents passed away, several years ago in that first life, they had left the house to her. In fact, we still owned it, and lived in it, until my dying day.

I knocked on the front door and waited on the porch for an answer. Her mother came to the door.

"Oh hello, Sam. Is college on break right now? Elizabeth didn't mention it," she asked me.

"Um, no. I am just taking some time off. Is Lizzie…Elizabeth home?" I corrected myself. I didn't start calling her Lizzie until later.

"Yes, she's home. Come on in." Her mother stepped aside and I walked into the house and to the living room ahead of her. "I'll go get her."

While she was fetching Elizabeth, I looked around. Boy, I had completely forgotten what our house looked like so long ago. Elizabeth and I had upgraded it considerably since we had owned it. New carpet, new paint, an added bathroom. Even a swimming pool in the backyard. At the moment though, it looked like something out of the 1940s, which is how long they had owned it.

"Sam! What are you doing here?" Elizabeth ran into my arms and kissed me on the cheek. Her mother was watching and that was all she dared do.

I gave her a quick hug. "Can we go for a walk and talk?" I asked her.

"Okay, sure."

I followed her outside. I had forgotten how pretty she was back then. Her light brown hair was up in a pony tail and she wore slim fitting pants and slip on shoes. She turned to me as we reached the sidewalk and took my hand, leading me down the street, away from her house.

"Elizabeth, I wanted to talk to you," I began.

"How come you aren't in school?" she interrupted. "Are you on a break I didn't know about?"

"What? No. I quit school, but that's not why I'm here…"

"You quit school!" She stopped short, pulling me to a stop with her. Turning to face me, she continued. "Why in the world would you quit school? If you don't get your degree, and a good job, how are you going to support our baby?"

"Our what?" I looked her straight in the eyes and then down at her slightly pudgy belly. Her hand rubbed that spot tenderly. "You're…you're…" I couldn't make the words come out.

"Sam? Are you all right? Your face is turning white." She took hold of my hand once more and pulled me over to the curb. "Sit down. You look like you are going to pass out."

I sat down on the curb and she took the spot next to mine.

"Take some deep breaths," she ordered, and I obliged.

When I finally had my wits about me, I spoke up. "You're pregnant?" I looked down at her belly again.

"Yes Sam, I'm pregnant. You know that. We've already

had this discussion." Elizabeth gave me a look of incredulity. "I know you didn't forget. What's going on?"

"I…well I…I don't know. I guess I've had a lot on my mind lately. I didn't forget. I just…put it out of my mind. Sorry, that didn't come out like I meant it to." I sounded like an idiot.

"And you dropped out of school? I don't understand," Elizabeth continued.

"I decided that this time school was not for me. I don't want to go," I told her honestly.

"This time? What do you mean?"

Oops. I needed to watch what I was saying. "I just mean that I don't want to go to school. That's all. I'll get a job," I told her.

"A job without college is not going to pay that much. What about our baby? And we are supposed to get married soon, before I really start to show. I know we were going to do that over your Thanksgiving break home, but since you are here, we can do it now." She smiled at the thought.

Oh no. What had I walked into? I hadn't done the pregnancy math. I should have known that she was already expecting. God, what an idiot I was.

"Elizabeth, I…I…I'm sorry, but no, I can't marry you." I could barely get the words out. I felt like such an awful person for doing what I was doing. She was pregnant with my child after all, and here I was, kicking her to the curb, so to speak.

"What! What do you mean you can't marry me? I'm pregnant. You have to marry me!" She jumped up off of the curb we were still sitting on and began yelling.

I followed suit and stood up also. "I'll send you money for Walt.., um, for the baby. But, no, I can't marry you."

I knew that I was the biggest jerk on the planet at that moment, but it couldn't be helped. I had already spent 60 years with Elizabeth. Sixty unhappy years, and I wouldn't do it again. No matter what. That was something that I was sure of.

I braced myself for the inevitable screaming and crying to come. But it didn't. She actually stood in front of me, calmly. She said nothing for probably a full minute.

Elizabeth's lips thinned and trembled. "I hate you, and will never forgive you for this."

She was very calm. No screaming. No hysterics. The words came out slowly and eerily. Then she turned and walked away.

"Well, that's done," I said out loud to myself.

I stood there on the sidewalk for several minutes trying to decide what to do. The sun was beginning to set over the houses and I needed to get back home. I didn't dare walk past her house. If she had told her father what had happened, I was a goner. So, I took the long way home, and walked all the way around the block. It was the coward's trek home, and I knew it. When I stepped into my own house, there were other problems waiting for me.

"Samuel Wells, what the hell is this that I hear about you quitting school?"

It was my father. Obviously, my mother had already clued him in to my plans. My father was exactly as I remembered him. Tall and scary. He had a booming voice and ruled the house by yelling. Still, I missed him very much. Just like my mother, I hadn't seen him in over 25 years. Yelling at me or not, all I wanted to do was hug him.

I didn't dare though.

I stood my ground and looked up at my father meekly. He was taller than I remembered. And still scary as hell.

"Dad, school just isn't for me. I want to get a job instead. I'm going to look for one first thing in the morning."

I was hoping that by telling him I was going to get a job

right away, that it would calm him down. I knew he would not put up with me freeloading for any amount of time.

"Do you know how much money I spent to send you there?" His face, and his voice, were both stern.

I lowered my head. "I know, and I'm sorry. But I just don't want to go. I will pay you back every cent. I promise."

"Yes, you will," he responded.

I glanced over to see my mother standing in the doorway between the kitchen and the living room, watching our exchange.

"Boys, dinner is ready."

Other than that, she didn't mention college again. She didn't need to. My father spent the entire dinner telling me how disappointed he was with me. I understood his position. I really did. I had a son of my own…or least I used to have one, and he is currently on the way now. I wanted Walter to go to college. Even though I didn't want to go, I knew it was the best course of action.

"Well, since I've already dropped one bombshell on you today, I have another announcement," I added.

Both of my parents had that 'what now' looks on their faces, and I took a deep breath before speaking.

"Elizabeth is pregnant."

I was startled when my mother's fork hit her plate.

My father said nothing and continued his dinner. He didn't even look up at me. Somehow that was much worse than being yelled at.

Ten minutes later, my father finally spoke. "When is the wedding?"

"What? No, there will be no wedding," I told him as I steadied myself for the inevitable lecture. I was not disappointed.

"There will be a wedding. You impregnated her, now you will marry her. We are friends with her parents and will not allow you to shirk your responsibilities," my father explained.

"No, Dad. Elizabeth and I have already discussed it. We are not getting married," I told him.

"Is that right? Elizabeth told you that she doesn't want to marry you? Is that what you are trying to tell me?" he asked.

"Um, well, no. She didn't tell me that. I think she wants to get married. I'm the one that doesn't." There was no point in lying. The truth would come out eventually.

"That's what I thought," he responded. "You will marry her. Do I make myself clear?"

"No."

"What did you just say to me?" My father stood, looming over me. For the first time in my life, I thought he was going to hit me. He didn't.

I stood also. "I said no. I'm going to bed."

With that, I walked up the stairs and slammed my bedroom door.

CHAPTER 5

Early the next morning, I waited until my father had left for work before skulking down the stairs. It was my intention to sneak out the front door without my mother noticing. No such luck.

"Sam, come in the kitchen. I've made you some breakfast," she called after me.

I sat down at one of the kitchen chairs. My mother set a plate in front of me with fried eggs, fried potatoes, toast with loads of butter, and pancakes topped with a dollop of butter. They certainly weren't concerned about their cholesterol back in the sixties.

"It looks delicious, thanks Mom." I dug in. At 18 years old, I didn't yet need to worry about my cholesterol or my weight. It was great to be young again.

While I ate, my mother set about cleaning up the breakfast dishes. She never said a word about my declarations from the previous evening. Not that I expected her to.

"Well, I think I'll go for a walk. And maybe job hunting." I wiped my face and stood up.

"Okay, dear. Will you be back for lunch?" she asked without skipping a beat on her task of dishwashing.

"I'm not sure. Please don't make anything special. If I'm back by then, I'll just make myself a sandwich."

There was only one place in the world that I wanted to go. And that was to find *her*.

Ruby. She was the one. She was the love of my life. We had dated for a short while in high school. Then I met Elizabeth. Elizabeth was pretty, and vivacious, and something had drawn me to her back then. I messed it all up with Ruby by getting Elizabeth pregnant.

The second that Ruby found out, she refused to speak to me again. Who could blame her? It was my fault. I was a stupid kid back then and thought I could have both girls. The fallout from that had never occurred to me, until Ruby walked away.

I was devastated when that happened. Ruby was beautiful, with her long, jet black hair and dark brown eyes. I have regretted what I did to her for sixty years. Back then, I did the right thing and married the girl I was about to have a baby with. I never saw Ruby again, and that gnawed at me. But I had made my bed, as they say.

I remembered exactly where Ruby lived. That house had been forever burned into my mind. I made my way over there.

Standing in the park across the street from her house, I tried to come up with a game plan. My first thought was to just go up and knock on the door, ask for Ruby, and see what happened.

Was that a bad idea? Does she know about the baby? She probably did. She walked away from me once already. What made me think there was even the slightest chance that she would want to talk to me.

My second thought was to just hang out in the park for a

bit, and watch. Maybe she would come out of her house. Maybe she would see me across the street, smile, and come over.

No, that was a dumb idea. What if her father saw me? He probably already knew about the baby and would kill me on sight. That was the most likely scenario. Getting another girl pregnant, while dating his daughter, was quite likely to get me killed.

While I stood partially behind a tree, contemplating my next move, a car drove up. It was one of those big, loud, muscle cars. The 1960s was full of them. And it was shiny red. I was sure it didn't belong to Ruby. So, who did it belong to? Her brother, perhaps.

I watched as Ruby's front door opened and she flew down the steps of her front porch, her long dark hair flying behind her. The boy in the muscle car jumped out just in time for her to leap into his arms. Their passionate kiss made my face turn red. Not with jealousy, well…maybe a little jealousy, but mostly red with anger. Okay, obviously he was not her brother.

The anger was with myself. I was the one to blame for the scene unfolding in front of me. No one else. I moved back behind the tree as she walked around the car and made herself comfortable in the front seat.

Now what? She clearly had a boyfriend. I wondered how serious it was. Had they been dating long? Maybe they just started a very short time ago. Hence the passionate kiss.

None of it mattered to me though. I wanted Ruby back. I just needed to figure out how to make that happen.

No point in standing around in the park. I began walking and headed for downtown Red Lake. I spent the day completing job applications. Everything from fast food restaurants to auto shops. I would take any job that was offered to me. At least that would make my father a little bit happier with me. Though I'm pretty sure that me dropping out of college would never smooth completely over, in his mind anyway.

That evening, after a tense dinner with my parents, I walked back over to Ruby's house. As I walked up the sidewalk, I saw her sitting on her front porch reading. She didn't strike me as the reading type. That's when I realized that I really didn't know her very well at all. We had only dated a few weeks during my senior year of high school. It was all hot and heavy. Not a lot of conversation. I didn't even know her birthdate.

I began to wonder if she would know me. Had we even dated in this lifetime? So far, things seemed to be pretty much the same as last time, but I knew they could change. The fact that I had dropped out of college this time, and the world didn't end, proved that.

I figured that the only way to find out the answer to the question of whether she knew me or not, was to just take the plunge. I stopped on the sidewalk, right in front of her. She was still reading and hadn't noticed me.

"Um, hi," I stupidly blurted out.

Ruby looked up at me with only her eyes, not moving at all.

"What do you want?" Her eyes went back to her book.

Okay, so that question is answered. We clearly did date and she definitely knew who I was. By her demeanor, this was going to be tougher than I had imagined.

"I just wanted to see you," I told her honestly.

Wow. Up close she was just as beautiful as I remembered. Even with her long, dark hair all pulled up into a bun on her head. She also wore no make-up. Somehow, that seemed to make her more beautiful. She wore a polka dotted short sleeved top, and shorts. Her feet were bare.

Ruby let out a sigh, picked up the bookmark that was

lying on the porch step next to her, and put it in her book. Closing it, she looked up at me again.

"Why do you want to see me? Is that girl still pregnant? Aren't you married by now?"

Yikes. She was not going to make this easy for me.

"Yes, she's still pregnant, and no, I'm not married to her. In fact, I'm never going to marry her. You are the one I want," I blurted out.

Her laughter carried up into the trees, dissipating somewhere high above us.

Not to be dissuaded, I took a few steps toward her.

"You want me? Now you want me? After getting some slut pregnant? Are you serious right now?"

I could almost see the anger rising within her.

"Don't call her that." Elizabeth was still the mother of my child. "If you want to be mad at someone, be mad at me."

"Oh, I have no problem being mad at you. We were dating and you went off and got someone else pregnant. How do you think that makes me feel?" Ruby looked like she was about to cry.

"I know. I'm a horrible person. And believe me, I have regretted that stupid decision my entire life...I mean since it happened." Be careful what you say, I told myself.

"I have a boyfriend now," she told me.

"I know."

Ruby's eyes widened. "How do you know? Miguel and I haven't been seeing each other long." She lowered her head and looked up at me with suspicion in her eyes. "Have you been watching me?"

I put my palms up in front of me. "No, nothing like that. I was...was...just walking yesterday, in the park over there, and I saw him pick you up, in that shiny, red car of his." I was doing my best not to sound like a stalker.

"Oh. Well, I have to go." Ruby stood up. "You should leave now," she told me point blank.

I needed to think fast. I was about to lose Ruby again. I couldn't bear another lifetime without her.

"Ruby, why don't you come for a walk with me? We can go get some ice cream. I just want to talk. Really." I was doing my best to keep the pleading part of it out of my voice. "Come on. You don't have anything better to do, do you?"

She shrugged. "I guess not. Okay, let me go tell my mother that I'm leaving."

With that, she disappeared into the house. My face was all smiles. My hands instinctively shot up and slammed over my mouth. The smile needed to be gone by the time she returned. Otherwise, I would be standing there looking like some sort of idiot. That was no way to get the girl.

CHAPTER 6

When Ruby returned a few minutes later to that front porch, I noticed that she had changed into long pants, slip on shoes, and had added a yellow sweater over her polka dotted top. It was early fall, and the evening was turning cool. I suddenly wished that I had thought to bring a sweatshirt.

We walked side by side to the ice cream shop. Ruby did most of the talking. She told me all about what she had been doing over the summer, and of course, all about that boyfriend of hers, Miguel. I did my best to sound interested. That was a tough one to pull off. Talking about her boyfriend was the last thing I wanted to do.

We sat in a booth at the shop and both ordered a malt. Man, it had been a really long time since I had one of those. It was fantastic. I wondered why Elizabeth and I had never done this.

Why was I thinking about Elizabeth, when I had the most beautiful girl in the world sitting right in front of me? Idiot.

"So, Ruby, I wanted to talk to you about something important," I began.

"Okay, what?" She took a long draw of her malted shake.

Okay, here goes, I thought. I'm just going to lay it all out on the line and see where the rocks fly.

"Elizabeth is not the one for me. You are. You are the one I want to be with. The one I want to marry. The one I want to have my babies with. All of it. I want all of it with you." Whew, I said it. I wasn't sure whether to brace for a face full of ice cream, or a passionate kiss from the one I loved.

As it turned out, neither of those things happened.

"You know what, Sam? Your loyalty is elastic, and I don't know what to believe." Ruby took a drink from her shake and watched me for a reaction.

What could I say to that? She wasn't wrong. The old Sam was exactly how she described him. That Sam jumped from woman to woman and didn't take into account that they had feelings. Even when I married Elizabeth, it wasn't for true love. It was because Walter was on the way. Her feelings never factored into my decision.

And now Ruby was calling me out on it. I deserved that.

"Ruby, I know it seems that way, but…"

"Seems that way?" she interrupted. "No, it doesn't seem that way. It is exactly that way. You were dating me, and apparently I wasn't good enough. So, you started seeing her. When you found out that you had gotten her pregnant, you wanted to be with me again, but your family pressured you into marrying her. Am I right so far?"

I nodded.

"Now, you can't go through with it. So, here you are again, with me." She pushed her half empty shake over to the side. "Do you think that I want to be with someone so…so…"

"Elastic?" I offered.

"Yes. Why would I want that in my life? And why would I want to be with someone that would just walk away from the mother of his child? Don't you think that I have more self esteem than that?"

She was letting me have it, and I deserved every single thing that she threw at me.

"I know, I know." I threw my hands up in front of me. "You are right. About everything. I deserve for you to get up and walk out of here and never talk to me again. But," I reached across the table and took her hands into mine, "please don't do that. Please stay and hear me out. Then when I'm done, if you still want to go, then I will sit here and just watch you leave. And, I swear that I will never bother you again." I gave her a slight reassuring smile, pulling one hand from hers and doing the 'cross my heart gesture.' "Will you please stay and hear me out?" I took both of her hands again.

She looked down at my hands holding hers, and she squeezed gently. "Yeah, I will listen. No promises though." She pulled her hands from mine and put them in her lap.

"Okay, thank you. Well, what I wanted to say is that I know I made a huge mistake. We were in high school and I did a stupid thing. Being young makes you do stupid things," I told her.

"Sam, we are still young. High school was literally four months ago."

I nodded. "Yeah, I guess it was. Well, I like to think that maybe I've matured a bit since then." I gave her a cheesy grin and she smiled back.

"Anyway, Elizabeth was a huge mistake. I don't want to be with her. I know that now. You are the one I love. Really, I mean that. I love you. I have for a long time," I admitted.

"What about the baby?" She scowled when asking the question.

My gaze dropped down to the table top. Walter, my son, my only child. Even though Walter was a grandfather himself when I saw him last, he would always be my child. I couldn't imagine life without him, and I would do my best to make sure that never happened.

"Well, he is my son…"

"Your son? How do you know it's a boy?" she asked.

Oh yeah, how could I even begin to explain that to her? There was no way I could tell her that I've already lived this life before. No, she would never believe that in a million years. And DNA hadn't been invented yet. Or discovered yet, is probably the right term. Either way, how could I explain…

"Oh, well, it's just a feeling. Of course, I have no way of knowing for sure," I answered. "What I was about to say is that the kid is my child. I will take care of him…or her, but I want nothing to do with Elizabeth. So, you don't have to worry about that." I sat back in the booth to contemplate for a moment what all of that might entail.

"What the hell is going on here?"

We both looked up to see Miguel standing at the head of the booth, glaring at both of us.

Ruby blanched and jumped up out of her seat, to stand next to Miguel. I wasn't quite sure how to react. Miguel looked like he wanted to kill me. And if we hadn't been in a public place, he might have done just that.

"We were just talking, baby," Ruby said in a sultry voice. "This is Sam. Remember, I told you about him?"

"Yeah, I remember. He's the one that cheated on you and knocked up some other girl. Right?" He looked right at me as he was speaking.

"Yes, but I'm over it," Ruby told him. Somehow I didn't believe her.

"I think we should talk outside," Miguel said to me between clenched teeth.

Aw crap. Just what I needed. I hadn't been in a fight in… well, many decades. I wasn't sure if I could even defend myself anymore.

Thankfully, Ruby intervened.

"Miguel, baby, just let it go. All we were doing was talking. It's nothing. You are my man, not him. He just wanted to tell me about the baby." She looked my way. "Right Sam?"

I nodded. "Right."

I sat in the booth and watched the two of them walk away. Well, that's probably the last of her I'm ever going to see.

~

Over the next few weeks, I did my best to get Ruby's attention. I kind of became a stalker, which wasn't my intention at all. And I would never hurt her.

Yes, I know that I wasn't an innocent person when it came to hurting young women, but Ruby was safe with me. She would always be safe with me.

One day, I was walking past her house, like I did almost every day, and she was sitting on her front porch, crying. Normally, I just walked on past her house, without slowing, but not that day.

"Ruby, honey, are you all right?" I walked up and sat down next to her.

She laid her head on my shoulder. "Miguel and I had a fight."

My insides were dancing, but she would never see that on my face.

"He accused me of wanting you, and not him," she told me.

Yes!

"Really? And is that true?" I asked her before I had a chance to chicken out.

She shrugged.

I lifted her chin up off of my shoulder with one finger and looked her in the eyes. "Is it true?"

"Yes, it's true."

My heart sang. It was all I could do to not leap up and break out in a dance.

"Why now? You didn't want me before. What changed?" It was probably stupid of me to even ask. I knew I was taking the chance that I might talk her out of wanting to be with me by reminding her of what a jerk I had been.

"Nothing changed," she admitted.

My brows knit together. "What do you mean?"

"I mean, that I always wanted to be with you. But my pride, and my mother, told me that you were bad for me. After that whole baby thing, you know," she admitted.

I knew.

"Soooo," I dragged out nonchalantly, "are you and Miguel broken up?" I could only hope.

"No, I don't think so. It was just a fight," she told me. "But, I'm going to break up with him anyway. I'm tired of his jealousy and controlling ways."

"And then we can be together?" I asked. "I still have a child to take care of though." Ruby or not, Walter would always come first with me.

"Well, you should take care of your child. I just don't ever want to have anything to do with his or her mother. Got it?" Ruby told me.

I sat up straight on that front porch step, eyes wide. "Does that mean what I think it means? You will marry me?" My face was hopeful.

"Whoa, just hold on a moment, Romeo. I didn't say that. Let's just take this slowly, okay? Maybe go on a few dates. Nice, innocent dates, to the movies and stuff. No shenanigans, if you know what I mean?" She pointed her finger at me when she said it.

"Yeah, I know what you mean."

I didn't care. I was thrilled. I had another shot at being with my true love. I wouldn't do anything to screw it up this time.

"So, when is this breakup with Miguel going to happen? I'm not interested in sharing you," I told her honestly.

"He and I aren't really serious anyway. Not as far as I'm concerned. I'll let him know that we aren't dating anymore." She waved her hand in the air dismissively. "It'll be fine."

CHAPTER 7

I was walking on clouds after that. Ruby was my girl. She got rid of Miguel and we became inseparable.

Over the next few months, I got a job in the local tire shop. Nothing fancy, but it would do for the time being. I continued living with my parents, though my father didn't like the idea at all. He didn't hesitate to tell me often that if I wasn't going to college, then I needed to be out on my own, paying my own way. Thankfully, Mom helped smooth things over between us. And I did intend to move out as soon as I could.

I didn't remember it being so difficult to save up money and get out on my own back in that first lifetime of mine. Was that because I was four years older and had a college degree at the time? When I let myself admit it, then yes, that was probably why. Trying to start out straight at 18 years old, with nothing more than a high school education, was much more difficult. But I would make it work.

A few months into my new life, my mother approached me one day.

"Sam, did you hear that Elizabeth got married?"

"She what?" I was shocked, to say the least.

"I guess you didn't hear then. I still talk to her mother, you know," she announced.

"No, I didn't know that. Who did she marry?" I asked, genuinely curious about the man who would be raising my son.

"Some boy from out of town. No one you know. I guess his parents are friends of the family and she's known him forever." My mother didn't seem to have any opinions on the matter at all.

"I see. And did Elizabeth's mother tell you what they plan to do about my baby?" I asked her.

"What do you mean?" She knit her eyebrows together when asking the question.

"You know what I mean. Are they going to raise my child together, or is she going to put him up for adoption?"

"Apparently they are going to raise the child together. Her new husband will be on the birth certificate," she explained.

"The hell he is," I blurted out. "Walter is my son and always will be. I'm going to go have a talk with Elizabeth." I stood up.

"Walter?" she asked.

"Yes. Walter. That's what I want to name him…if it's a boy anyway," I told her.

"That's a very nice name," I heard her say behind me as I headed for the front door.

I walked straight to Elizabeth's house and pounded on the front door. Her father answered. Oh great, I thought to myself.

"Is Elizabeth home?" I asked him.

"Elizabeth is a married woman now. She doesn't live here anymore. She lives with her husband." He slammed the door in my face.

I deserved that.

Now what? No point in knocking on the door again. Her father would not respond favorably. Okay then, I would wait.

I went back to Elizabeth's house the next morning, after her father had left for work. Perhaps her mother would be more forthcoming with information.

I heard her mother call from inside the house in response to my knock on the front door. "Come in!"

What? Really? Oh yeah, it was the 1960s. People did that back then.

I walked into the house and toward the kitchen in the back. When Elizabeth's mother looked up at me, her eyes widened.

"Oh, Sam. Hello. How are you?" She obviously didn't expect to see me walk into her kitchen.

"Well, to be honest, not so great. I'm sure you know why I'm here," I told her.

She nodded. "You know that I can't tell you where Elizabeth lives. That's between the two of you. Or the three of you actually. She does have a husband now and he's part of this."

"I understand. Really I do. But how can I have a conversation with her about my child if I don't know where to find her?" It was an honest question.

"Well, I can give her a message for you," she offered.

"What good is that going to do? If she doesn't want me to know where she is, and doesn't want to talk to me, a message isn't going to…"

We were interrupted by the slamming of the front door and both turned to see who it was.

"Sam, what are you doing here?" It was Elizabeth.

"I came to see you."

I looked down at her huge belly and she instinctively rubbed it with her right hand.

"About what?" she asked.

"You know about what. I heard you got married and I want to talk about my baby," I said.

"Sam, it's not your baby anymore. It belongs to my husband and me now. You didn't want anything to do with us, remember?"

"No, you have it wrong. I didn't want to marry you, that part is true. But, I want to be in my child's life. He's still mine." I took a deep breath because I could feel that my voice sounded agitated.

"I don't think that is going to work out. Sam, we don't want anything from you. No child support, no visitation, nothing. My husband will be his true father, in every sense. The baby will not know that you even exist."

I honestly thought that I could feel my heart actually breaking at that moment. Not being part of Walter's life would be devastating. Though I didn't want his mother, I still wanted to be his father.

"Whose name is going on the birth certificate?" I asked, as if it was the first time it had occurred to me.

"My husband's," she responded, with no emotion whatsoever.

"No. I can't let that happen," I responded.

"You don't have a choice. I will tell everyone that my husband is the child's father. You can't prove it one way or another. And if you cause us any trouble, I will have you arrested for harassment. Do I make myself clear?"

She had me there, and she knew it. Without DNA testing being available, there was no way I could prove that the child was mine.

"Elizabeth, why are you doing this? It's not like you," I asked her, feeling as if my world was crashing in around me.

"You are the one who rejected us. I'm just reacting to it. I have to do what is right for my child. And having a loving husband and father is the right thing. Having an absent father is not the way I want to raise my child. Him being bounced around from my house to yours, and back and forth over a bunch of years, would be a terrible upbringing. Can't you see that?" she explained.

I hated to admit it, but yeah, I could see that. And it wasn't something I wanted for my son. It tore me up that another man would be raising him. I had no idea if I could come up with a better solution, one that would be right for all of us, but I would continue to think about that.

The problem was that even if I wanted to get back together with Elizabeth, so that I could raise my son, that was never going to happen now. She was married to another man. Though I might have had a chance to change that in another decade, in the 1960s it was almost impossible. For the most part, when someone got married, they stayed that way. Especially when there were children involved.

So, I told Elizabeth that I would back down. It was the best thing for my son.

"I do have a favor to ask of you though. I just ask that you name him Walter, after my grandfather. If you do that, then I won't contact you. I will let you live your life. And I will let Walter live his." I almost broke down right there in her parents' kitchen when I said that.

"Walter is a nice name. I will talk to my husband about it, but it probably won't be a problem. You promise to leave us alone?" she asked, staring daggers into me.

"I said I would." I turned and walked out the door. Neither Elizabeth, nor her mother, saw the flood of tears on my face as I closed the door behind me.

That night as I laid in my bed, staring up at the ceiling, I thought about Elizabeth's husband. I didn't even know his name. I thought about killing him. It wasn't as if I lacked experience in that department. I had killed many people. Killing didn't weigh heavily on my conscious. It was just something I did.

The problem was that I had never killed a man before. It was always women. I had no burning desire to kill a man. Not even Elizabeth's husband. I just didn't think it was something I was capable of doing.

Almost as if it were an automatic function of my body, I climbed out of bed, got dressed, and headed out the front door, latching it quietly behind me. My parents were sleeping soundly down the hall.

It was around one a.m. and I wandered the streets of Red Lake. It was so quiet at that time of night. I made my way down to the lake and sat on a log at the shore.

The moon was bright and it gleamed across the surface of the flat, undisturbed water. I watched the moonlight shimmy on the surface when a fish jumped. It calmed my mind.

Why was I out there in the middle of the night? I really didn't know. I just knew that I needed to get out of that house and I needed to be in the fresh air. It calmed me somehow.

I was startled out of my daydream when I heard a giggle come from a nearby car. I hadn't even noticed the car when I walked up, as it was partially hidden behind some bushes. That was probably on purpose. When I stood up and walked closer, they were making out, hot and heavy in the backseat.

The hairs on the back of my neck stood up. A tingling sensation worked its way through my core. Oh no. I recognized the feeling. I willed my feet to walk away. They refused. I stood there, watching the couple for a few minutes, unable to leave.

I ducked down behind some bushes when the car door opened. The man, no more than 20 years old, stepped out of the car and walked over to the lake. When he opened his fly and began relieving himself in Red Lake, I made my move.

I picked up a baseball sized rock that was lying at my feet and I sneaked up behind him. He never even saw me coming. When the rock connected with his skull, the thump was loud enough to be heard by the girl. He landed in a heap at my feet, his fly still open. I didn't think I hit him hard enough to kill him, but he would be out for a while.

The girl scrambled out of the backseat of the sedan. She screamed when she took in the scene before her. Her eyes went directly to her date, then back up at me.

She turned and ran. She had bare feet and it made it difficult for her to run fast, her skirt flying in the wind behind her. It didn't matter. She was no match for me. My 18 year old legs were lightning speed compared to hers. I caught her before she had gone no more than twenty feet.

I grabbed her around the waist and the two of us fell in a heap on the shore of Red Lake. The water was cold on my bare skin. The girl was a fighter. That was something I wasn't used to.

She kicked, bit, and scratched her way out of my grasp. When her teeth locked onto my left forearm, I instinctively let go, and yelled.

"You bitch! You bit me!"

Before I had the words out, she had jumped up and was on the run again. I was right on her trail though. She was much faster this time. She wasn't letting the pain of her bare feet over sharp rocks slow her down. I can only imagine the adrenaline that was pumping through her body at that moment.

Just as she reached the road, I caught up to her. I grabbed a handful of long blonde hair and yanked her down to the ground, covering her mouth with my free hand, just as a car was approaching. The driver apparently didn't see us though, as he never slowed his pace.

Once the car was past, I yanked her to her feet.

"Shut up and come with me," I said through clenched teeth, pulling her back toward the lake.

My fingers were entangled in her hair. She was not going to get away from me this time. She whimpered while we walked.

"Why are you doing this? Did you kill Hank?" she whined.

"I said shut up," I told her. "And no, I didn't kill Hank. He'll survive, but he will have one hell of a headache when he wakes up."

We both looked over at him. He was still unconscious near the water's edge. In the moonlight, I could see his chest rising and falling. I turned my attention back to the girl.

"You, on the other hand, will not survive," I told her in no uncertain terms.

Her eyes widened and she cried out. The moment her scream began, I reached my fist back to gain momentum, and then slammed it into her nose. It was broken. There was no doubt about that. The blood poured down her face and onto her pretty blue dress.

It looked as if she was going to lose consciousness, and I couldn't let that happen. Killing her was not going to be satisfactory if she weren't awake to experience her own death.

"Hey, wake up!" I shook her.

Her eyes opened and she stared at me. "Please don't hurt me," she pleaded.

I reached over and picked up the very same rock that I had knocked out Hank with. It would do very well.

I slammed it into her temple. She cried out and slumped to the ground. I bashed the rock into her head a total of seven more times. When I could see that her pretty head was smashed beyond recognition, I stopped. That was enough. My task was completed.

I threw the rock into the lake and walked back home.

It was after two a.m. when I walked into my front door. When I got to the bathroom, I realized that I was covered in blood. I don't know why that hadn't occurred to me until that very moment. Of course I would be covered in blood. How could I not be?

That was the first time anything like that had happened. Though I had killed in a variety of ways over my lifetime, strangulation was my usual go-to method. It produced no blood.

I was thankful that it was the sixties. The science of forensics was barely getting started then. Besides, there would be no need for them to look for blood in my home. I was never a suspect at any point.

I took a shower. A long one. I was disgusted with what I had done, and needed to scrub every last bit of that girl's DNA from my body. My skin felt raw and scratchy by the time I was done. But I felt clean again.

When my shower was complete, I cleaned everything with bleach. I then put my bloody clothing in with the trash that would be picked up around six that very morning, long before anyone would come knocking on my door. Though I didn't expect that to happen, ever.

Then the remorse set in. It always did. During the act of killing, I was in such a zone, that nothing and no one mattered. I had a one track mind and almost nothing would be able to stop me.

But once the deed was done, remorse and regret squirmed their way inside me.

The next day, the news of a young woman's body being found by the lake was out. And her boyfriend was in jail for the crime.

Did I feel guilt that someone was going to spend their life in prison for something I did? Absolutely. Was I going to do anything about it? Hell no.

There was no way that I was going to confess to killing her. I wasn't about to spend the rest of this life in prison. It was horrible that he probably would spend the rest of his days locked up, but I doubted that I could do anything about it.

I had to put that unfortunate tragedy out of my mind, and move on.

CHAPTER 8

A sort of depression set deep into my soul after that. I knew that I would never have a relationship with my own son. That was a loss all it's own. It was almost as if he had died.

The only thing that kept me sane was the fact that I did have at least one lifetime with him. I did get to see him grow up, date, marry, and have children and grandchildren of his own. Those were the only thoughts that sustained me.

I walked around in almost a daze for probably a year after that last meeting with Elizabeth. I had heard from my mother when the baby was born, and that she had kept her word, and named him Walter. That part made me happy.

And I kept my word. I left them alone. It was the fairest thing I could do for my son. Let him have a normal family life, with a full time mother and father. I certainly wouldn't be the first man, or the last, to let another man raise his child.

Once Walter was born, and I had made the decision to leave them alone, I did just that, and I moved on with my life. Ruby and I stayed together for a couple more years, but I knew it wasn't working. That was probably my fault too.

I had immortalized her in my mind in that first life of

mine. Back then, we hadn't been together long, when Elizabeth became pregnant, and we split up. This time, Ruby and I were together for a few years. She wasn't the fun, vivacious girl that I had remembered. Our relationship had still been so new that first time, that we never got to the point when things inevitably changed.

You know, when the thrill of a new relationship wanes, and you settle into something more mature. A respectful, adult relationship. Ruby and I had never had that before. Now we were past the thrilling stage, and she started getting on my nerves.

Her wild and vivacious ways were no longer cute and exciting. They were just annoying. Around the time that Walter turned 3 years old, I knew that Ruby and I needed to part ways.

But how to do that? I had promised her love and marriage in those early days. And a house full of kids. I no longer wanted any of those things with her. Ruby was not the love of my life, as I had imagined for all of those lonely decades, when I was unhappy with Elizabeth. My bad marriage with Elizabeth had been all my own doing, because of my longing for Ruby. What an idiot I had been. And I screwed things up all over again.

Walter's third birthday was rapidly approaching and it was all that I could think about. Would I be a terrible person if I tried to see him? I was positive that he had no knowledge of my existence. I would be okay, sort of, if they just called me a family friend or something. I wondered if Elizabeth would even begin to consider it. No, probably not.

I could probably find out where they lived though. I was sure that my mother knew. She and Elizabeth's mother were still friends. In fact, I was pretty sure that my mother had seen Walter. She never told me directly, but there were clues.

My mother once opened her purse and a photo fell out. In

a quick glance, I could see that it was a baby. She grabbed the photo quickly from the living room floor, where it had landed, and stuffed it back into her purse. Her eyes refused to meet mine, and I didn't say a word. I just let it go. If Walter couldn't have a relationship with me, then at least he could get to know his grandmother. I was okay with that.

"Mom," I began one day. "Where does Elizabeth live?"

She looked up at me with a surprised look on her face. "Oh, Sam, I don't think that would be a good idea."

"You don't think *what* would be a good idea? I didn't even tell you anything. I just asked you a question," I responded.

"Yeah, I know. But I can tell where that question is leading. You want to go over there and stir up some trouble. Honey, Walter is doing just fine. He has his mother, and his... father. They love him. Do you really want to shake up that little boy's world?"

I knew in my heart that my mother was right. Still...I needed to see my son. In my world, it had been many decades since he was 3 years old. I wanted to be there for that milestone. I just had to.

I assured my mother that I just wanted to have a conversation with Elizabeth, which was the truth, and I eventually pried the information out of her.

When I knocked on her front door, Elizabeth looked like she had seen a ghost. I'm sure that I was the very last person she ever expected to see at her house.

She looked behind her and then walked out onto the porch, closing the front door. Apparently she didn't want whoever was in the house to hear our conversation.

"What are you doing here?" she asked me. I could hear the disdain in her voice.

"My son is about to turn three and I want to see him."

"We had an agreement," she announced.

"I know we did. But things change. He doesn't have to know who I am. Just tell him I'm an old friend or something. I just want to meet him, that's all. Please." I prayed that she would feel something for me. Anything at all, for the man who gave her a son.

"No."

When she turned back toward the front door, I knew that it was my last chance. I took her by the arm. When she looked down at her arm, and then back up at me, I let go immediately.

"Sorry. I just want you to stay out here and talk to me. Please, talk to me about this. I have abided by your wishes for three years now. Don't you think that Walter has the right to know his father?"

"He does know his father. He is the man that is raising him. The man that has been here every single day of Walter's life. That man is not you."

Man, that stung.

"I've only been absent from his life because those were your wishes. I thought I was doing the right thing," I told her honestly.

"You were doing the right thing. The right thing for Walter. Not for you, and not for me. Now, please just go and leave us alone."

That time I let her turn and walk back in the house. I flinched when the front door slammed.

CHAPTER 9

I cried on Ruby's shoulder that night. Though I wasn't really sure what to do about our relationship, Ruby comforted me. She let me cry it out, without judgment. She knew that not having Walter in my life was rough on me. It had been from the moment that I agreed to let Elizabeth raise him. Without me.

The next morning, Ruby found me sitting at the kitchen table with a mug and a full pot of coffee on the table next to it.

"Hey, how are you feeling today?" she asked me, sitting down and pouring herself a cup of coffee.

"Like shit. I don't think I got any sleep last night. This coffee here is the only thing that is keeping me sane right now." I poured more of the thick liquid into my mug.

"Well, why don't we go to the mall today? Just the two of us. We can do some shopping and get some lunch," she suggested. "It might help get your mind off of things."

"Yeah, sure." Anything was better than fretting over my circumstances all day.

Two hours later, we were carrying our purchases and

wandering through the mall, just to kill time until lunch, when we ran into Elizabeth and Walter. The moment she spotted us, Elizabeth took Walter's hand and tried to steer him down another row of shops, away from us.

"Elizabeth!" I called. I probably should have let them go, but I thought that it might have been my only chance to engage with my son.

She ignored me and quickened her pace.

"Mommy, that man is yelling for you," I heard Walter say as we caught up with them.

Elizabeth turned to face Ruby and me. When she looked down at her son, and then back up at me, she gave me a very slight shaking of her head back and forth. I understood her meaning. I wasn't about to tell Walter who I really was. Though it broke my heart to stand there with him and not be able to hug him.

"Hi," Elizabeth said first.

After our initial greetings, Walter began tugging at his mother's skirt. "Mommy, who's that?"

"Oh," Elizabeth responded, "these are my friends, Sam and Ruby."

Ruby looked at me. I could tell that she had no idea that Elizabeth even knew her name. But, my mother and Elizabeth's mother were still friends. I was positive that our names came up in conversations between the two women.

"What do you want, Sam?" Elizabeth confronted.

"Mommy, can I go in the store?"

I looked up then and realized that we were standing right by the entrance to the toy store.

"Sure, honey. Just don't go anywhere else, okay?"

She knew that as long as we were standing there at the entrance, that a 3 year old would be fine in the store alone. And it was the 1960s after all. People did that sort of thing back then. I couldn't imagine anyone doing it decades later.

We all watched Walter bound into the store and disappear down a row of toys.

"I would like to know why you are keeping Sam away from his son?" Ruby asked. She didn't even try to keep the accusatory tone from her voice.

Elizabeth's jaw clenched and she stared daggers into Ruby. "This is really none of your business."

"That's where you are wrong. I'm with Sam. That makes it my business. You are being selfish by not allowing them to have a relationship," Ruby spat out, as she took a step closer to Elizabeth.

"That was his choice. He is the one who walked away," Elizabeth responded.

"Only because you told him to walk away. You pretty much forced him to cut all ties with Walter." Ruby got right into Elizabeth's face then. "You know that when Walter grows up, he is going to resent you for this. Even hate you maybe. You will have no one to blame but yourself!"

"Ladies, please." I tried to interject into their argument, but was too late.

Elizabeth had just about enough of Ruby's interference at that point. She dropped her bags and her purse, and shoved Ruby as hard as she could.

Ruby was taken off guard and flailed just a bit, before landing on her backside, on the mall floor. The shopping bags she had been carrying scattered haphazardly across the hard tile floor.

Ruby was stunned for just a moment, but didn't stay that way for long. She jumped up and ran at Elizabeth with everything she had, slamming the woman into the store front wall.

I tried to get in between them, but they ignored me. Between the screaming, the slugging, and the hair pulling, I couldn't do anything to stop them. The fight was on.

Before I knew it, they were on the floor, with Ruby on top of Elizabeth. Ruby was pounding her in the face, and all Elizabeth could do was try to protect herself. She was in no position to fight back at the same time.

However, Elizabeth was no slouch. She somehow managed to grab onto Ruby and roll them both, so that neither were on top then.

With all the shouting, their fight drew in quite a crowd. No one was helping though. It was as if they got some sort of perverted thrill out of watching the two women beating on each other.

I couldn't take it anymore and yelled to one of the men watching to help me pull the women apart. I was closest to Elizabeth, so I grabbed her around the waist, and the man grabbed Ruby's waist and we broke them up.

Still, the screaming and insults persisted.

"Shut up! Both of you!" I yelled at them. "Do you want Walter to see this?"

The name Walter, seemed to snap them out of it. I watched as Elizabeth looked around. "Where is he?" she asked me.

"He's still in the toy store, I'm sure," I explained.

Elizabeth pulled herself out of my hold on her and started walking toward the store.

"You have blood all over your face and blouse," I told her. I pulled a handkerchief from my pants pocket and handed it to her. "Clean yourself up a bit before he sees you."

Elizabeth took the handkerchief from me, without comment. Her face looked mostly presentable by the time she was done. She found her purse, pulled out a hairbrush and fixed that too.

The crowd was still watching our exchange.

"Don't you all have something better to do?" Ruby challenged them. "There's nothing more for you to see here. You all need to go away." She flicked her wrists at them in a shooing motion.

The embarrassed faces turned and went on with their shopping. I could hear excited chatter from them as they dispersed. That fight was probably the most interesting thing to happen in their dull lives in a long time.

Elizabeth glared at Ruby, then at me, and disappeared into the store to get her son. Our son.

"Come on Ruby. I think we've done enough damage around here for today. I just want to go home." I took her hand and we headed for the exit.

"Walter!" I heard Elizabeth yell.

It made me stop and turn back.

"Walter! Oh my god, I can't find him!" she yelled again.

I picked up the pace toward the store.

"Where are you going?" Ruby called after me.

"I'm going to help Elizabeth find my son. He's probably hiding, but I just need to make sure before we leave," I explained over my shoulder, without slowing my pace.

I pushed through the throngs of people converging on the store in response to Elizabeth's frantic cries.

"Lizzie, where's Walter?" I asked.

She didn't even look my way, but continued running up and down each of the toy store aisles. I followed close on her heels.

"I don't know where he is. Walter!" she screamed.

The people outside the store went dead silent. A handful of them entered the store to help, but most stayed outside. I don't know if they wanted to stay out of the way, or just didn't know what to do.

"I'll help," I told her. "I'll go see if anyone noticed him in the store, or walking out."

She ignored me. I stood there for just a moment and watched a mother frantically search for her child. It was a sad sight. I could see the terror in her face. Turning, I ran to the front of the store and began questioning the crowd. Not a single person remembered seeing a 3 year old boy walking around on his own.

Wanting to branch out into the mall, for a wider search, I glanced around for Ruby to help me. I couldn't find her in the large crowd that had gathered. I figured she was out there already searching.

An hour later, Sheriff Jay Mitchell had cordoned off the store and was already questioning everyone in sight. He didn't have any better luck with the crowd than I had.

"Mr. Wells, I would like to ask you a few questions," the sheriff said to me.

"Okay, sure."

"I understand that you are the boy's father?" he asked.

I was positive he already knew the answer to that one, but I replied anyway. "Yes sir."

"Where were you when the altercation was taking place between the boy's mother and your girlfriend?" The look on his face was judgmental.

"I was outside the store, trying to break up the fight," I told him honestly.

"Who was watching the boy?"

"No one, I guess. He was in the store while we were all talking just outside. We figured he was fine in there for a few minutes. He couldn't have gotten past us," I explained.

"But he did get past you, didn't he?" The sheriff looked down on me. I could see the look of disapproval in his eyes.

"Well…yes. I guess he did. But we didn't anticipate that a fight would break out and distract everyone," I answered.

"I see. Did you have anything to do with the disappearance of your son?" he asked me point blank.

"What? No. Why would I do that? I told you where I was

when he disappeared." I was shocked that I was being openly accused of something I had nothing to do with.

"You could have had an accomplice," he told me.

"Well, I didn't. I would never take Walter from his mother. I told her she could have full custody and raise him, without me in his life," I tried to explain.

"Then why are you here today?"

I had a feeling that the sheriff already knew the answer to that one.

"We were just shopping and ran into Elizabeth and Walter. It wasn't planned. At the spur of the moment I asked Elizabeth if I could talk to him."

"Why did you want to talk to your son, Mr. Wells?" he asked.

By the look on his face, he didn't believe a word I said.

"Because I miss him. I want him in my life. I tried to explain that to his mother," I told him.

He nodded. "Where is your girlfriend? The one that was fighting with Walter's mother."

"Yeah, I know who she is." The words came out snarkier than I meant them to. "I don't know where she is. After Elizabeth started yelling for Walter, I ran to help. I haven't seen Ruby since."

"I need to question her," he told me.

I shrugged. "I just said that I don't know where she is. When I see her, I will let her know that you want to talk to her. But honestly, she was kind of busy fighting with Elizabeth. There's no way that she knows anything about where Walter might be."

The sheriff nodded at me and wrote something in his notebook.

"Sheriff, if that's all, I would like to get back to searching for my son. I'm very worried about him." I shifted back and forth nervously from foot to foot. He didn't seem to notice.

"That's all for now. I'm sure I will have more questions for you later."

I took that as my cue to leave.

I spent the next two hours searching every nook and cranny in the mall, along with the deputies and many volunteers. Walter was nowhere to be found. Of course, there were no security cameras for us to look at for clues. Those were many years away.

Elizabeth and I ran into each other when we both returned to the toy store. It had been set up as a sort of central place for everyone to meet.

She walked up to me and I braced myself. The look on her face scared the hell out of me. Her husband joined us and stood by her side. I had never met the man, and right then was not the time for pleasantries.

Elizabeth leaned in so that she was no more than a few inches from my face. When she spoke, it was slowly and deliberately. "I'll never forgive you for this. If we don't find Walter, alive and well, then I will kill you. Do I make myself clear?"

I knew that the hyperbole was just out of fear. Fear of what the outcome might be for Walter. But I took her threat seriously anyway. She was capable of carrying it out. Any mother would be.

CHAPTER 10

I would like to report that everything turned out just fine. Walter was found playing in one of the stores and had no idea that anyone was looking for him.

Unfortunately, I can't say that.

Walter was never found. Eight years later, we still had no idea what had happened to him. There were a few tips called in to the sheriff's office, and they followed up on every single one of them. But not a single one of those leads turned out to be anything significant.

Depression hit me, and it hit me hard. With that, I started drinking. Though I felt that Ruby and I were doomed anyway, the drinking definitely accelerated that issue. She walked out on me one day and never looked back.

It didn't matter. By that time, I was so deep into the daily drinking that I would not have even noticed if she was there or not.

Over those eight long years, I killed several more women. I don't even remember how many. Six or seven of them would be my guess. I didn't keep track. I just didn't care.

After each kill, I felt better for a short while, and then the depression would hit me again.

The town of Red Lake was on high alert by that time. The news of Walter's disappearance was long forgotten. Everyone assumed he was dead. He probably was. The news of a serial killer loose in Red Lake was all anyone talked about. At that point, I no longer cared. If I got caught, then I did. Nothing but my boy mattered to me any longer.

Whenever I could drag myself out of bed, I spent all of my waking hours looking for my son. I questioned people. I harassed the sheriff's department into looking harder for him. I even called Elizabeth at least once a week for several years. At some point, she finally told me to never call her again. And I never did.

Years after Ruby left me, I began to blame her for Walter's disappearance. If she hadn't started that fight that day in the mall, Walter would be safe and sound. Yes, it was all Ruby's fault.

I spent about a year watching Ruby. She had met and married another man, and completely forgotten about me. I was sure of that. I don't know why I was watching her, to be honest. What was the point in it all?

One night, while I was skulking in the bushes near her home, I watched her with her two small children. And it pissed me off. My son was gone because of her, and there she was with her own children. Two little girls. She had no right to have a family of her own after what she had done.

That night, I felt the urge to kill start bubbling up inside me. I wanted Ruby to suffer the same way I had. The best way to do that would be to go after one of her daughters. But I couldn't do that. No matter what kind of a monster I was, I didn't have it in me to harm a small child.

But I could kill Ruby. I could do it slowly, making her suffer. I could make her daughters watch. I could stab her repeatedly, causing her to bleed to death. I laughed at the thought.

I watched as Ruby walked into her house, with her small girls leading the way. That's when I knew that I would never let myself harm her. I had actually loved her once. That was a fact. And I couldn't leave those girls motherless. I just couldn't let myself do it.

I took off running and vowed to never go to her house again. I knew that I might not be able to stop myself next time.

That was the night I told myself that I would stop killing. I had to stop it completely. Cold turkey. But it wasn't as easy as all of that. I struggled with my impulses. I struggled with everything in my life. Especially the part of my life that missed Walter.

My life moved on to a downward spiral, and kept falling fast. If I was going to continue, I needed to get help. But did I really want help? That was a good question. I didn't really want help. I wanted to wallow in my grief. And that's just what I did.

I had lived a long life the first time, making it to 79 years old before the lung cancer took me. This time, I made it to 31 years old.

On what would have been Walter's 12th birthday, I drank an entire bottle of whiskey and stepped in front of a train.

PART 2

CHAPTER 1

I braced for the train barreling down on me. My body jumped in response, causing a loud ruckus, and I heard laughter. As my vision cleared, I found myself sitting in a classroom, with at least a hundred students. All eyes were on me.

"Mr. Wells." I heard a booming male voice come from the front of the room, and I turned toward it. "I know that algebra is not the most riveting of subjects, but sleeping in my class is discouraged."

The entire room howled with laughter. I didn't know what else to do but run. I left everything on my desk and bolted out the door. No doubt, with a hundred pairs of eyes following my every move.

Once out of the room, I was greeted by an overcast, dreary sort of day. It had clearly been raining, as puddles littered the campus.

I walked, not knowing my destination. It didn't take long for me to figure out what was going on. It had happened again.

I had been hit by that train, though I don't remember

actually being hit. It must have happened so fast, and I must have died instantaneously. The impact didn't even register in my brain.

How in the world could this be happening? So far, I've died twice and awakened younger, twice. I don't understand it. Would it happen again? I guessed that I would find that out eventually.

I found a bench and sat down. I needed to collect my thoughts, and figure out if it was the same date as the last time I awoke from death. I knew that the day was different, and the circumstances were different.

Last time I woke up from dying, it was a bright, sunny day, and I was walking on campus. I collapsed almost immediately, not knowing what was happening to me.

This time, I knew what was happening. My life was beginning again. What I didn't know was *why*. I guess my life wasn't technically beginning again, since I didn't start again by being born. I must be just jumping into my life at a different point. A life that was already being lived, but I didn't remember any of it from before I awoke. I couldn't think of a better word.

"Hey man." I called out to a young student walking by. "What is the date today?"

He told me the date and continued walking. Now this is interesting, I thought. It was spring time, which meant that it was several months later than when I woke up last time.

Walter should have already been born by now. If he existed at all. I had no idea if he did or not. It was entirely possible that Elizabeth and I never got together in this lifetime.

I needed to find out. But how? Cell phones didn't yet exist. I could go to the administration building and ask to use their phone. I had no idea if they would let me or not. It probably had to be an emergency. I think finding out if I had a son or not, constituted an emergency. I started for the building.

Then it hit me. A payphone. I couldn't remember the last time I had used one. But I knew they were around. I scanned the campus and spotted one a few yards away. I jogged over and picked up the receiver. Reaching into the right pocket of my trousers, I found some change and promptly deposited it into the phone.

That's when I realized that I had no idea what Elizabeth's phone number was. I replaced the phone into its cradle. I heard my nickels drop into the return slot as I began searching my clothing for a scrap of paper. Anything at all with her number on it. Nothing.

Maybe in my dorm room? I remembered exactly where it was this time. I headed right for it.

In the top drawer of my desk, I found what I was looking for, my address book. Back to the payphone for me.

Elizabeth's mother answered on the second ring.

"Oh, hello Sam. Yes, she's here. Just a moment."

While I waited, something dawned on me. How was I going to ask her if we had a son or not, without sounding like I had lost my mind.

'So Elizabeth, do we have a baby together?'

No way was that going to fly. Especially not in the 1960s. I could get flogged for even suggesting something so sordid.

"Sam! I wasn't expecting you to call until tonight."

Well at least she was happy to hear from me. That was an encouraging start.

"Hi. I just wanted to see how you were? Is everything...all right there?" God, I sounded like an idiot.

"Yeah, everything here is great. Walter didn't sleep very well last night. I think he misses his daddy," she told me.

I let out a deep breath. Well, that answers that. I thought I would jump for joy at the news that my son was alive and well.

"And I miss my husband. Are you coming home this weekend?" she added.

Husband! Oh boy. I definitely didn't expect that.

"I…uh…I'm coming home soon. I think. Let me see what my…schedule looks like and I'll…call you back. Okay?" I stuttered my way through that entire exchange, having no idea how to proceed.

"Yeah, okay. Call me soon," she added.

"Will do. Well, I have a class, so I have to go."

"I love…" I hung up before she said anything further.

Married. Holy cow. I looked down at my left ring finger. No ring. I wondered why. It didn't matter, I guess. Being married certainly complicated things. How was I going to get out of a marriage with Elizabeth? I didn't want to be married to her any more than I wanted to be married to her in my last two lifetimes. Or in my next hundred. I had a lot of things to think about.

It was late afternoon by then and the sun was going down. What I could see of it anyway. It was pretty much covered by dark, ominous clouds. I started walking, not really sure of my destination, when the rain hit. And it hit hard. Normally, rain didn't bother me. Just a little water, so what. But, the torrential downpour that hit was too much, even for me. I ran for cover into the nearest building, which was the school's library.

That was not a bad thing. I enjoyed libraries. However, the moment I stepped inside, I could see several young women, engaging in animated conversations, albeit quietly.

That was when I felt it. That ache in my gut. I wanted to kill someone. I had been back in this life for a couple of hours by then, and it hadn't even crossed my mind. That was strange, all on its own.

I didn't know what to do. Continue on into the library, and stay out of the weather, or leave, and hope that the feeling in the pit of my stomach left also.

Standing there, unsure of myself, I probably looked a sight. My hair and clothing were all drenched. I had no books or papers with me. That's when a young woman walked up to me. I recognized her as the girl in the pink sweater from my last life. We had such a brief encounter then, that I was surprised I remembered her, but I did.

The churning in my stomach literally made me double over in physical pain. I almost didn't know if I was feeling the need to kill someone, or if I had food poisoning. Almost.

No, I knew exactly what it was. This body of mine needed to do what I had fought my entire life...lives actually...to stop. It didn't seem to matter what my brain, and my rational thought wanted. My body seemed to have a mind all its own.

"Hello. I work here. Can I help you find something?" She looked at me from head to toe. "Or get you a towel?"

When she smiled, she was beautiful. I grabbed my stomach as it lurched.

"I...uh...I just need to...sit down for a moment. I'm not... feeling...well." I managed to spit out the words between cramps.

"There's an empty table right over there," she told me with a look of concern on her face.

I looked up and my eyes followed the line of her pointing finger. When she touched my back, in an effort to guide or comfort me, I'm not sure which, a surge shot through my body. It was indescribable. I reacted as if her hand was on fire, lurching forward, out of her reach. I knew that if I had done anything differently, I might have strangled her right then and there. In front of everyone.

"Are you all right?" The worry was etched into her young, smooth forehead.

"I'm…uh…I gotta go."

I bolted out the front door and right into the storm. My face was re-drenched within a second or two. I didn't care. The cold, pelting rain, seemed to work a miracle. I felt better almost immediately, and the horrible cramping was gone. I'm not sure if it was the coolness of the rain and wind on my face, or just the fact that the distance between me and the young woman had increased.

CHAPTER 2

I ran straight for my dorm room. At least I would be alone there. I laid down on my bed and thought about what was happening to me. It seemed that with each life my urges…or compulsions, or whatever they were, got worse. And they seemed to manifest themselves into actual physical pain. That didn't happen the first time around.

Back then, I just had the need to hurt someone, but I didn't feel actual pain because of it. It was a lot different this time around. The problem was that I didn't think there was anything I could do about it. I certainly couldn't go to the doctor. No, that wouldn't go over well at all. I would end up with a one way ticket to the loony bin. And in the 1960s, mental hospitals were a whole lot different than in the 21st century. So, so different. I didn't want to end up in one of them even in the 21st century, but certainly not at this point in history. I had read the horror stories. The inhumane conditions and treatment were unfathomable, and I wanted no part of it.

When Henry, my roommate, walked in, I was startled. I don't know why, really. It wasn't totally out of the ordinary that he would show up at some point. It had been 13 years since I had seen him last and I was happy he was here. There was something new that I thought I would try.

"Man, it's cats and dogs out there." Henry pulled off his sweatshirt, shoes and socks, and plopped onto his bed. He laid there on his back. "History class was hell today. Who can remember all those dates from way back when? And who even cares? I hate history."

"Funny you should mention that," I told him, sitting up on my bed, so I could see Henry.

"Why is that funny?" he tilted his head at me, without moving from his position on his bed.

"I need to tell you something. You are going to think it's crazy…that I'm crazy. And hell, maybe I am. But I don't think so. It all seems very real to me. You know what I mean?" I asked him.

Henry sat up on his bed, letting his bare feet touch the floor, and faced me. "No, I don't know what you mean."

I took a deep breath, exhaled courage, and began. "I think I'm dying and reliving my life over and over." There, I said it. I held my breath.

Henry stared at me for a moment, then his lips curled up at the edges, finally resulting in a full blown smile and laugh.

"Yeah, that is crazy." He picked up his pillow and threw it at me. I caught it mid-air and tossed it back.

"I'm not kidding," I told him with as serious a look on my face as I could muster.

"Oookaaaay," he drawled out. "What makes you think you are living your life over and over? You know that's not possible, right?"

"If you had asked me that the first time, I would have agreed with you. But I'm currently on my third life," I said, bracing for more ridicule from Henry.

"Your third life? Are you listening to yourself?" He shook his head, proving that he didn't believe a word I was saying.

"Yeah, I know how it sounds. Believe me. But it's the truth. I just can't prove it," I admitted.

"Sure you can." Henry smiled. It was a mischievous sort of smile.

"How?" I asked.

"Tell me something that happened in one of your 'lives' that hasn't happened yet."

He used air quotes around the word *lives*. I rolled my eyes. I hated it when people did that.

"Hmmm." I looked up at the ceiling, thinking about history, a subject I also hated. But this was different. I had actually lived through this time period in my life. Twice so far, and was on the third time. There must be something that happened about this time. Something significant. If I could just remember…

"Okay, here's something. Martin Luther King, Jr. will give a famous speech, called 'I Have a Dream.' But I can't remember exactly when that was. It's sometime this summer though. That I'm sure of. Summer of 1963, yes." I gave him a satisfied smile.

"Summer is still a few months away. You are going to need to give me something sooner than that," Henry told me.

"I know that President Kennedy is going to be assassinated in November. But that's still months away also."

His eyes grew wide. "How can you possibly know that?" he asked me. "That's really big. Huge." He threw his arms up in the air dramatically as he spoke.

"I told you how I know." I raised my eyebrows and gave him the 'I'm really serious' look.

"I guess we'll see about that." His face told me that he didn't believe any of it. "Anything sooner?" he asked.

I thought on it a moment. "No, not really. Those are the

big historical moments that we all remember from this year. I couldn't tell you what's going to happen tomorrow."

"I see. Well, I gotta go see a girl about a date." He stood up and changed into dry clothes.

His face told me all that I needed to know. He didn't believe a word I was saying. I had no idea how to fix that.

"Anyone I know?" I asked him.

"No. She's new. Her name is Polly. I really like her, so try not to steal her away from me." Henry pointed at me and smiled.

I shrugged. "What?"

"You know what. My girlfriends can't seem to resist your charms, for some reason. Why couldn't I get an obese troglodyte as a roommate, instead of Adonis?" Henry asked with a serious look on his face.

"I don't think you know the meaning of troglodyte," I told him in all seriousness.

"Yeah, whatever. If it means hideously ugly and grotesque, then that's what I meant." The door slammed behind Henry.

"Well, okay, so that's how it's gonna be," I said out loud to no one.

About four hours later, I awoke to not so quiet whispers and laughter just outside my dorm room door. I pulled my pillow over my ears, to no avail. Several minutes later, I looked up as the door opened. I caught a glimpse of blonde hair just as Henry shut the door behind him. I felt my insides cramp.

I was glaring when Henry glanced over.

"Oh sorry. Did we wake you?" he asked, not sounding one bit sorry.

"Uh, yeah. It's after midnight. Is she even allowed in our

78

dorms at this hour?" It had been so long since I had actually lived in the dorms, I couldn't remember the rules.

"No. You know that. But she didn't want to leave me. She wanted to walk me back to my room. Isn't that cute?" he asked me, seriously.

"Isn't it the gentleman who is supposed to walk the lady to her dorm?" I asked. "Aren't you worried for her safety?"

He waved his hand in the air. "Nah, she's fine. It's not far, and there are plenty of students wandering around campus right now. It's Friday night, you know."

"It's Friday?" I had no idea what day of the week it was.

"Yeah, how could you not know that?" Henry's brows scrunched together. "What's with you lately?"

"I've got a lot on my mind, I guess," I told him honestly. "Maybe I should have gone home for the weekend." The cramping in my gut stopped.

"Yeah, your wife and kid might want to see you, for a change," Henry snarked.

"For a change? What do you mean by that?" I was pretty sure I knew exactly what he meant by that.

"You know what I mean." He didn't need to elaborate further.

A thought struck me. "Hey, do we have a recent edition of the newspaper around here somewhere?"

"Um, yeah." Henry lifted up a stack of textbooks and papers from the top of his desk, and pulled a newspaper out. "This one is from a couple days ago. Here." He handed it to me. "Some light reading in the middle of the night?"

"I guess. I just want to see if there's any local news. Like around campus. I haven't been paying attention lately," I told him.

"You mean like the two girls who got murdered in the last couple of weeks?"

My head jerked upward, toward Henry. "Murdered? Like here on campus?"

"Yeah. You know that. We even talked about it. You can't possibly have forgotten." He was scratching his jaw as he spoke. "What is going on with you? Forgetfulness is not like you."

"No, I haven't forgotten…okay, maybe I did. I've had a lot on my mind lately. How did the girls die?" I asked.

"They were both strangled," Henry replied. "At least that's what the newspaper said. Why are you so interested all of a sudden?"

"I told you why. I've just been preoccupied with school and Elizabeth and stuff lately. I just want to get caught up," I explained.

"If you say so." His tone was disbelieving.

I couldn't really blame him. I'm sure that I sounded like an idiot. But why stop then?

"Did you know either of the girls?" I asked him.

"I had English with one of them, but didn't really know her. She said hi to me once," he answered. "I don't remember the other one at all."

"Did they catch the killer?" I asked him.

"I don't think so. At least I haven't heard anything. Why? Did you kill them?" He laughed at his own comment.

I didn't laugh.

"Um no, of course not." I wasn't sure who I was trying to convince.

I had no recollection of the killings, since they were before I found myself in this life. But there was no point in lying to myself. I was probably the killer. I read the newspaper story, but didn't recognize either of the girls by name or photo. That didn't mean anything, of course. Lots of times I didn't know the identity of the girl I killed until I read about it in the newspaper afterward. This time was no different.

"So, you know that a killer is on the loose around here, and you let your girlfriend walk home alone? What is wrong with you?" I was the one asking him the questions this time.

"She's not my girlfriend," he replied.

"That is so not the point." I gave him an incredulous stare.

His shoulders slumped. "No, I guess not. Do you think that I should go see if she's okay?" He was looking to me for answers.

I thought for a moment. "No, she's probably back at her dorm by now. Or dead." That last comment wasn't intended to be a joke.

"Very funny," Henry replied.

"Sorry. That was in poor taste," I told him. "Really, I hope she's okay. I'm sure she is."

Strange thing was that I was almost positive that she was fine. I was in the dorm room the whole time. So, since I was probably the killer, she would be safe from me.

CHAPTER 3

I tossed and turned that first night back in my new life. The whole ordeal was tough on me. I had done this twice. Would it happen again? And again? When would it stop? I figured there was no way of knowing the answer to that, until I died again. Last time I stepped in front of a train, on purpose. I wouldn't do that again. Not ever. I was sure of that.

Since I wasn't getting any sleep anyway, I got out of bed around dawn. I quickly dressed in the dark dorm room, not wanting to wake Henry, and slipped out the door. Henry never stirred. I had forgotten what a heavy sleeper he was.

I wandered aimlessly around campus for about an hour, only seeing the rare student. One boy was sitting on a bench, reading a textbook. He glanced up as I passed, giving me a slight smile, then his attention promptly went back to his reading. Last minute test cramming was my guess. It was Saturday morning, no classes, but he must have had a test to make up. I put him out of my mind and continued walking.

Two more young men passed by me on the way to the dorms. By the looks of them, and the potent smell of alcohol wafting in their vicinity, they weren't up early, but were up very late, just arriving back from an eventful night out.

I thought of returning to my dorm room, but decided against it. Henry would almost surely still be asleep. I couldn't make any payphone calls as it was much too early for that.

The cafeteria always opened very early, so I headed there. After sitting down with my tray of oatmeal, toast, and orange juice, I looked around. There were more students in the cafeteria at that hour than I would have expected. Especially on a Saturday morning. Most were sitting alone with their breakfast. Perhaps they were all avoiding waking up their roommates, like I was.

I heard the commotion outside, before I saw it. Someone yelling, another person yelling back. There was an entire wall of the cafeteria that was made out of glass. It gave us a spectacular view of the courtyard on the campus, an area where many of the students hung out. The area was very green, with an abundance of trees and flowering plants. It was very peaceful and a favorite spot of most of the students. There were several benches and patio tables, which were perfect for gatherings. And that is exactly where you would probably find someone you were looking for.

A young woman, no more than 18 or 19 years old, was stopping people as they walked past her. She was average looking, nothing special. But I found her interesting nonetheless. She was dressed in what one would call 'hippie clothes.' Someone several years from now would call it that. In 1963, it was just odd clothing. People didn't dress her way just yet. Her dress was long and flowing. She wore a headband and sandals. She was quite different than the conservative dress of the 1963 crowd. And she was certainly catching the attention of those around her.

I watched as she reached out to grab a boy's arm and he

jerked it away from her and yelled something. I could tell that he was yelling, but I couldn't hear the words through the glass wall.

By that time, everyone in the cafeteria had abandoned their breakfasts, in favor of the entertainment going on in the courtyard.

My curiosity got the best of me and I felt the need to leave my breakfast, completely uneaten, to head out to the courtyard. Upon my arrival, I found that the boy who was just yelling at her, had already moved on. The young woman was calling out to those around her.

I walked up to a couple standing nearby, watching the commotion unfolding in front of us. "Hi. What's going on?"

Both of them turned to me. "That girl over there has lost her mind," the boy told me.

"What do you mean?" I asked, looking back in her direction.

"She's telling people that she died and came back to life," the girl responded.

"She what?" I couldn't believe what I was hearing. Could it be possible that someone else was also reliving their lives? It was almost too good to be true.

"Yeah, she's crazy. She's stopping people and telling them about the future," the boy added. "I think someone has already called the cops. I don't think she even goes to this school. I find it pretty funny though."

"Wouldn't it be great to be able to relive your life?" the girl asked. "You know, and fix all of your mistakes?" She laughed.

Her boyfriend took her arm. "Come on, let's go. I've got better things to do than stand around here all day."

I watched the two of them walk away. When I heard more yelling, my attention snapped back to the girl holding court.

A few people stood and engaged with her. Very few actually. Most made a wide berth as they passed her, not wanting to be the one that she focused on.

"President Kennedy is going to be shot and killed in a few months. Don't any of you care?!" she yelled to the crowd.

Quite a few eyeballs looked like they were going to roll out of people's heads.

"This is serious! You all need to listen to me," she continued. "Big things are coming up and I know all about them."

The hippie girl grabbed another girl by the arm, causing her to drop an armload of books.

"Oh, I'm so sorry," the crazy girl told her, dropping to her knees and retrieving the books.

"What is your problem?" the young lady asked her. "Give me my books and don't ever touch me again."

I still stood there, watching the exchange. That's when a group of four boys started walking toward the girl. I knew that I needed to do something, before she was arrested. Or worse. Those boys looked like they meant business.

"Whoa. Hey everyone," I said to the boys when I reached the girl. Standing in front of her, I continued speaking. "This is my sister. She has a few problems, if you know what I mean." I gave them a look as I tilted my head toward her.

The girl walked around and stood next to me. "This isn't my brother. I don't know this person," she told the boys.

"See what I mean? Just let me handle this. Okay guys?" I put my palms up, facing them. "I'll get her out of here. She's harmless, I promise."

I took the girl by the arm. "Come on. We need to go."

She pulled out of my grasp and stood her ground. "I don't know you. And I'm not going anywhere with you." She narrowed her eyes at me.

Leaning in, so that I was only an inch or so from her ear, I whispered, not wanting anyone but her to hear. "I believe you. I also relive my lives. Can we go somewhere to talk?"

She backed up, and looked me straight in the eyes. She said nothing for perhaps a full minute. I just stared back, giving her time to assess me.

"If you believe me, then you are the very first one. I think you are just trying to get me out of here." She crossed her arms in front of herself. "I'm just not sure why though. You don't know me, so why would you care if anything happens to me?"

"I told you why," I responded. "Now keep your voice down. Let's go over somewhere quiet to talk. Somewhere outside. Somewhere safe. I'm not a lunatic." That was debatable.

"Okay, fine." She dropped her arms to her side. "Let's go."

She followed me to a table that was out of the courtyard, and away from prying ears. We sat.

"Would you like something to drink?" I asked her. "I can go get us something from the cafeteria."

"No, I'm fine."

"My name is Sam." I stuck my hand out. "And you are?"

She left my hand hanging, mid air. "Olive."

"Olive. That's a nice name," I told her.

"So, why are we here? I don't think you really believe me." She got right to the point.

"Actually, I really do. And I wasn't kidding when I told you that I am also reliving my lives. I'm on my third one right now," I admitted.

"Don't play with me. I'm not going to sleep with you." She leaned back in her chair, folded her arms in front of her chest, and glared at me.

I shook my head slightly from side to side. I would say it was in disbelief at what she had just said to me. But honestly, I couldn't really blame her. She had absolutely no reason to believe a word I said. I wouldn't be the first man who said something ridiculous just to get in a woman's pants, and I certainly wouldn't be the last. Though she was no beauty, I was sure she had been hit on many times in her young life.

"That's not what this is about," I answered. "I'm here because you are the first person I have found that has claimed to be reliving their lives, just like me."

She gave me a look. No words necessary. It was obvious that she wasn't going to take my word for it.

"Would you like me to prove it?" I asked her.

She didn't move a muscle. "Yes, please do."

I smiled. "Well okay. Now we're getting somewhere."

"We'll see about that," she responded.

"Okay, um, JFK will be assassinated in a few months," I told her.

"Yeah, I was just saying that in the courtyard. You were standing there I'm sure when I was talking. Come on, you are going to have to do better than that."

I shrugged. "Fair enough. Let me see…" I had to think about it. What major world event would she know about? "Okay, how about this. Ronald Reagan, the actor, will become President of the United States."

She sat up in her chair. I could see interest on her face then. "What year?"

"You tell me," I responded.

"1980," she told me.

"And again in 1984," I told her.

"What else?" Olive asked me.

"Why don't you tell me something?" I asked her. "I don't have any proof that what you are saying is true."

"Yeah, good point. I have a good one." She looked straight into my eyes and took a deep breath. "9/11."

I gasped.

"You believe me now?" she asked, stretching her arms out wide in a satisfied sort of way.

I nodded. "I do. Oh, I have another. Our first black president, Barack Obama."

"Who?" she asked.

"Oh. How come you don't know that one?" Then something dawned on me. "Wait, when did you die?"

"We are going to have a black president?" she asked. "That's fantastic. With this time in history that we are living in, with all the racism and such, knowing that we are going to have a black president is really the best news ever. When is that going to happen?" she asked.

"You didn't answer my question," I deflected. "When did you die last time?"

She looked down at her hands and was bending each back, one at a time. I could see that it was a nervous gesture.

"Olive?"

"9/11. I was in the first tower that was hit." I watched as a solitary tear slid down her cheek.

"Oh no. I'm so sorry." I really had no other words for her. What could I say that would make that better? Nothing. Nothing at all.

"Then I woke up here, in my dorm room, two days ago. For the eighth time."

"Eight times!" I responded louder than I meant to.

"Yeah. No matter what I do, I keep dying and coming back. Sometimes I die in the tower, like I did two days ago. But not always. A few times I managed to avoid it. It's weird though. Even though I know it's coming, sometimes I still ended up in that damn tower. Once I tried to warn everyone. I yelled for them to evacuate the building."

"You did? What happened?" I was fascinated by her story.

"No one believed me. They all just stood around looking at me like I had lost my mind. Kind of like just a bit ago in the courtyard. No one ever believes me. Until you came along at least," she explained.

"Oh, I'm so sorry," I told her honestly.

"Then the plane hit us. Just like it did before. That never seems to change. I didn't even try to warn anyone this last time. I didn't see the point."

"That had to be really hard on you," I responded.

She just nodded.

"Yeah, many of those people were my friends. And I still couldn't save them."

The sadness on her face told me everything about how she felt recounting the events of her lives.

"I don't always come back here at school though. A couple times I was a teenager when I came back, and once I was married and had three kids. That was weird. I was only there for a few weeks, until I got attacked when out walking alone one night."

My heart began racing. "Tell me about that. What happened?" It was important that I knew more about how she died. For obvious reasons.

"It was not far from here actually. I guess I had met my future husband here at school and we stayed in town and had kids. I went for a walk one evening, because the kids, two boys and a girl, were out of control and driving me crazy. Someone attacked me from behind and strangled me. I never did see his face."

I gasped.

CHAPTER 4

"My parents think that I have lost my mind." Olive looked up to the sky. "Hell, maybe I have. I don't know for sure."

"No, you haven't. If you had, then we would be sharing the same delusion. That's not the case here. We are both reliving our lives, and neither of us knows why…or even how it is happening. But it is definitely happening," I told her.

"All of that may be true," Olive responded. "But it doesn't change the fact that my parents want to have me committed."

She looked back at me, to gauge my reaction. No need. I was positive that if I ever told my parents what was happening to me, that they would have the same reaction.

"Hey," Olive jumped in. "Let's make a pact, since neither of us knows how long we will be here this time."

I knit my eyebrows together. "What kind of pact?"

She smiled at me. "In our next lives, let's promise to meet up somewhere, at a specific date and time."

"Hmmm. What if our lives don't overlap next time?" I asked Olive. "Cause I still don't know how any of this works."

She shrugged. "I guess that's just a chance we will have to

take. But in case we do overlap, like we are now, when do you want to meet? And where?"

"How about right here? Right at this very table, at this very time." I looked at my watch. "It's 8:05 am. Will this date and time work for you?"

"Sounds good to me. It's a date," she agreed, sticking out her hand to seal the deal.

We both smiled at the thought of having a friend…or cohort, in our time travels.

"So, do you plan to keep going to school here?" I asked Olive. "I quit immediately after waking up in my last life. Didn't see the point."

"Yeah, I guess so. I don't want to go back home. Been there, done that. You know?" Olive admitted. "Maybe I can actually make something of my life this time."

"Good point." Then I decided to fill Olive in on my home life, such as it was. "Apparently I have a wife and son back home. I called yesterday when I arrived in this time period. My wife, Elizabeth is her name, answered and confirmed it all."

Olive leaned forward in her seat. I could see that she was quite interested in my story. "Oh boy. Did you ever have a wife before?"

"Well yes, actually. In my first life, Elizabeth and I were married for 60 years. And we raised our son, Walter, together."

"Oh, I see. But you don't sound like that's what you want. It's the tone in your voice, I guess. You sounded melancholy when you told me about her. Almost like you are resigned to live that life again. You don't want to be married to her, do you?"

Olive was quite astute. I was surprised that she could get all of that out of the short telling of my story. She was absolutely right. I didn't want to be married. But I was, and had no idea what to do about it.

"Truth? No, I don't want to be married. I don't love Elizabeth. Never did. Now don't get me wrong, she's a really nice person. I can't really say anything bad about her. I just don't love her. And I believe that married people should be in love. Don't you?" I told her truthfully.

"Absolutely." She nodded. "I was married the first time too. Twice actually. Neither of them stuck though. And thank goodness, there were no kids involved. This last time where I woke up and had a husband and three kids, well it was torture. I was almost happy that someone strangled me and put me out of my misery after only a few weeks here. I wouldn't have been able to survive years of that. No way."

She laughed at her story. I tried to laugh along, but didn't find the fact that she was strangled, and I was probably to blame, very funny.

I felt the need to change the subject. "So, tell me about your hippie garb here." I gestured toward her long flowing dress. "You do know that you are years ahead of your time?"

She looked down at herself and laughed. "Yeah, I guess I am. I just never was, at least after my first life, the type to wear all of that formal, clean cut stuff they wore back in the sixties. Or now in the sixties, I guess," she corrected herself. "I always loved this type of clothing and now I wear it all the time. Besides, I hate all the materialism and whatnot of the button down type. After my first life, I've kind of stood out with this clothing." She shrugged. "That wasn't my intention. I just love the freedom of it all."

"I can understand that," I replied.

"Do you plan to stay in school this time?" she asked me. "Or are you going to quit and go back home to your wife?" Olive's eyes followed a butterfly that was flitting around us as she spoke.

"You know, I hadn't totally made up my mind yet, until now. I think I'll stay here. I won't be happy back home with Elizabeth, and I don't have any other plans. Maybe I'll get my degree and be a productive human being this time."

"How did you die last time. Or the first time?" she asked me.

"The first time I died I was 79 years old and had lung cancer. It was not a pleasant way to go. I'll never smoke again," I explained.

"Yeah, I get it. I smoked the first time too. Haven't picked one up since. Even if it didn't kill ya, it's a disgusting habit," Olive told me. "And how did you die this last time? It was just a few days ago, right?"

"Two days ago, yes. I became a drunk and stepped in front of a train," I admitted.

"You did? Why?" she asked.

"My son was kidnapped and…" I felt a hitch in my throat and paused for a moment. Olive sat quietly. I'm sure that she could sense that I needed that. "We… never found him. I still don't know to this day if he was alive or not."

I looked down at my feet, trying desperately not to cry.

"Was there a ransom demand?" she asked. "Oh, if you don't want to talk about it, I understand."

"No it's okay. There was no ransom demand. That's the weird part. Elizabeth and Ruby were fighting in the mall and we all lost sight of Walter. It seemed as if he just disappeared," I explained.

"Who's Ruby?" Olive asked.

"Oh, she was my girlfriend. Elizabeth and I weren't together in this last life. I was with Ruby. The whole thing was a mess, to be honest. I don't want to be with either one of them this time," I told her.

"Yeah, I get that. I've had several relationships over my lives. Some were good. Most weren't. I may just stay single this time. It might be a refreshing change of pace." She looked off in the distance as she spoke. Olive appeared to be thinking about the past. I wondered what it was that was drawing her attention.

"You know," she reached over and took my hand in hers, "that part of your life is over. Your son is alive now. It is the same kid, right? What did you say his name was? Walter? Is he the same kid? I know it can change."

I thought for a moment. "You know, I'm not sure. Since his name is Walter, I assumed it was the same kid. But I don't know that for a fact. I guess it is possible that it's not him this time. Just another kid that we happened to name the same. Hmmm. Maybe I should go home and find out."

"That's probably a good idea," Olive agreed. "If you find it is the same child, then it might make you feel better about his kidnapping. That's over, and Walter is with you again."

I nodded. "Yeah, maybe."

I jumped on the next bus to Red Lake. After my conversation with Olive, it was imperative that I find out if this Walter is the same Walter. My son. The one that I raised and loved. And lost the last time around.

I was so antsy that I could barely sit still in my bus seat. I was going to get to see Walter again. At least I hoped so. I couldn't bear the thought that he might be a different child. It was something that had never occurred to me, until Olive brought up the possibility. Then it became something that I needed to know. I needed to know for sure if this Walter was the same person. It wasn't a question that I could call Elizabeth, or anyone else for that matter, and ask. They would have no idea how to answer that. I needed to see him for myself. And that is exactly what I intended on doing.

I found myself thinking about Olive, when something odd struck me. I realized that the desire to kill never even entered my mind when I was with her. I wondered if it was due to the fact that we were so engrossed in our conversation about our past lives that I was too preoccupied to think about killing. Or perhaps, even better, she just wasn't on my radar to kill. I never even felt a pang of desire to kill her when we were speaking. I thought of that as a good sign. And if it did hit me later, I would do everything in my power to not hurt her. I still didn't know if I was the one that strangled her in her last life. It's something I would probably never know. But no matter what happened, I would not let myself hurt her. Not ever. I would kill myself before I let that happen.

CHAPTER 5

Elizabeth jumped into my arms, when she answered my knock on the door.

"Sam! What are you doing here?" She kissed me passionately.

I gently pulled out of her grasp. "I just wanted to come home. Is that okay with you?" It came out harsher than intended.

"Yeah. Of course," she replied, with what sounded liked trepidation in her voice. "Why are you being so cranky with me? It was just a question."

Her face drooped when she asked that last question and I instantly felt like a heel.

I looked around the living room and peeked into the kitchen. "So, where are your parents?"

"They went to a movie. Why?" she asked.

"No reason." There was a reason. I wanted to talk to Elizabeth alone. No prying ears and all.

I reached up and brushed the back of my hand across her cheek. "I'm sorry. Really. That was not my intention. It's just been a long day and I'm tired. Okay?" I gave her a slight smile to show her that I really meant it.

"Okay." She smiled. "I'm glad you're home. Walter and I missed you."

I looked around, my heart beating faster. "Where is Walter? I want to see him."

"He's taking a nap, but should be up shortly."

As if on cue, a wail belted out from down the hall.

Elizabeth smiled. "I guess he's up now. You go get him. I'll make us some tea."

"Sounds good."

I followed the crying that got louder as I made my way down the hall. I had no idea which room he was in, but he let me know, loud and clear. Opening the last door in the hallway, I saw his crib across the room. Taking a deep breath, I crossed the room in what seemed like an instant and looked down into the red face of my son.

He stopped crying when I smiled down at him. It was Walter. My Walter. The same one that I had raised, all those years ago. There was no mistaking those dimples. Reaching into the crib, I lifted him up and held him to me. That's when the flood of tears hit. I couldn't help it. I had my Walter back.

The last time I had seen him was in the mall on that fateful day, all those years ago. The day he disappeared and was never seen again. I knew right then that I would never let that happen this time. Walter was my priority. I would make sure that he lived to grow up and have a family of his own.

My grandchildren. It had been a long time since I had thought about them. Ivy and Parker. I would get to see them again. Hopefully. I would do whatever it took to live this life and grow old, and give Walter the chance to grow old and give me my grandchildren back. How I missed them. I hadn't even realized how much, until that moment.

"What's going on in here?"

I turned toward Elizabeth. She walked over and wiped my tears with the sleeve of her shirt.

"Are you okay? What's the matter?"

Her concern comforted me. Though I had never really been in love with her, Elizabeth was a kind person. And she had always been kind to me, even when I couldn't return the favor. I began to think that maybe I should stay with her this time. It would give me the chance to raise Walter, and not be an absentee father, like I was the last time. I knew in my heart, and in my head, that his disappearance was at least partly my fault. If I hadn't been so selfish in wanting Ruby, instead of Elizabeth, then that fight between them that day at the mall would never have happened, and Walter would never have disappeared. So, the entire thing was probably my fault. Not a little bit. Not partly. But entirely.

"Yes, I'm okay. I just miss him. It feels like it's been years since I saw him last. He's growing so fast," I told her.

"Yeah, he is growing fast." She gently rubbed the baby's bald head. He smiled in response. "And I'm sure that he misses you too. But you need to tell me what's going on and why you are really here."

She looked me directly in the eyes when she said that. Elizabeth was one of the smartest people I knew. I never could fool her.

"Come on, give me the baby." She took him from my arms. "We can talk while I give him his bottle."

I followed her down the hall and to the kitchen.

Once we were all seated and Walter was happily sucking away at his bottle, she asked me again to tell her why I was home, in the middle of the semester.

"I missed Walter here. I told you that." I reached over and stroked his bare foot while speaking.

"Is there a problem at school? Something I should know about?" she prodded.

I turned my head and rolled my eyes, so that Elizabeth couldn't see me. When I turned back to face her, she was watching me intently.

"Seriously, Lizzie, can you please stop grilling me? Nothing is wrong at school. It's the weekend. I just wanted to come home. Now, can we move past this topic?" I didn't smile. I didn't even hint at a joking tone.

"Whatever," Elizabeth told me, as she looked down at Walter in her lap.

"You know, I came here to see my son, and now I've seen him. I really do have a lot of studying to do this weekend." I stood up. "I'll try to make it back next weekend."

I guessed that my conversation with Elizabeth would have to wait for another time. I no longer wanted to hang around and talk.

As I walked out the front door, grabbing my car keys from the hook just to the left of the door, I didn't dare turn to look at Elizabeth. I was sure that she was staring daggers into my back. My car was parked in the street in front of the house. I must have left it for her to use. No, not anymore.

Just as I climbed into my car, I heard her scream my name from inside the house, causing me to cringe. I didn't hesitate though. I started up my car and hit the gas hard.

CHAPTER 6

Pulling into the parking lot, I was never so relieved to be back at college. The first thing I did upon arriving at school was to walk around campus, looking for Olive. I needed someone to talk to. Someone who would understand what I was going through.

I found her sitting alone at one of the many benches on campus.

"Hey there. What are you reading?" I asked, sitting down next to her.

She looked up at me and smiled, lifting up her book so that I could see the title. I smiled in response.

"The Time Machine? Interesting reading," I told her.

"Yeah, I thought it was appropriate. Considering our circumstances and all," she replied, laying the closed book on the bench between us.

"So, do you think we are actually time traveling?" I asked her. "We aren't staying in the same body and jumping through a portal somewhere, and landing in a different time. Isn't that pretty much what time travel is?"

"Well, no. It isn't happening like that. But if it isn't time travel, then what is it?" Olive asked me.

"I really don't know what to call it," I responded honestly. "Since we are actually dying, and then just coming back at a different point in our lives, and reliving it all over again, then it doesn't sound like actual time travel. Not in the way we know it anyhow. Does that make sense?"

"Yeah, I guess." She shrugged.

Olive and I spent the next hour and a half chatting on that bench. I couldn't remember ever enjoying someone's company as much. It was a great feeling to have someone else around that knew what I was feeling and going through. In fact, she had much more experience with it than I did. I was sure that I could learn a few things from her.

While the two of us were sitting there, deep in conversation about having the same relationships over and over again, the pretty girl in the pink sweater walked by. This time, she wasn't wearing a pink sweater though. It was a warm day, and she had on no sweater at all. But I recognized her from my first time coming back to life, and she was the nice girl in the library in this life.

Suddenly, I couldn't breathe. I gasped several times, while my hand flew to my chest.

"Sam? Sam! What's wrong?" Olive's eyes grew wide.

I couldn't answer her. The breath wouldn't come. And my heart was beating so fast that I thought it might explode right out of my chest. When my arms started flailing in an effort to explain to her that I thought I was having a heart attack, Olive jumped up off the bench.

"Your face is turning red! Oh my god, Sam! Someone help us! Someone call the nurse!" she began screaming to anyone who would listen.

Several students gathered around us to see what all the

commotion was about. In my moment of severe distress, I heard someone say that they would go get the nurse.

Then, just as quickly as it had begun, it stopped. Just like that. I could breathe normally. My heart rate returned to normal. I just needed a moment to collect myself, and everything was fine.

"I'm okay," I told Olive.

"What happened?" She put her arm around my shoulders as she spoke.

I knew exactly what had happened. It was that blonde girl, the one that I called 'the girl in the pink sweater.' The moment she walked past us, was the moment that I was overcome. It was as if I didn't kill her right then and there, then I would die myself. And I felt like I almost did. It was the most intense feeling I had ever had.

"Are you all right?" It was another student that I didn't recognize.

Suddenly, I felt like I was in a fishbowl. At least a dozen students were all standing in front of me, staring. It was the oddest feeling.

I leaned over and whispered in Olive's ear. "Would you mind getting rid of all the people?" My eyes traveled from her, back up to the crowd.

She also looked up at the crowd. "Oh, of course."

Olive stood up and gestured for everyone to disperse. "Please, everyone, he is fine now. Nothing to see here. Time to go."

A couple of the boys hung around, kind of gawking. I was still trying to get my bearings. I still was just a bit short of breath.

"I said to go! Now! Do I need to kick your asses myself?" Olive threatened.

I smiled. She certainly wasn't the shy type. Maybe reliving your life several times did that to a person.

"Everybody stand back." The nurse had arrived and turned to me. "Young man, can you tell me what hurts?"

Though it had been several years since I had last seen her, on my first day back, last time, I recognized the nurse immediately. It was the same middle aged woman that had helped me when I found myself back in my previous life. She was still wearing that old starched, white nurse's uniform, and that old fashioned nurse's cap and white pumps. Obviously, they weren't old fashioned for the 1960s, but they certainly were in later years.

Within a minute, I felt my heart rate quickening and my breath came back in shallow gasps. I reached for Olive. Grabbing the sleeve of her dress, I pulled her down to me and looked her right in the eyes.

"Get her out of here. Please." My breath was labored and raspy.

"But the nurse is here to help you."

"Now! Please!" I tried to yell, but it didn't quite come out that way. It came out even more raspy and gurgling.

She threw up her hands. "Okay, okay." Turning to the nurse, "Ma'am, please. He's fine. We don't need you anymore. But thank you for coming."

"I need to make sure that he is all right. I can't just leave him if he is having a medical emergency," she argued.

"No, he's fine." Olive leaned in to the nurse. I heard what she said though. "He's had a little too much, if you know what I mean?"

Olive made some sort of drinking gesture, and it worked.

The nurse looked over at me and I wrapped my arms around my stomach, in an exaggerated sort of gesture, to get Olive's point across. "I'll be okay," I old her.

"Well, if you're sure." She turned to Olive. "Please bring him to my office if he isn't feeling better by morning."

Olive saluted her. "Will do."

The nurse huffed and stormed her way back up the sidewalk, toward the administration building. Olive turned back to me. She looked very worried.

"Are you sure you are okay?" she asked, stroking my shoulder in a soothing way. It was more sisterly than anything else.

The last few hangers on turned and left. I guess the excitement wasn't so exciting anymore. There was nothing I hated more than being the center of attention. Well…almost. I hated that I hurt people. I really hated that. But I hadn't figured out how to stop it. Not yet anyway. And I wasn't entirely sure that I ever would.

Thankfully, Olive didn't bring out the need in me to kill. I didn't understand why, but I was thankful nonetheless.

"Um yeah, I'll be fine. I think it might just be a panic attack. Maybe from having so many people around. I'm fine now." I wasn't sure that my attempt at an explanation would work or not, but I had to tell her something. Otherwise, she might think I was having a heart attack and insist that I go to the hospital for tests. Nobody has time for that.

"Really? You have panic attacks? I didn't know that about you."

The look of concern on her face was heartwarming. I wondered if maybe the reason that I didn't have the desire to hurt Olive was because she was someone that genuinely cared for me. That was an interesting thought and something that hadn't occurred to me before. We had only met very recently, but there was an instant connection between us. It was as if we had known each other forever.

Hell, maybe we had know each other forever. Who was to say that we hadn't each lived a hundred lifetimes. Maybe a thousand. Maybe we just didn't remember them. I know that we didn't remember our lives until the moment we jumped back in to them, right after dying.

CHAPTER 7

That very night, I couldn't sleep much. There were so many things going on in my life, that they just whirled around in my brain, refusing to give in and let me get a good night's sleep.

After a few hours of just lying there, listening to my roommate, Henry, snoring, I gave up and left the dorm room. I needed to go for a walk, get some fresh air, and clear my head. That should do the trick.

Almost immediately upon exiting my dorm building, I heard laughter drifting up into the sky above me. It was definitely from a group of girls. The giggles and high voices seemed to come out of nowhere. I looked around and couldn't see a single person anywhere near me.

I continued walking. Without even realizing it at first, my legs carried me in the direction of the voices and laughing. After only a couple of minutes, I rounded a corner of one of the student housing buildings and there they were. I couldn't see their faces, but could make out three girls, all smoking and laughing. I stopped, backed up, and peered at them around the corner of the building. They hadn't noticed me.

My gut started to ache.

About five minutes later, the girls began to disperse.

"I'll be inside in a minute. As soon as I finish this smoke," I heard one of the girls say.

"Okay, see you then," one of the other girls responded, as the dorm building door closed behind her.

I stayed there for another few seconds, before I made my move. I would have to act fast, before the girl finished smoking and went back inside. I promptly turned around and made my way around the side and then to the back of her building. I didn't want her to see me coming.

My breath quickened.

Just as she was stepping on her cigarette butt to put it out, I pounced. Though it was the middle of the night, we were still in a public place. Students tended to wander the campus at all hours.

I stepped up quietly behind her, clamped my hand over her mouth, and wrapped my other arm around her waist, pinning her arms to her side, and pulling her into me. She began to struggle immediately, but she was no match for my strength.

I dragged her behind the building, where there was just a small alleyway, for parking and dumpsters. The only lighting was a single yellow lamppost. It was just enough to help me see where I was going, but not enough for anyone at a distance to make out who we were.

"Don't make any noise, and I won't hurt you," I ordered. "I'm going to pull my hand away from your mouth now. Okay?"

It was a lie, and I knew it. She probably knew it too. I'll bet she thought she was going to get raped that night. She wasn't. That was not something I had ever done, nor will ever do.

She didn't have much range of motion, with me still holding her tightly, but she managed to give me a slight nod.

The second I pulled my hand from her mouth, she let out a blood curdling scream.

"Damnit!" I slammed my hand back over her face. "You stupid bitch. Now I have to do this fast."

I heard her whimper.

There was no longer any time for strangulation. That took way too long, and the chance of us getting caught was now very real.

I reached up with the hand not clamped over her mouth and grabbed the top of her head, at her forehead. One quick motion and I heard the familiar sound of her neck snapping. She hadn't even had the chance to struggle. Her body slumped. The moment that she hit the ground, the ache in my gut subsided. Funny how that worked.

I didn't need to check her for a pulse. I knew she was dead. I glanced down at her lifeless body, her face planted in the soil, next to a rusty dumpster. A single, tan sandal, laid on its side next to her barefoot.

I took off running and got to my dorm building in seconds. I never even looked back. I was still breathing hard from my sprint, when I quietly let myself back into our dorm room.

"Where the hell have you been? It's the middle of the night."

I jumped when Henry began speaking, completely not expecting him to be stirring at all.

"I...uh...I couldn't sleep. Just went for a quick walk. Go back to sleep," I told him.

"Yeah, okay." I couldn't see him in the dark room, but I heard him turn over in his bed. Within seconds his snoring resumed.

Lying in my own bed, I suddenly felt dirty. Remorse

spread over me and I thought I might break down. My eyes filled to almost overflowing and I wiped the dampness away with the bedsheet.

It didn't happen every single time, but quite often I felt this way after killing someone. Killing wasn't something that I wanted to do. In fact, it was an almost unconscious act. Almost. Unfortunately, I can't claim that it all happened while I was sleepwalking or something. No, I can't do that. I was always aware of what was going on. But, I was mostly powerless to stop it.

Thankfully, I drifted off in short order.

I was startled out of grogginess a little after dawn, to the sound of an approaching siren. I wondered if that was because of me. Of course it was. What else could it be?

I looked over at Henry's bed and found it empty. That was odd. I thought about getting up and going outside to see what all the commotion was about. Or to actually confirm my suspicions, but thought better of it. I had seen enough true crime TV shows over the years to know that the killer often went back and stood in the crowd, watching the investigation. I wouldn't be stupid enough to be that person.

I did get up though, about a half hour later, and began getting dressed anyway. I was hungry. A trip to the cafeteria wouldn't seem suspicious at all.

Looking up at Henry when he entered the dorm room, just as I was tying my shoes, his face was red and swollen from crying. That was not something I expected.

"What's going on down there?" I asked him. "I heard a siren."

"It's…it's…Polly. She's been…murdered," he managed to stutter out, between sobs.

My eyes grew wide, and I turned away from him. I didn't want Henry to see the look on my face. When I turned back, he was sitting on his bed, facing me.

I kicked my acting into full gear. "Polly? Someone murdered her? What happened?"

"I...don't know exactly. The cops wouldn't tell me anything," he told me.

"Why were you down there so early? Did you hear the sirens?" I asked him.

"No. Polly and I were set to go running at dawn. It's something she's been doing for a while, I guess. Yesterday, she invited me to go with her this morning. When I got to her dorm, she wasn't there. Her roommate said she never went in after they left her outside late last night. I guess they fell asleep and didn't realize she wasn't there until I knocked on the door," Henry told me.

"Who found her?" I asked, fearing the answer.

"I did. She was right behind their building, next to the trash. Oh my god, Sam, it was horrible." He dropped his face into his hands. I could see his body shuddering, even though I heard no sound coming from him. "I could see right away that she was dead. She was so pale. I ran for the administration building. It wasn't open, but the janitor let me in to call the ambulance."

"I'm so sorry that happened," I told him truthfully.

"You know, we hadn't been dating long, but I think I was starting to fall for her." The tears fell then.

I felt horrible. How could I not? I had just killed my best friend's girlfriend. If I had known at the time, I would have done anything...and everything...that I could to not do it. Unfortunately, it was too late now. What was done, was done. I vowed right then and there that if I got a chance at a new life, somewhere down the road, I would stay as far away from Polly as I could possibly get. I would never do that to her, or to Henry, ever again.

"Hey," I said to Henry, "why don't you come with me to the cafeteria? Maybe getting some food in you will help you

MICHELLE FILES

feel better. Maybe a little better, at least." I stood up from my bed.

"I don't know. I don't think I can eat right now," Henry said to me softly.

"Yeah, I understand. Well, I'm going to go get some breakfast. Maybe I'll see you down there?"

"Okay," Henry replied. "Let me get my wits about me and I'll be there in a few."

I nodded and headed out.

CHAPTER 8

That morning turned out to be dark and dreary. No actual rain just yet, more of a drizzle. Just enough to put a coating of dampness on my red hair. I'm sure I looked a sight by the time I reached the cafeteria. I ran my fingers through my hair in an effort to put it back into some semblance of order.

"Hey, Red. You're out early."

I turned to see Olive standing behind me in line.

"Red? Is that my new nickname?" I asked her with a smile.

She gave me a one shoulder shrug. "It suits you."

"Isn't every single person on this planet who has red hair called 'Red'? I think it might be a requirement at birth," I told her jokingly.

"Probably." She pulled a tray off of the stack and set it down on the counter in front of her. "But I like it."

And that was that. I don't think she ever called me anything else for the rest of the time we knew each other. I thought about it for a second and realized that no one had ever called me that before. I kind of liked it.

Olive and I sat down for breakfast together.

"Did you hear about the girl that got killed last night?

Right here on campus?" Olive asked me, taking a big bite out of a buttered biscuit. Her face was about as serious as I had ever seen it.

"Yeah," I nodded. "She was dating my roommate, Henry."

Her face blanched. "What? Really? Is he okay? Did you know her?"

I put my palms up toward her. "Whoa, that's a lot of questions. No, he's not really okay. But he will be." I knew he would be all right eventually. "And no, I didn't know her. They hadn't been dating long."

"That is just so crazy. I remember there being a killer on campus the last time I was a student here." She leaned forward and whispered, "You know, in a previous life."

I nodded. "Yeah, I got that."

The last time I was a student at the college, I didn't kill anyone, though I wanted to. I was only at the campus for a day before I quit and went back home to Red Lake. However, I did kill a few young women at the school my first go 'round in life.

Once the deed was done, I usually forgot about it and moved on. I rarely knew the identity of the woman, and most of the time I never even saw her face. That was because the killings took place late at night, in a dark, quiet area. The darkness was great cover, and it made it easier for me to kill someone. If I couldn't see her face, then it was just some anonymous person that didn't matter to me. I didn't know her. I didn't want to know who she was. I didn't care.

Until it was all over, that is. Once the woman was dead, that's when remorse set in.

I think I was a unique serial killer in that way. Reading quite a bit on the subject, and watching crime shows on TV, I learned quite a bit. Serial killers didn't usually feel guilty for what they did. They just did it. And many liked to take trophies from their kills. In addition, most of them knew exactly who their victims were, and where the bodies were buried.

I never buried the bodies. It was too much trouble. Though I had to admit that I probably should have. Thankfully, I had never been caught.

Sitting there in the cafeteria with Olive, I realized that I had killed Polly at least once before. Once that I could remember anyway. It was during my first lifetime. And it was at this school, under very similar circumstances. I didn't remember her exactly, but I remember killing someone outside of those dorms, in the dark alley. I strangled her that time, after she begged for her life. I wondered if she was destined to die by my hands again, in a later life. No, I wouldn't let that happen. I couldn't let that happen.

None of that mattered right now though. Polly was dead and there was absolutely nothing that I could do to change that.

"I'll bet that if we put our heads together that we could figure out who the killer is. I mean, between us, we have several lifetimes of memories to access. What do you think?" Olive looked at me with hopefulness in her face.

"I have to go." I jumped up and ran out of the cafeteria before Olive could say anything to stop me.

I found Henry sitting at one of the tables in the courtyard. The day was still dreary, but the drizzle had stopped, for the time being anyway. From his seat at the table he had a perfect view into the cafeteria. He must have seen Olive and me having breakfast together.

"What are you doing out here?" I asked my friend, wiping the dampness off of a chair with my bare hand before sitting down across from him.

"I don't know. I just didn't feel like eating," he responded. "Besides, you looked like you were otherwise occupied."

I scrunched up my face. "What do you mean?"

"The girl you were with. Isn't that the crazy one who has been accosting people and trying to tell them their futures?" Henry asked me. "Why were you having breakfast with her? Have you lost your mind? She's nuts."

He sounded confrontational when speaking about Olive. Due to the recent circumstances, I let that go.

"We've become friends. She's really nice. And she's not nuts." I tried to speak in a friendly tone, not wanting it to escalate into an argument about Olive.

"Whatever. I don't care. Do what you want," Henry responded.

"Hey, I know a terrible thing has happened, but are you all right? You seem angry with me and I don't know why," I told him.

He paused for what seemed an eternity before responding. "I'll be fine. I really liked Polly, but it wasn't like we were married or anything. It's just really raw right now." He looked down at his feet as he spoke. "But something struck me just a little while ago, when I was still in my room going over the events of last night."

"Really? What's that?" I asked. I had no idea where he was going.

He looked up at me with a hard glare. "You were out wandering around campus in the middle of the night. That's when Polly was killed. Don't you think that's quite the coincidence?"

He didn't actually accuse me, but I could hear the accusatory tone in his voice. It rang loud and clear.

I took a deep breath, while trying to come up with a viable response. "I didn't see anything. In fact, I hardly saw anyone. The campus was pretty sparse last night. Besides, we don't even know what time she was out. Or what time she was killed."

"The coroner said that it was at about 2:30 a.m., which is right after her roommates said that they went inside and left her outside alone. Isn't that about the same time you went out?" Henry was staring at me, as he spoke.

"How do you know what time I left our room?" I asked him. "You were sound asleep."

"Actually, I wasn't," he responded. "I heard the door close and glanced over at the clock. It was 2:18 am. Exactly. I don't know why I remember that, but I do. That's too much to be a coincidence."

"No, it's not. I frequently walk around at night, when I can't sleep. Last night was no exception," I offered as an explanation. "It just happened to be around the same time. So what? That doesn't mean anything."

"Doesn't it though?" Henry asked. "In fact, we've had a couple other girls killed around here lately. And you just admitted that you frequently go out in the middle of the night."

I threw my hands up in front of me. "Whoa, what are you saying? You can't possibly think that I had anything to do with Polly's death. Or of those other girls." God, I really hoped I wasn't sounding too defensive.

"Well, did you?" he asked me point blank.

"You know, I've had enough of this attack on me for one day. You're very emotional right now, understandably, and I'm leaving until you calm down and can think rationally."

"No. Sam, I'm sorry," Henry called after me as I walked away. I didn't stop.

CHAPTER 9

Henry and I avoided each other all that week. The moment classes were over on Friday, Olive and I jumped into my car and drove straight to Red Lake.

"Hi Mom." I greeted my mother with a hug. "I brought a friend home with me. I hope that's all right."

My mother released me and looked over at Olive, standing behind me. She gave Olive the once over from head to sandals.

"Mom, this is Olive."

My mother was a hugger, and this time was no exception. She pulled Olive into an embrace. By the look on Olive's face, I could see that she was surprised by the maneuver. It made me smile.

"It's so nice to meet you, Olive. You two must be hungry after your long trip. Come on in. I'll re-heat the lasagna your father and I had for dinner."

She didn't wait for an answer and walked to the kitchen. We followed. The two of us sat down at the kitchen table while my mother went about heating up the dinner. She loved taking care of people.

"Are Elizabeth and Walter coming over for dinner also?" my mother asked.

For anyone who didn't know my mother, that innocent sounding question would come across as her making sure that Olive knew I had a wife and son. But that wasn't my mother. She genuinely believed that Olive and I were just friends, and really wanted to know if Elizabeth and her grandson would be eating with us too.

I could see in Olive's face that she thought my mother might be trying to protect me from Olive's wiles.

"I haven't called her yet, Mom. I'll call her in a few minutes. I would like to see her and the baby," I replied.

That answer satisfied my mother.

Microwave ovens technically existed in 1963, but were still very new, and my mother was an old fashioned cook. She did everything by scratch. So, we waited while the oven heated up and then the lasagna heated. It took a while. So we talked.

"Where's Dad?" I asked my mother.

"Oh, he went to see an old friend. Someone he used to work with. He'll be back in a bit," she explained. "If he had known you were coming, I'm sure he would have stayed home. Should I call him?"

"No, Mom, that's fine. We'll be here all weekend. I'll see him when he gets home."

"Okay, if you say so. So...Olive," my mother began, "your parents aren't expecting you home this weekend?"

"No. They are off visiting with some relatives. I'll see them next time." I knew that wasn't the truth. Olive didn't want my mother to know that her parents wanted to have her committed.

"I see," my mother responded.

"I really hope I'm not intruding here," Olive added. "I can go stay at a motel..."

"Don't be silly, dear. There is plenty of room here. You can have Sam's room and he can sleep on the sofa." My mother looked at me when she said that. It was a defiant sort of look, that told me there had better be no shenanigans in the middle of the night.

"That's fine, Mom. Thanks."

∿

Right about the time the dishes were done being cleaned from dinner, in walked Elizabeth, carrying Walter. Her eyes immediately landed on Olive. Shock, and possibly a bit of hatred, showed through.

I jumped up and walked over, taking Walter from her arms.

"Elizabeth, this is Olive. She's a friend from school."

"Hi." Olive stuck out her hand and smiled. "It's nice to meet you."

Elizabeth just stood there and glared at her.

"Elizabeth, we are just friends. That's all. I swear. She had nowhere to go this weekend." I did my best to diffuse the situation before it got out of hand.

"Sam," Elizabeth turned toward me. "I'd like to talk to you. Outside." She tilted her head toward the front door.

"Yeah, okay." Let me get my mom to watch the baby. "Mom!"

"Of course I'll take him." My mother had appeared out of nowhere.

As I followed Elizabeth out onto the front porch, I turned to Olive and gave her a look that I hoped would convey how sorry I was. She nodded.

The moment that the front door closed behind me, Elizabeth spun around and got in my face.

"What the hell is going on here? Are you two sleeping together?!"

"What? No. It's nothing like that." I backed up a bit. She was invading my personal space big time. "We just met a few days ago. She's having family issues and had nowhere to go this weekend. I thought it would be nice to show her Red Lake. I thought you two might hit it off," I explained.

"Hit it off? Are you kidding me? I'm not hanging out with some girl when I have no idea what is going on between the two of you!" she almost screamed.

I lowered my voice down to a whisper, in an attempt to calm the situation. "Lizzie, I told you nothing is going on. Do you think that if there was something going on between us, that I would be stupid enough to bring her here?"

"Yes. I think you would be exactly that stupid," she answered, crossing her arms defiantly in front of her chest.

I stood back and stared at her in shock. I couldn't even come up with the words to respond to that.

"What? You have nothing to say to me now? Can't think of another lie?" she goaded.

"No, I can't think of any lies," I answered. "And you know what? That's it, I'm done. We are done. I want a divorce." Whew, I couldn't believe those words came out of my mouth so easily.

Her mouth dropped open. That was obviously not something she ever expected to hear from me.

"Sam, no." Her tone changed instantly from anger to pleading. "That's not what I want." She reached for my arm and I jerked it back away from her.

"Well, you clearly don't trust me. We should never have gotten married. We are way too young. I'll contact a lawyer on Monday." There was no way I was giving in then. I had managed to get the words out and I wanted them to stay that way.

I walked past her, into the house, and straight to my mother and son. Kissing Walter on the forehead, I told him I loved him. I hugged my mother and told her I loved her too. Then I took Olive's hand and walked out the front door. I didn't give a damn what Elizabeth thought of that.

The moment we got into the car, a wave of relief washed over me. I was free. Or at least I would be soon enough. I wouldn't be tied down to Elizabeth for the next sixty years, and that was a great feeling.

CHAPTER 10

Three years passed before I saw Elizabeth again. I did see my son as often as possible, thanks to my mother. She was a great go-between for Elizabeth and me.

Our divorce wasn't exactly cordial, but I wouldn't call it ugly either. We didn't own anything together, so the dividing of assets was not a problem. The only issue we really had was Walter. I wanted joint custody, and Elizabeth wanted full custody. I ended up relenting on the full custody portion, until I was out of school anyway, as long as she let me visit with Walter whenever I was in town. She agreed.

By the time I was in my senior year in college, my life had stayed on a pretty even course. I was going to graduate soon. I would like to say that it was with honors, but I can't say that. Truth is that I barely squeaked by. That was fine by me.

Olive and I remained friends. Only friends. Best friends actually. We had decided years ago not to tell anyone about our life and death experiences, mainly to keep us safe from those who would not understand. We did keep our eyes out for anyone else that seemed to also be reliving their lives. We never did come across anyone else.

Though I was sure that it had to be happening to someone, somewhere out there. What was the chance that Olive and I were the only two human beings on the planet who were reliving our lives? And we happened to be going to the same college, at the same time?

Neither of us thought that was very probable. We just didn't know where to look for others. So, we continued on with our lives.

I decided a while back not to seek out Ruby this time. I knew she wasn't the one I wanted, though I wasn't sure at all who that actually was. I dated some, but not that much.

In the three years since that fateful day when I announced my divorce intention to Elizabeth, I had killed only two people. As hard as it was, I had managed to keep my impulses intact. Mostly.

After my fight that day with Henry, about Polly, Henry moved out of our dorm room. He didn't hate me, I think, but he probably still had suspicions that I was responsible for Polly's death. I was responsible, but he didn't know that for sure. We saw each other around campus here and there, and we were cordial, but we were never friends again. If I got another chance, in another lifetime, I would try harder with Henry. That chance had already passed this time.

One Saturday morning, Olive and I were just hanging around at my parents' home in Red Lake, waiting until Elizabeth was scheduled to drop off Walter that afternoon.

"Hey, let's go to the mall," I suggested. "It'll kill some time while we wait. I need some new shoes anyway."

I propped my feet up on the coffee table so that Olive could get a good look at my worn shoes.

"Get your feet off my table," my mother ordered as she walked through the living room. Her timing was impeccable.

I grimaced. "Sorry, Mom."

Olive giggled in response. "Yeah, let's go. Nothing to do here anyway."

Twenty minutes into our shopping trip, we were heading toward the shoe store, when we ran into Elizabeth. She was holding three year old Walter's hand.

"Daddy!" Walter broke free from Elizabeth's hold on him and ran into my arms.

I hugged him tightly, grateful every single day for his existence. My own existence wouldn't be worth it to me, without him.

When Elizabeth walked up to us, she stood with her stare set on Olive. I knew that she thought all along that Olive and I were an item. But that didn't matter to me. Elizabeth's opinion of my life was none of my concern any longer.

Walter turned toward his mother. "Mommy, can we go shopping with Daddy and Olive?" He turned to smile at Olive as he spoke.

Elizabeth broke her gaze from Olive, long enough to speak to our son. "No. They have their own shopping to do, and we have ours. I'll drop you off at Grandma's house in a little while, so you can visit then. Okay buddy?" She reached over and rubbed his back as she spoke. I still held him in my arms.

Walter scowled at Elizabeth and I laughed. No one else did.

"Would you mind if we just took him with us now?" Olive asked. "It will save you the trip later."

Elizabeth turned back toward Olive. "You are not taking my son anywhere. Not now. Not ever."

"I just thought we'd save you the trip. Sorry." Olive threw her hands up in the air as she spoke.

"You aren't sorry. You have been trying your best to get in the middle of my marriage from the beginning. We don't need your help. We don't need you involved." The air was almost palpable with the hatred that dripped from Elizabeth's words.

"What marriage?" Olive replied. "You two haven't been married for years. Besides, I'm not trying to get in the middle of anything. Sam and I are friends and that's it. I don't know why you refuse to believe that."

I set Walter down and tried to interject before the conversation got too heated.

"Ladies, ladies, no need to fight over me." I tried humor. It didn't work.

Both women stared daggers into me.

Olive ignored my comment and continued. "You know what? It doesn't matter at all what you think of me, or of our friendship. Believe what you want. Sam has the right to be friends with, or date, anyone he wants. It's none of your business at all."

"Oh yes it is my business. Anyone who is going to be around my son, is my business. And I don't care if you like it or not," Elizabeth spat out.

"Come on, Walter, let's go. I don't need to deal with this." Elizabeth looked around us. "Walter?" She looked up at me. "Where's Walter?"

I looked around the area where we were standing. "I don't know. He was just here."

"Walter!" Elizabeth yelled. No response.

I looked up at the stores around us and my blood froze when my eyes landed on the store sign. The toy store sign. The very store that Walter had disappeared from all those years ago. Never to be seen again.

"Let's split up and look for him."

I took off for the toy store, praying with all my heart that he had just seen the sign and gone in to play with the toys. I didn't wait to see if the women had listened to me and split up. I didn't care either. If the two of them wanted to stand there and fight, so be it. I was going to get my son.

I searched the entire toy store in about two minutes, checking every single aisle and asking the clerk if she had seen him. Negative on both counts.

"Walter!" I yelled at the top of my lungs. I knew I sounded frantic. It didn't matter. I was frantic.

I gave explicit instructions to the toy store clerk to hang on to Walter, if he turned up. I would be back to check in a few minutes.

Back out in the mall, I ran up and down the walkway, checking every single store. That's when I saw something that made my heart almost stop.

Walter. There he was, at the candy store at one of the mall intersections. He was standing in front of a display of large, multi-colored lollipops. My knees almost gave out under me as I stood there trying to collect myself before I walked into the store and retrieved my son. I sat down on a nearby bench for just a minute, watching my son. Once my emotions were collected, and the moment passed, I walked into the store and took Walter by the hand. As we were walking out of the candy store, I turned the corner, and we ran into Elizabeth.

"Oh my god, Walter! I was so worried." She knelt down and hugged him tightly, looking up at me with hatred, as she did so.

She stood back up, holding onto Walter's hand for dear life. "Where were you taking my son?"

My face tightened. "What do you mean? I was bringing him back to you. Where else would I be taking him?"

"Then why were you heading that way?" She pointed and I turned to follow her finger. She was pointing right at a nearby door that led to the parking lot.

"Oh, I must have been turned around. I wasn't leaving

with him. I can't believe you thought I would," I explained. "I wouldn't do that."

"I don't believe you. I'm finding security," Elizabeth announced, turning to walk away with Walter.

My eyes grew wide. "Lizzie, what are you doing?" I followed right behind them.

Ten minutes later, she had found security and they had called the sheriff. Olive had found us by then and I filled her in on what was happening.

"Sir, what were you doing with this boy?" the sheriff asked me.

"He's my son. He had taken off. Then I found him in the candy store. We were looking for his mother when she found us," I tried to explain.

"His mother told me that you were trying to leave with him."

"No, I wasn't." What else could I say?

"You weren't heading toward the mall exit when his mother stopped you?" the sheriff asked.

"Well…yes, I was. But it was on accident. I was actually trying to find Elizabeth. Like I told you I was." It wasn't going well. Olive stood by my side, silently.

"And who are you, young lady?" he addressed Olive.

Her eyebrows shot up. "Me? I'm just a friend."

"And were you involved in the attempted kidnapping of Walter Wells?" he asked her.

She shook her head. "Look, Sheriff, Sam didn't try to kidnap his son. We were all looking for him."

He looked her up and down before speaking. "I see." Turning back to me, he continued. "Do you have custody of the boy?"

"No. His mother does. But I have visitation rights. We are changing that as soon as I graduate from college," I tried to explain.

"So let me see if I've got this straight. Your ex-wife has full custody of the boy. She and your girlfriend here," he glanced over at Olive, "were having a heated disagreement in the middle of the mall, when your son went missing. Does that sound about right?"

I nodded.

"Then you all split up to look for him. You happen to be the one who finds him and then are spotted heading for the parking lot. Do I still have that right?" He stared at me, unblinking.

"Yeah, I guess. I might have been technically going toward the exit, but that wasn't where I meant to be going. I was turned around. I was trying to find Elizabeth." I knew how it all sounded. And it wasn't looking good for me.

"Your ex-wife has expressed her desire to press charges against you for kidnapping," he told me matter-of-factly.

My eyes widened. "She what?!"

"Sir, turn around." He motioned for his deputy to come over.

"Sheriff, you have this all wrong."

"Do what I say, and this will go a lot easier on you, son."

I did as I was told. The deputy handcuffed me and led me to their car, parked right in front of the mall entrance. Olive stood there motionless. And silently. I did hear her call to me just as the sheriff's car door closed behind me.

"I'll call your mother!" Olive shouted.

CHAPTER 11

I spent about a week in the Red Lake Jail.

My entire stay, I spent stewing about what Elizabeth had done. How could she? She had to know that I would never do what they were accusing me of.

And believe me when I say that the irony was not lost on me. I had gone to jail for something I really didn't do, when in actuality I was a serial killer.

That was hard for me to say. Just the thought that I was a serial killer sickened me. I didn't want to be lumped in with those disgusting people. Not now and not ever. Most serial killers, those that I was familiar with anyway, either hadn't killed yet, or hadn't been caught yet. I'm talking about those men who were active in the 1970s and 1980s. They were infamous. That was the last thing I ever wanted to be.

In fact, I desperately wanted it to stop. All of it. I didn't want to kill anyone. It hurt me down to the core every single time it happened. I just didn't know what to do about it.

"You're outta here, Wells." It was the sheriff with the key to my freedom.

"Why? What happened?" I asked.

"Son, just be thankful that it's all over, and just go home."

That's exactly what I did. My mother was waiting in the front lobby for me.

Olive had gone back to school the week before. I let her take my car. I figured that I could catch the bus, if the time ever came that I was let out. Maybe it was stupid, but the first thing I did upon release, and arriving at my parents' house, was to head straight for Elizabeth's house.

"How could you?" Those were the first words that left my mouth when Elizabeth answered her front door.

She attempted to slam it back in my face, but my hand shot out and stopped it.

"What are you doing? I don't want you here," she responded.

"Where is Walter?"

"He's at the lake with my parents. What do you want?"

"You know what I want. I want to know why you did what you did?" The anger in my voice was not disguised.

"I'm sorry," Elizabeth said to me, not sounding sorry at all. "But I didn't want Olive around my son and I was afraid that now that you are graduating, you would want to get custody of him."

"So you thought you would have me go to prison for the rest of my life for attempted kidnapping? That's a horrible thing to do." I was in shock, and I'm sure it showed on my face.

She looked down at her feet. "I'm sorry."

"The hell you are," I responded.

Then a furious anger took over me. And a punch in the gut. That familiar punch in the gut. I knew what that meant.

I knew that I had better get out of there, and quickly. If I didn't, then Elizabeth would be in serious trouble. As much as I hated her at that very moment, she was the mother of my child. No matter what, I wouldn't leave my son motherless.

"I did tell the sheriff that I was wrong. That's why he released you. I told him it was all a big misunderstanding," she admitted.

"You think that makes up for what you did? I spent eight days in that cell. And you didn't care. You just left me in there. I didn't get to see my son. You know that makes you a horrible person, right?" I looked over to the side as I was thinking. "You know, it would serve you right if I did fight you for custody. I could certainly use this whole incident against you. I might even win."

"Please don't do that," she begged. "I said that I'm sorry. It was stupid and impulsive. I swear that I will never do anything like that again. Please Sam, I'm the only mother that Walter has. He has lived with me his entire life. Do you really want to upset his life by ripping him away from his mother?"

"It's not like he doesn't know who I am," I replied. "And I would let you see him. Under supervision." I spoke through gritted teeth. I was still furious at her for what she had done. I didn't know if it was something I would ever be able to forgive her for.

I doubled over in pain when the next cramp hit me like a ton of bricks.

"Are you all right?" Elizabeth asked. I could see the worry on her face.

"Don't act like you care," I told her, barely able to keep myself from passing out from the pain.

"Look, I know you hate me right now. And I deserve it. But I don't want you hurting. Should I call someone? Your mother?" she offered.

"No, don't call anyone. I'll be fi…awwww!" I screamed out in pain, not finishing my sentence.

"Sam, come sit down. I'm calling your mother," Elizabeth announced.

"No you are not!"

Then it hit me and I couldn't stop myself. I reached up and wrapped my hands around Elizabeth's throat. It was wrong. It was something I really didn't want to do. Though my mind was screaming at me to stop, my hands had a life of their own.

Elizabeth's eyes widened as the reality of what was happening hit her. I could see that she was in shock. As I was. I had never had the desire to hurt her before. Not ever. No matter what, she had always been safe with me.

I tried to pull my hands away from her throat. It didn't work, they only squeezed tighter. Tears spilled over and down my face as I watched her face turn red, and the ability to struggle began to leave her body.

Just as her eyes were closing and her body began to go limp, I heard the front door open. Walter and his grandparents were having an animated conversation.

Finally, and involuntarily, my grip released from her throat. Elizabeth began gasping for air. I turned and intercepted the trio before anyone could see Elizabeth. Though she was breathing again, she slumped to the floor, and continued gasping from that spot. She put her arm out to keep from falling over.

"Hey everyone. Walter, how are you, my boy!" I scooped him up into a bear hug.

Elizabeth's parents were obviously surprised to see me there. Both walked past me without speaking to me.

"Elizabeth! Are you all right?" her mother ran over to her. "Your face is bright red."

Elizabeth looked up at me before responding. When my eyes narrowed at her, she got the point.

Elizabeth cleared her throat and spoke with a bit of

hoarseness. "Um…yes…I'm fine. I just swallowed something wrong. I'm okay."

I watched as Elizabeth covered her throat with her hand.

"You sure, honey? Let me go get you a glass of water." Her mother disappeared into the kitchen.

"What's going on in here?" Her father finally chimed in. "What are you doing here, Sam? And why are you out of…" He looked over at Walter and whispered, "Why are you out of, you know where?"

"I'm out because Elizabeth decided to do the right thing and tell the truth," I answered.

"Here, honey, drink this water." Elizabeth's mother handed her the glass and Elizabeth drank it down thirstily. We all stopped to watch.

"Um, do you mind taking Walter?" I asked her mother.

She walked over and took him from my arms. "He needs a nap anyway. Come on, sweetheart."

Once they were out of earshot, I continued my conversation with her father.

"I hope you know that I never tried to kidnap Walter. I wouldn't do that. Just ask your daughter."

I looked at her father's face for some sort of reaction.

We both turned to Elizabeth. She looked away. I could see the shame written all over her face. She couldn't look either one of us in the eyes. Her chin began trembling.

"Elizabeth, is this true?" her father asked her.

"I'm sorry, Daddy." She looked my way, but spoke to him. "I know it was wrong."

It wasn't lost on me that she wasn't apologizing to me. She was apologizing to him. She was caught not being the upstanding citizen her parents had raised her to be. That was something she was sorry for. Not for what she had done to me.

Thankfully, the desire to strangle her had been abated.

For the time being anyway. I felt like I should probably stay away from my ex-wife, for the foreseeable future at least. And if I did see her again, I should never be alone with her. That was something I was sure of. Next time it might not turn out so favorably for Elizabeth.

CHAPTER 12

Graduation day had finally come. It also turned out to be one of the hottest days of the year. At well above 100 degrees, we were all sweltering in our dark graduation gowns.

I didn't see Elizabeth after that fateful day when I almost strangled her to death. I have to say that I can't blame her for avoiding me.

Olive and I remained best friends. Somehow I knew that if it hadn't been for her friendship, I would never have survived college...and my tumultuous relationship with the mother of my child.

Olive had been dating a young man from school. I didn't care much for him. I found him controlling and jealous. He didn't like the fact that she and I were friends. I told her once how I felt about him, and she matter of factly told me that it was none of my business. So, I stayed out of it.

His name was James. While we stood in line to walk across the stage, Olive brought up the fact that James was not there. We both looked around, but couldn't find him.

"That's weird, don't you think?" she asked me.

"Yeah, I do. Who goes through four years of college and then doesn't want to go to their own graduation?" I asked her. "You know, I wouldn't worry. He's probably somewhere around here. Or maybe he's just running late. He'll probably show." I pulled at the collar of my gown. The sweat was dripping down my neck, and into the collared shirt I wore underneath. It was quite uncomfortable.

We moved forward as the line progressed toward the stage.

"It really doesn't matter anyway. We had a big fight this morning and broke up," she admitted. "I just wanted to make sure he was all right."

"You broke up with him? Or the other way around?" I asked.

"I broke up with James. I was just sick of him always wanting to know where I was and who I was with," Olive told me. "I need to find someone more even tempered, and trusting. You know," she looked my way and smiled, "someone like you."

She smiled when my eyes widened.

Then she patted me on the shoulder. "Relax. I'm not interested in you like that. I just mean that you are a nice guy. When you have a girlfriend, she is important to you, but you don't make her your whole life. You each have your own lives to lead. That's what I want."

I tried not to look too relieved. I loved Olive, but just as friends. It would never be more than that.

We continued moving in line and both of us were almost to the steps leading up to the stage. I thought the sun beating down on us was going to make me pass out. It was all I could do not to rip off the gown and throw it as far as I could. Whose stupid idea was it to have an outdoor graduation in June? I couldn't think of a single reason why it couldn't have been held in the cafeteria or gym. Anywhere with air conditioning.

I put that thought out of my mind. Too late now. Soon we would be walking across the stage, and would be graduates. Finally.

Olive was in front of me in line. Just as she took her first step up, a shot rang out. I instinctively turned toward the sound and I gasped.

It was Olive's boyfriend, James. I watched as he turned and ran, gun still in his hand. I spun back around to ask Olive if she had seen who it was, and realized she was lying on the ground in front of me, one foot still on that bottom step.

I knelt down to try and stop the bleeding coming from her chest, as chaos ensued around me.

Everyone was screaming. I did my best to tune them out. I could hear scrambling feet, and cries of terror. It seemed as if no one but me had noticed that there was only one gunshot and the perpetrator had already run from the scene.

Another graduate, a young woman that I did not know, sat down on the edge of the stage and began crying. She didn't even seem to notice Olive and me.

"Hey," I called. No response. "Hey you!" She looked up that time. "Go into the administration office and call an ambulance. And see if the nurse is inside. I have a gunshot victim here." She just sat there, staring at me as if she didn't comprehend a word I said. "Did you hear me?" I yelled louder over the cacophony going on around us.

She nodded, still saying nothing.

"Then go! Now!" I screamed.

That seemed to do the trick. She jumped off the stage and ran for the building. I didn't have the time to watch her progress. I just hoped that she was able to complete her task. She seemed to be in shock.

I flung off my graduation gown, tore off part of it, and used it to press on the wound, doing my best to stop the bleeding. It seemed to help a little, but not much. The bleeding continued.

"Olive. Don't you dare die on me. Do you hear me?" I said it calmly. She was unconscious and couldn't hear me. "Olive!"

I checked her pulse. I couldn't find one. The bleeding had slowed down considerably. Normally that would be a good thing. This time, I didn't think that was the case.

"Okay, what do we have?" It was the very same nurse that had met me during my first 'rebirth,' when I landed there at college, completely unaware of what was happening to me.

"Gunshot. She's bleeding from her chest. Can you do anything to help her?" My words came out frantic sounding.

The nurse got down on her knees and felt Olive's neck for a pulse. She then paused for a moment and checked her wrists. Then she bent down and put her ear in front of Olive's mouth.

"I'm sorry, but I'm afraid she's gone," the nurse said, straightening up and speaking directly to me.

"Nooo!" I screamed.

Bending back down to where she lay, I wrapped myself around my best friend and sobbed into her shoulder.

"Sir, we need to check on her." I felt a hand gently touch my shoulder.

Turning, I saw that the paramedics had shown up. I knew by then that there was no chance to save her, but I let her go anyway, and stood up, to give them room to work.

Within seconds, the same paramedic stood up and confirmed what the nurse had told me. Olive was gone.

I would never see my best friend again.

Or would I? I wondered if I would see her in my next life, and if I did, would she know me? It really didn't matter at that point though. It might be years before any of that happened. If ever.

Without any conscious effort on my part, I turned and ran. I had no idea where I was going, and I didn't care. I just wanted to run.

CHAPTER 13

Was this karma? For all the people I had killed during my three lives? For saving Walter before he was kidnapped? Did I bring on Olive's death?

It would serve me right.

I don't regret saving Walter's life. I would never regret that, no matter how many times I lived, and someone had to die.

I told the police what I saw that day of our college graduation. James was arrested shortly thereafter. His arrest did absolutely nothing to make me feel any better. I had no idea how I was going to navigate life without Olive. She had become my rock, in an otherwise twisted world. I needed her. There was absolutely no one else that I could turn to.

But, life had to go on.

When my life went from bad to unbearable, I wondered what in the hell I had done to cause whatever it was that was happening to me. I didn't want it. I didn't ask for it. Somehow it was all thrust upon me.

About a week after Olive's untimely death, I picked up Walter for the weekend. Elizabeth didn't like it, but she relented when I told her that this was about Walter, and not about me. Thankfully she had never told anyone that I tried to strangle her. Though I don't know why.

The day was dark and dreary, and it was pouring rain by the time I collected Walter. That was okay though. We could find plenty to keep us busy at home. I just wanted to spend some time with my boy. I didn't get to see him nearly as much as I would have liked.

"Where are we going, Daddy?!" Walter squealed as he ran outside and made a big leap into a huge rain puddle in the front lawn.

I cringed at the thought of him drenching the seats of my car. "You are getting soaking wet, Walter. Hurry up and get in the car."

Walter jumped into the front seat of my car, dripping everywhere. After a moment of thought, I realized that it didn't matter. I was just happy to have him with me.

"Put your seatbelt on. Okay partner?"

"Mommy doesn't make me wear my seatbelt. Why do I have to in your car?" he asked, as he connected the lap belt, like I had demonstrated.

"I don't know the answer to that, sorry."

Unfortunately, I did know the answer to that. It was the 1960s. People didn't wear seatbelts in those days. It would be another two decades before it was standard practice to wear a seatbelt. I had no idea how to explain that to a small child.

"Where are we going?" he asked me again.

"Let's go get some burgers, then we'll go to my house and play some games. Does that sound good to you?"

He threw his arms up into the air. "Yay!"

I guess it sounded good to him.

Pulling up to the Red Lake Cafe, I parked across the street. There were a couple other cars out front, but it looked pretty slow. That wasn't surprising, given the soggy weather.

Before I had the chance to climb out and go around the car to help Walter with his seatbelt, he had already unbuckled it and gotten out of the car, all on his own. When I saw that he was running around the front of the car, I quickly jumped out myself.

When I saw the pickup truck coming toward us, I dove to grab Walter.

I was too late.

Walter had already run into the street. The screeching pickup truck's brakes were indescribable. In the pouring rain, with the wet, slippery roads, he couldn't stop. I watched as my boy was catapulted what seemed like at least ten feet into the air. Even over the rain and the truck engine, I heard his little body hit the pavement with a thud.

I screamed without even realizing what I was doing. When I reached Walter, he had a massive head wound from his impact. There was nothing I could do. So, for the second time in about a week, I held someone I loved while they died.

The man in the pickup truck ran up to us and dropped to his knees when he saw what he had hit. I could tell by the look on his face, that he was devastated by what he was looking at. He began crying alongside me on that road, in the rain, in front of the cafe.

A few people came running out of the cafe. I saw that some were wearing uniforms and others who were probably customers.

I looked up at an especially friendly looking face, that looked pained at the scene in front of her. "Can someone please call an ambulance for my son?"

I said it calmly. There was no need for hysterics. No need for chaos. Walter was already gone.

She nodded at me and turned to go back into the cafe. I waited. No one spoke to me. It was as if they all respected my need to sit there in the rain in silence. Tears ran down my face, though I was sure no one could tell, as we were all soaked to the bone. Despite the weather, and the chill we for sure all felt, no one moved.

The ambulance arrived a few minutes later. I allowed them to collect the body of my son. I climbed into the ambulance with him. I would not leave him alone. As the ambulance headed down the road, I looked out the back window and saw the man who had hit Walter speaking with the police.

I didn't think that the man had been speeding, but was still probably driving too fast for the wet roads. I would later speak with the police and tell them what I had witnessed.

CHAPTER 14

The paramedics took my son into the hospital. They asked me to wait in the waiting room while the doctor took a look at him. A nice nurse escorted me to the chairs and waited while I sat down.

She was a large woman and her white nurse's uniform was pulled tightly against her frame. It was clearly a couple of sizes too small for her.

"Sir, will you be all right out here alone? Is there someone I can call for you?" she asked me.

"Huh?" I looked up at her, barely able to concentrate on what she was saying. I rubbed my eyes and pinched the bridge of my nose.

"Do you have a wife, or someone else, that I can call? What about the child's mother?" I wouldn't have blamed her for sounding impatient with me, but she didn't. She was calm and nice and comforting. "I'm happy to make a call."

"Oh! Of course. His mother…I completely forgot to call her."

She handed me a notepad and pencil. "Please write her

name and phone number down here. I'll let her know what happened."

I wrote down the information that she asked for and handed the items back. "Thank you. I really do appreciate it."

She nodded and disappeared into a door across the hall.

I sat there, unmoving, for what seemed like an eternity. Eventually I heard the outer hospital door open and looked up. When I saw the look on Elizabeth's face, I knew there was going to be a scene. But she was his mother. Who could blame her for being devastated? I knew that I was.

"Sam! What the hell happened? You killed my son!"

I stood up to speak with her.

Before I had a chance to answer, I felt the sting of a powerful slap across my left cheek.

"Ow, damnit!" I put my hand over my cheek. Glaring at her, I didn't say anything else about the slap. It wasn't the time.

"How could you let this happen? I trusted you with my son!" she yelled.

"Elizabeth." I looked around at the curious faces in the waiting room. "Can you keep your voice down?"

"I'm not going to keep my voice down. I want you to answer me!"

"Okay, okay. Please sit." I gestured to the chair next to mine and we both sat.

Taking her hand in mine, I was surprised that she allowed that. I spent the next five minutes explaining to her exactly what had happened, from the moment we parked in front of the Red Lake Cafe, to the moment we drove away in the ambulance. She sat silently as I spoke.

"He is…was…so young. How could you let him out of the car without you?" she asked. She was calm, but I could still see the hatred in her eyes, through the tears that were streaming down her face.

"I told you, I didn't let him out. He got out before I had the chance to stop him. You know how he can be," I tried to explain.

"I'll never forgive you for this. If I could kill you right now, I would."

I recalled almost those exact words from her in my last life, when Walter went missing at the mall. And I knew she meant every single word.

The night after my son's horrific accident, unable to sleep, I needed to go out and walk. It didn't matter that it was after midnight. I just needed to get out. I had no specific destination in mind, just anywhere away from my house, that didn't remind me of my son.

I had probably walked over an hour when I came upon a couple in a car, overlooking the lake. They were just sitting in the car, listening to the radio, and talking. The scene was very familiar. I had killed many people sitting at the lake late at night. Still…it didn't seem to deter everyone from continuing the practice.

I began shaking and felt faint. I thought I might pass out, so I sat down on a log that was probably thirty feet or so from the car. It was dark and I was in the shadows, therefore neither of the occupants noticed me. For the next few minutes, I caught my breath and collected my thoughts. I knew what was happening to me. I couldn't pretend that I didn't. It always seemed to happen right before I killed someone. This time it was going to be different. I would not let that happen. I didn't want to kill anyone. Especially not after what had happened to my baby boy. I just couldn't do that to someone else's child.

Before I had a chance to consider what was happening,

my legs seemed to spring to life, all on their own. I reached over, picked up a baseball sized rock and made a beeline for the driver's side door. I tried to stop myself. I couldn't. Yanking open the door, I registered the surprise on the young man's face as I grabbed the front of his shirt and pulled him from the car. The moment he hit the ground, I smashed the rock into his skull.

A scream came from the car. Dropping the rock, I walked around the front of the car to the passenger side. The girl had already started opening the door and took off in a sprint. Unfortunately, she never had a chance. I was much faster than she was and caught up with her in a mere three or four seconds.

Wrapping my left arm around her neck, I dragged her to the water's edge. She screamed the entire way. It didn't matter. There were no houses within hearing distance. She could scream all she wanted. Even so, it was annoying. Throwing her down, she landed on her back and I climbed on top of her, with my knees on each side of her hips. My fist slamming into her face stopped the screaming abruptly. With the little bit of moonlight that we had, I could see blood trickling from her cut lip.

"What are you doing? Please don't hurt me," she cried out.

It was rare for any of my victims to speak. I usually put them out of commission before they even realized what was happening to them.

"I don't want to hurt you," I told her honestly. "I have to."

I reached for her neck.

"No, you don't. Please. I have parents that love me. And I have a little brother. Please don't take me away from them." Her voice cracked as she spoke.

I hesitated. I truly didn't want to kill her. I just didn't think my body, or my mind, or whatever it was that drove me, would let me stop.

My body shook, and I reached for her again.

When an arm wrapped around my neck from behind, I was startled. I was yanked off of the girl. I thought that my neck would snap from the violent way he was wrenching my body.

The fact that the boyfriend was alive, and alert enough to pull me up, was shock enough. That was something that had never happened to me before, and I was temporarily caught off guard.

I struggled and managed to free myself from his grip. No matter what, I knew that I couldn't let him see my face. Rather than fight back, and risk fighting both of them, I ran.

It was the coward thing to do. I knew that. But I couldn't risk being recognized. I heard the boyfriend shout after me, but couldn't make out exactly what he said. I ran like my legs were on fire. I needed to put as much distance between them and me as I possibly could.

I didn't stop until I reached my parents' place. I had gotten away. This time at least. It had been a close one. A very close one. And it had left me terrified of being caught. I would never make the mistake of assuming someone was dead again.

The following weekend, Elizabeth held a memorial for Walter at her house. Surprisingly she invited me. I'm positive that others had a lot to do with that. Left up to Elizabeth, I have no doubt that I would never have been told.

After the service, I grabbed a bottle and a glass from the open bar and settled into a corner of the couch. I didn't want to speak to anyone, and it was pretty obvious that no one wanted to speak to me.

My parents, and a smattering of other relatives attended, but my parents felt unwelcome, causing them to leave early.

I don't want to admit it, but I drank too much. By the time everything was winding down, I was feeling quite woozy.

"Sam, why don't you stay a while?" I looked up through bleary eyes at Elizabeth standing in front of me.

"Huh?" I asked.

"Stay a while. Everyone is going home. You need some time away from all of these people. Here," she reached for my glass, "let me get you something to drink. Your bottle is empty."

I handed the empty bottle and glass to her. I was too drunk to comprehend that Elizabeth had just offered more booze to me. That wasn't like her. Maybe Elizabeth didn't hate me so much after all.

She returned a couple of minutes later with a beer.

I held it up. "What is this? It certainly doesn't look like whiskey to me," I mumbled out.

"It's beer. Just drink it."

I complied, not caring what I was drinking, as long as it kept me drunk. That's all I wanted on the day of my son's memorial service, to stay as drunk as possible.

"This tastes funny," I slurred after taking a long pull on the beer.

Elizabeth waved her hand in the air. "Oh, it's fine. You're just drunk."

"You got that right," I laughed. Though I knew there was nothing laughable going on that day.

Within just a few minutes my head began swimming. I figured that I had just reached my limit of alcohol. Well, gone way past my limit, if I'm being truthful.

"Lizzie, come sit here beside me." I grabbed her hand and pulled her down onto the couch next to me.

"You know, I should have married you," I told her.

"You did marry me. Then we divorced. Remember?"

"We did?" I searched my memories. "Oh yeah, we did. Why did we do that?"

"Sam, you're drunk. That is a conversation for another day," she told me.

"I'm really sorry that I killed them. I killed all of them. I shouldn't have done that," I told her.

Through my blurry eyes I saw Elizabeth scrunch up her face at me.

"Killed who? What are you talking about?" she asked me.

"Them. All those girls. I don't know their names...except Polly. I remember her name. She was Henry's girl. But I didn't know that until after I killed her. He hates me now."

"You killed Henry's girlfriend?" Though I could barely keep my eyes open by then, I registered the shock on Elizabeth's face.

"Yeah, I just said that. And all those others. I shouldn't have killed them. I didn't want to kill them. I couldn't help it."

"Oh my god, Sam. Are you telling me the truth? You are the one who killed those girls at the college, and the others here in Red Lake?" Her mouth hung open.

"Ugh, I..I...can't...breathe. What's...happening?" I could barely speak.

"You killed my son. That's why you can't breathe."

Elizabeth stood up and left me on that couch. She didn't call anyone. She didn't even look concerned. As I began to pass out, everything around me grew dim, until I was no longer conscious.

PART 3

CHAPTER 1

My head felt like it would explode at any moment. Even before I opened my eyes, I could feel them burning.

My head was still swimming from the enormous amount of alcohol that I had consumed at Walter's memorial service. I didn't know why I had done that. Drowning my sorrows didn't work. I could still feel the pangs of agony in my gut. That was something that I was sure would never fully go away.

Through my foggy brain, I heard someone making odd sounds, like choking maybe. I couldn't hear any voices around me though. Elizabeth and her family must have still been asleep. I was passed out on the couch.

As I was coming to, I felt a cold breeze on my bare arms. And something wet. It sent a chill up my spine. That confused me. Where was my blanket? I reached for it in the dark.

The moment that I became aware of my hands, I froze. My eyelids popped open and there was someone below me. I was straddling her hips. Focusing on her face, I gasped and dropped whatever it was that I had been holding.

The face in front of me was Polly, Henry's girlfriend. I recognized her immediately this time. I had killed her too many times in the past to not know who she was.

She didn't fight back. It was too late. She was gone.

I hadn't been strangling her though. That was odd. I had been holding something. What was it? I looked down and saw blood. A lot of blood. And a knife was lying in the dirt next to her body.

"What the hell?"

I jumped up and stood next to her.

"Damnit! Not again!" I yelled. Then I looked around to make sure no one had heard me.

I had been stabbing her when I woke up. I had never stabbed anyone before and that was a completely new sensation. So why was I stabbing her now?

"How did I get here?" I was speaking out loud. "I didn't die. I was only drunk."

"Wasn't I?"

"Well…I must have died." I was still talking out loud to myself. We seemed to be in a secluded spot, so I didn't worry about being overheard. "I'm here with Polly. She already died in my last life. So yes, this is most definitely a new life."

I stood there staring at the young lady lying below me, covered in blood. A bunch of possibilities were rummaging around in my brain. But only one stood out.

Elizabeth.

It had to be her. I was at Walter's memorial service. Everyone left, and it was just me and her. She brought me a beer. That had to be it. I remembered feeling very odd and not being able to breathe. Right before I passed out, Elizabeth said something about me killing her son and that was why I couldn't breathe.

Oh my god, Elizabeth murdered me. I sat down on a bench, while I contemplated that fact.

I knew that she blamed me for Walter's accident. But to actually murder me over it? Even that seemed completely out of character for Elizabeth. I had lived with her for sixty years, and had a difficult time believing that she was capable of something like that. But could her grief over the death of Walter have pushed her over the edge?

Sitting there, with Polly's blood all over me, I couldn't get the idea that Elizabeth had murdered me out of my mind. I looked around at my surroundings. Grass, trees, benches, a medium sized pond. We were at the park down the road from campus. And much too close to just be sitting there doing nothing to hide my crime. Yet, I couldn't move. My mind was reeling.

Then it hit me. "Oh no." In my drunken state, I had blabbed to Elizabeth about killing all those young women.

Did that matter now? I suppose not. But what were the consequences of my story telling in the last life? Even though I had died, the rest of humanity lived on. The world didn't stop just because I was gone. Did it? No, I was sure that it didn't.

Would Elizabeth have told people what I confessed to her? Did all of my loved ones spend the rest of their lives thinking that I was a serial killer?

Yes, I know that I was actually a serial killer, but I cringed at the thought that my parents would have lived out their lives with the stigma of what their son had done. There is no doubt that they would have been ashamed, and possibly ostracized.

That thought horrified me.

But I also knew that it was something I would never know for sure. I just had to tell myself that Elizabeth had kept her mouth shut and not repeated the ramblings of a drunk, grieving father.

If she had blabbed what I told her, now that my life has

started over, did that completely erase everything from before? I would have to say that the answer to that question was yes. But those people all still lived that life and may have known what I did.

It was all so complicated. It made my brain hurt.

A squawk from some creature on the pond jolted me back to the present.

My clothing was covered in blood. Polly's blood. I needed get changed as quickly as possible, before someone saw me. But how was I going to do that? I didn't have a change of clothes with me. Going back to my dorm was my only choice. It was late, thankfully. Maybe the cover of darkness would be my salvation.

Because the spot we were in wasn't as secluded as I had initially thought, I rolled Polly's body into the bushes that she had been lying next to. She was wearing that pink sweater that I remembered so well.

Walking back to campus, which was only a few blocks away, I tried to be casual. If someone did see me, they would probably not think too much about it, if I were just strolling home, as if I had just left a date at her door. If I had been running and acting erratic, that would be a whole different story. People remembered when someone acted oddly. I didn't want to be that person.

Of course, there was still the fact that I had Polly's blood all over me. I cut across the street whenever I came near a lamppost, trying my best to stay in the shadows. It seemed to work. Only one car passed me during my journey back to my dorm room, and it didn't slow down.

Campus was mostly deserted. I skulked around behind buildings and through the alley near my dorm, taking one last look around before peering into the main door of my building. No one was in sight and I hurried in and to my room. The next, and final, test, would be Henry. I prayed that he was not in the room.

I knew he wasn't with Polly, that was for sure.

CHAPTER 2

I heard the familiar sound of snoring as I gently opened the dorm room door. Working in the dark, I rummaged around the room, and in my dresser for a change of clothing.

"What are you doing?" Henry's sleepy voice mumbled from his side of the room.

"Just looking for something," I whispered. "Go back to sleep."

Almost immediately, the snoring resumed.

No one would ever know how much I wanted to stop and talk to Henry right at that moment. In my last life, he hated me because he thought I had killed Polly. The irony.

If he knew what I had done for sure in this life, he would hate me again. That's one of the reasons I needed to do whatever I could to hide the fact that I had stabbed the poor girl to death.

Yes, remorse hit me like a ton of bricks. I didn't want to kill that girl. And even more so because she was my roommate's girlfriend. I felt horrible that I took her away from him again. But this time I didn't even get the chance to avoid killing Polly. When I woke up in this life, I was smack in the middle of killing her, and it was too late. There was absolutely nothing I could do about it now.

I made it out of the dorm room and across the hall to the bathroom without being seen. It was a community bathroom, that everyone on the floor shared. Checking the stalls for any sign of life, I locked the door behind me.

I gasped when I saw my reflection in the mirror. I had a lot of blood on me. Even on my face and and in my hair. Thankfully I hadn't come across anyone. If I had, they would certainly have remembered me.

Twenty minutes later, I had stripped down, taken a shower, and redressed. Bundling all of my clothing, even my shoes and underwear, into a plastic bag, I exited the bathroom. I didn't go back to my dorm though. I headed for the dumpsters behind one of the dorm buildings, two buildings over. I may not be the brightest person out there, but I was at least smart enough to not throw everything away in my own dumpster. Because there were so many students, trash pick up was every morning, so I felt secure in the knowledge that everything would be gone before Polly's body was discovered.

And something great about the 1960s? No DNA testing. Even if they did find my clothing, there was no way to prove it was mine. It would be some thirty years or so before they could pin that on me. I doubted that I would still be in the current lifetime by then. But even if I was, they would have to catch me for another crime and get my DNA then. No, I wasn't really worried about it at this point.

Once everything was properly disposed of, I made my way back to my dorm and climbed into bed without waking Henry again. I was dead asleep within seconds.

A few hours later I was awakened by a knock at the door. Henry answered it, while I barely stirred.

"Hi Officer. Can I help you?"

I bolted awake, but stayed still in my bed.

"What is your name?" The officer asked.

"Henry. What's going on?" Henry was polite.

"Do you know a.." He consulted his notepad. "A Polly Sanderson?" The officer made direct, unblinking, eye contact with Henry. I could see how intense it was from my bed. The officer hadn't noticed that I was in the room.

I flinched when he mentioned her name.

"Yes, why?" Henry asked, genuinely perplexed by the question.

"I will ask the questions, if you don't mind," the officer snapped.

"Yes sir," Henry replied.

"What is the nature of your relationship with her?"

"Um…we've been out a few times."

Henry waited patiently while the deputy wrote in his notepad. He seemed to be taking an inordinate amount of time to write.

The deputy finally looked up from his written notes. "When was the last time that you saw her?"

"Yesterday. We stopped and talked on campus for a moment between classes," Henry told him. "Can you please tell me what this is all about?"

"Your girlfriend's body was discovered early this morning."

I could see the deputy watching Henry for a reaction. He was not disappointed.

"What? Her body? What happened?!" Henry's voice had gotten louder and definitely agitated sounding.

Turning toward me, Henry continued speaking. "Sam, did you hear that? Polly is dead."

I sat up and the officer turned toward me. There was surprise on his face. He hadn't noticed that I was there until that moment.

"Yeah, I heard," I told him, rubbing my face with my palms. "I'm sorry to hear that. She was a nice girl."

Once I said that, I realized that it was a mistake. Never volunteer information that is not asked. That is the first rule in the Criminal Handbook. Yet I had just volunteered that I knew Polly. Too late to say any different now.

The deputy pushed past Henry. They did stuff like that back in the sixties.

"Young man, what is your name?" He stood over me, looming.

"Who me?" I was stalling. Like that was really going to work.

"Yes, young man. You. What is your name?" The impatience in his voice was evident.

"Um...Sam. Sam Wells." I stood up to face him. We were the same height and looked each other right in the eyes. "Just so you know," I added, "I only met her once. We didn't know each other at all."

I was still running my mouth, even though I knew better.

"What happened to her, officer?" Henry chimed in.

The deputy turned to face Henry. "It appears that she was stabbed. Several times."

Both Henry and I flinched when he added the 'several times' part. You would think that someone dying by my hands would be just another day to me, but it wasn't. I never got comfortable with the fact that I had killed many, many people in my lifetimes. It still bothered me, every single time.

"Oh my god," Henry exclaimed. "Do you have any suspects?"

Funny how it hadn't dawned on Henry that we were probably their main suspects. Probably their only suspects.

"We are working on it. Can you tell me where you were between the hours of midnight and six a.m.?" He was speaking directly to Henry.

Henry's eyebrows shot up. "What? You don't actually believe that I had anything to do with it, do you?"

"Just answer the question, young man."

Henry's shoulders slumped in response. "Yes sir. I was here, asleep. And I never left this room that entire time, except to go to the bathroom, across the hall."

I grimaced and shook my head. Never offer any information that they don't ask. Unfortunately I couldn't say that out loud at the moment. Not in front of the deputy, that was for sure.

The deputy turned toward our closed dorm room door. "The bathroom is right across the hall, you say? And that is the only place you went all night?"

Henry nodded. "Yes."

He turned toward me. "And what about you? Where were you last night?"

My eyes jumped to Henry. I wasn't quite sure how to answer the question. Henry probably knew that I wasn't in the room when he went to sleep. Or maybe I was. I wasn't entirely sure about that. All I knew was that I came to in this life sometime in the middle of the night, and I was in the throes of stabbing Polly to death when I did so.

"I was here all night also. Never left the room." I didn't move. I didn't fidget. I didn't look around erratically. Those were the actions of a guilty person. I stood there perfectly still, waiting for a response.

He nodded. "I see. And is there anyone who can corroborate your stories?" He looked back and forth between the two of us.

We both shrugged. "Just him," Henry told him, pointing at me.

"Yeah, him." I tilted my head toward Henry.

"Mmm hmm. Anyone else?" he asked.

We both shook our heads.

He turned back toward Henry. "Were there any personal problems between you and Polly?"

Henry shook his head once more. "No sir. We had only been out a couple of times. I really didn't know her very well."

"A couple of times?" The deputy leafed back a few pages in his notebook. "A few minutes ago, you told me that you two had been out a few times." He looked back up at Henry. "So which is it? A few times, or a couple of times?"

Henry's eyes grew wide.

That was precisely why one should never offer information that is not asked. Never ever ever.

"Um...I don't know exactly. Two or three times, I guess," Henry tried to explain.

"Two or three times," the deputy repeated back.

"Yes sir."

"I see." He closed his notebook and stuck it in his shirt pocket. "You two stay in town for the foreseeable future. I'm sure that we will have more questions for you." He pointed at both of us. "Understood?"

We both nodded and answered in unison. "Understood."

The deputy turned and walked out the door.

CHAPTER 3

I could tell that Henry wanted to talk, but I didn't. There really was nothing for the two of us to discuss. I quickly dressed. "Gotta go do something," I told him as I practically ran out of the room.

I really needed to find Olive. She was the only person I could talk to. I wouldn't mention the part about stabbing Polly, of course. But I could talk to her about almost anything else going on in my life.

It took me about fifteen minutes to find Olive. She was in the cafeteria having breakfast with some friends. I walked up to her table.

"Hi Olive."

She looked up at me, furrowed her brows, and looked back over at her friends. When she gave me a small, uncomfortable sort of smile, I had a bad feeling. "Um, do I know you?"

Oh no. She didn't know me in this life. I had to think quick. "No, I guess not. We have a class together. I'll catch you later."

I couldn't get out of the cafeteria quickly enough. There

was a howl of laughter following me out the door. Great, just great.

I found a bench in the furthest corner of campus. I didn't want anyone I knew to see me there. I sat down to contemplate what was happening.

What did the fact that Olive didn't know me mean? She hadn't awakened yet? Would she ever awaken in this life to the Olive that I once knew? Or would she just be another girl living her life as if it were the first time. If she did wake to this new life, would she know me? I couldn't believe this was happening, and had no idea how to handle it.

"What do I do now?" I said out loud, just as a student passed by.

He looked over at me curiously, nodded my way, and kept walking.

I wondered about Elizabeth. Were we dating? Were we married? Was Walter on the way? Those were all good questions, and I needed to find out the answers.

It was still hard for me to believe that Elizabeth had poisoned me. I didn't know if I could ever trust her again.

I knew that there was no telling when Olive would jump back into this life. It could be tomorrow, next year, or even never. Hell, I didn't know how it all worked. Neither did she. I didn't want to sit around school waiting for her. Waiting for something that might never happen. I remembered her telling me that she once woke up with a husband and three children. So, it could be years before she came around.

One thing was for certain, I didn't want to go through college, yet again. I mean, how many times can someone possibly attend the same classes, at the same school, without going stark raving mad? I just couldn't do it again.

I got up off of that bench, walked straight to the administration office, and quit school. Again. Regardless of the fact that the deputy told me to stick around, I didn't. After packing up the few belongings I had in my dorm room, I headed home. Henry hadn't been there, so I didn't get a chance to say good-bye. It was just as well. I was afraid that the guilt I felt would be written all over my face. I did leave him a note though, saying something about my girlfriend needing me. Hey, maybe it was true.

My parents were not too happy to find out that I had quit school and was moving back home. They would get over it.

Through some discreet inquiries, I found out that Elizabeth and I were not dating. We had gone out briefly in high school, but it never went anywhere. I was actually happy about that, for a moment anyway. Then I realized that it meant Walter didn't exist. And never would.

The rational side of me figured that if Walter never existed, then he was never kidnapped, and was never hit by a car, and that meant that he never died.

The father side of me still mourned my son. It was a burden that I would have to bear alone. No one else in this lifetime knew of his existence. They had no one to mourn.

CHAPTER 4

Over the next several months, I drove to the college every weekend and hung out on campus. Luckily no one knew that I wasn't a student there, otherwise I would probably have been arrested.

I was keeping an eye on Olive. I wanted to be around when she woke up. I wanted her to be able to find me easily. If anyone had been paying close attention, I would probably have been spotted as some sort of stalker. In retrospect, following her to the cafeteria and around campus, and even when she left campus, was probably not a good idea.

During those months, the investigation into Polly's death continued. They questioned Henry several times. I found out from the newspaper that they had arrested Henry for her murder. I was horrified. The problem was that I had no idea what to do about it. I couldn't walk in and tell them that I did it. Otherwise, I would be the one in jail. But leaving my friend, Henry, locked up for life for something I did? How could I live with that?

For the time being, I left it alone. It was a shitty thing to do, but I just couldn't go to prison. Doing that to my friend was something I was going to have to live with.

Another interesting fact that I had gleaned from the newspapers was that there were no missing or dead young women in the Red Lake area in the past few years. No unsolved cases, at least. This was interesting, because it meant that I had not killed anyone in Red Lake during my current lifetime. It appeared that Polly was the first, and so far the only one I had killed in this lifetime.

One afternoon, the sky was a pale blue and there was just the faintest hint of a breeze out. It was a great day for a walk. I had nothing else going on, so off I went. The day seemed perfect.

Until I ran into Elizabeth, also walking alone.

"Oh, hi." She began the conversation. Her eyes drifted down to her feet.

I didn't know what to say. In this lifetime we barely knew each other. "Hi," I responded. "How are you?"

Looking back up at me, "Good, thanks," she smiled.

The conversation was stilted. Neither of us wanted to be there making small talk. I really did still hate her for poisoning me, and hoped that didn't show on my face. But of course, I knew that this Elizabeth standing in front of me was not the person who poisoned me. Not really anyway.

Before we got any further into the conversation, my stomach cramped. I actually doubled over in pain, holding my arms against my belly in front of me.

"Sam? Are you all right?" I could hear the concern in her voice.

"Yes…I…think so," I stuttered out.

It had been quite a while since I had that urge to kill someone, and almost had forgotten what it felt like. Almost.

The moment that my breathing became labored, I knew. It took everything I had not to strangle Elizabeth right there and then. Right on the sidewalk in the middle of the day. The odd thing was that in all of my lives, and all of our sordid history, I had never wanted to harm her. I did try to strangle her once, but we were interrupted and she was fine. I didn't think that I could have actually killed her though. She was the mother of my child after all.

I wondered if the fact that I hated her for poisoning me, and the fact that we had no child together in this lifetime, was the reason that I felt like killing her. We had no real connection this time. That had to be the reason.

I struggled to breathe and had to sit down on the curb to catch my breath.

"Sam, should I go get someone? You are really pale right now."

"No. Please just go. I'll be fine." The only thing that would make me feel better was if she was nowhere close to me. Distance from my intended target was usually the medicine that worked best.

"I don't know. I don't think I should leave you." Elizabeth leaned toward me.

When she placed her hand on my shoulder, I lurched out of her grip. "Just go!" I yelled, gasping for breath. "I don't want you here!"

She fidgeted, looking around us. The uncertainty on her face struck me as odd. I couldn't believe that me yelling at her caused her to not know what to do.

I started to stand up, finally unable to control myself. Walking toward her, the look on my face must have been the catalyst that made her turn. She didn't say a word, but ran. I stood there watching her until she was completely out of sight. The moment she was gone, my cramps subsided and my breathing returned to normal.

I took several deep breaths and headed straight for my house.

As difficult as it is to admit, late that night I went out and wandered a neighborhood a couple of miles away, looking for a target. I hit pay dirt, when a woman drove up to a dark house. I backed into some bushes to watch. I wanted to make sure that she was completely alone in the car, and in the house.

There definitely was no one in the car with her. I sneaked up alongside the house after she went in and watched through a side window to see if anyone else was around. It appeared that no one was. It was late and I watched as she washed a few dishes before heading upstairs. A half hour later I made my move.

I jimmied the back door open and crept through the house and up the stairs. I checked the first two bedroom doors that I came to, opening them quietly and peering inside. No one. The only bedroom left was the one at the end of the hall, which I assumed was the master bedroom.

Listening at her bedroom door for a couple of minutes, I could hear the familiar sounds of deep breathing that came with heavy sleep. I gently twisted the doorknob and opened the door just far enough to stick my head in. She was still breathing heavily and had not stirred.

I crept across the bedroom floor, stopping short when one of the floorboards creaked underneath my foot. She stirred for only the briefest of moments, rolled over and continued her snoring. I let out deep breath.

Before she realized what was happening, I climbed on top of her and wrapped my hands around her neck. Her eyes flew open and widened as she gasped for breath. Ten minutes later she was dead and I was sneaking out of the back door of her house.

I had a bit of time to reflect on my walk home. I was a horrible person and I knew it. I was under no delusion at all that I could blame any of my behaviors on anyone or anything else. Even still, I really had no control over my behavior at all. I had tried to stop myself many times in the past. Failing every single time. This time was no different. I'm pretty sure that my chance encounter with Elizabeth earlier in the day was the catalyst for the event that just took place.

Even so, it horrified me that I was the person that I was. I hated myself more than anyone or anything else in the world. By the time I arrived home, tears were free flowing down my face.

CHAPTER 5

The very next day, my mother sent me to the supermarket to pick up a few things.

"Sam Wells. What are you doing here?"

The voice was familiar and I turned around to see Ruby standing behind me.

"Oh, hello," I said to her.

She was just as beautiful as I had remembered. She still had that long, jet black hair and large brown eyes. Her curvy figure was hard to ignore. When she smiled, I couldn't help but smile back.

What were the odds that I would run into Elizabeth and Ruby both, one right after another? But that's what happened. I immediately tried searching my memory for how Ruby and I might have known each other in this life. Nothing. My memories before waking up were always a blank slate. I had no way of knowing whether we had just been friends or had actually dated. And if we had dated, when was that? Was it a year ago? Was it a month ago? I figured I would just try to let Ruby do most of the talking.

Perhaps during the conversation she would answer some of my questions.

"How have you been? It's been a while," she said to me.

That was helpful. We hadn't been dating anytime recently.

"Oh just fine. And you?" I asked.

"Pretty good, I guess." She looked around, as if worried that someone might be listening in. Then she gave me the once over, from head to toe. "Are you single?"

Wow, right to the point. But that was Ruby. Her red, flimsy blouse flittered in the slight breeze when a man passed by us. I waited until he was out of earshot.

I gave her a one shouldered shrug. "Yeah, I guess. Why?"

"I just thought you might want to have dinner sometime. For old time's sake, you know?" She smiled and her face lit up the room.

Hell, why not? What did I have to lose at this point in my life? Besides, I knew very well that people could change from lifetime to lifetime. Look at Elizabeth, for example. I was married to her for sixty years. She was nice, polite, a good mother. She was someone that could never hurt a fly. Then in another life, she poisoned me to death. That was something I never saw coming. Because of that, I knew better than to assume what someone might do or not do.

"Well?" she asked, sounding a bit impatient.

I snapped out of my daydream. "Oh, sorry. Sure, we can go out sometime."

"How about tomorrow night? Pick me up at seven." With that, she walked away, before I had a chance to respond.

"Hmm, I guess I have a date." I looked around and a woman smiled my way. I really needed to stop talking to myself. Out loud anyway.

∾

I knocked on Ruby's parents' front door promptly at seven. When she opened the door, my jaw dropped. She was wearing a clingy powder blue dress, that very nicely accentuated her curves. The dress might fit in just fine in thirty or forty years. But in the 1960s? No way. Though I personally had no complaints about her choice of wardrobe, I thought it might be a bit risqué for a simple dinner out.

"Wow Ruby, you look fantastic," I told her honestly.

She smiled and twirled for me.

"You like?" She already knew the answer. I'm sure it was written all over my face.

I nodded. "I like."

Taking a step toward me, I put up my hand to stop her.

"I really do like the dress, Ruby. But don't you think it's a little much for dinner?" I tried my best to say it tactfully, not wanting to offend my beautiful date.

She looked down at the powder blue. "What, this? No, it's fine. Come on, let's go."

And that was the end of the conversation. She took my hand and led me down the sidewalk to the car. I had no choice but to follow suit.

When we entered the Italian restaurant a few minutes later, heads swiveled. Not that I expected anything less.

During dinner, I found out that she was dating Miguel. She didn't feel like it was an issue that she was also dating me. She said that she and Miguel did not have an exclusive relationship. But she did admit, he did tend to get a bit jealous at times, even though the non-exclusivity was his idea.

I began to get the feeling that she only asked me out to make Miguel jealous. I wasn't sure why that bothered me, but it did a bit. Ruby and I had a tumultuous past. She was not aware of any of it, of course, as it had all happened in our past lives. I was a bit torn between staying with Ruby, and all the excitement she had to offer, or getting up and walking right out of that restaurant.

In the end, I stayed and we had a wonderful evening together. Ruby was beautiful, and engaging, and I couldn't take my eyes off of her. Everything else going on in my life, or lives as it may be, was completely forgotten. For a few hours anyway.

I headed back up to college that weekend to see Olive, like I did every weekend. I had no idea if she would ever come back to me. I just knew that I needed to be there when she became aware of this life. I figured that I was probably wasting my time, because I had no idea when, or if, it would happen, but it was just something I had to do.

Arriving at college, I climbed out of my car and put on my jacket, zipping it up high. The day was quite breezy and damp. I was just going to wander around campus for a little while, hoping to run into Olive.

"Sam!"

I turned to the voice, knowing full well who it was. Before I had a chance to respond, Olive jumped into my arms.

"You know who I am?" Dumb question. Of course she did.

"I woke up just this morning and found myself in this new life." She squeezed me harder as she spoke.

I pulled out of her embrace and looked her in the eyes. "Well, it's about time." I smiled.

"What do you mean? How long have you been in this life?" she asked.

"Several months."

"Really? How did you know that I wasn't aware of this life

yet?" She tilted her head to the side as she waited for me to answer.

"I found you in the cafeteria on the day that I came back, and you were with friends," I explained. "I said hi to you. You didn't know who I was. Then you and your friends laughed at me. It was pretty obvious at that point."

Olive made a grimacing gesture with her face. "Oh, I'm so sorry. I don't remember that." She took my hand briefly and squeezed it. It was a nice, comforting gesture.

"Of course you don't. I never remember anything in my life from before the moment I jump into it," I told her. "It's not your fault. I'm just really glad that you're finally here. I've been coming here every weekend for months, just waiting for you."

"Well, I'm back now," Olive said, spreading her arms dramatically.

"I'm really glad that you are," I told her.

"So who shot me?" Olive blurted out.

For a moment, I didn't know what she meant. Then it dawned on me. "Oh, you mean at graduation?"

"Uh, yeah," she replied with a stupid look on her face. I guess that was meant for me. "When else was I ever shot?"

"How should I know? You've been at this dying thing for a lot longer than I have."

"Ha ha, very funny." She gave me a gentle punch in the arm. "So answer my question. Who shot me at graduation?"

"James."

She nodded. "Really? That surprises me."

"It does? Didn't you break up with him right before that?" I asked. "He seems like the obvious one to me."

"Yeah, maybe. I mean, we did have a fight that morning. But I never thought of him as the type that would come after me." She shrugged. "Guess I was wrong."

"You were wrong big time, missy," I told her with a bit of a smile.

She smiled back. "I'll be sure to steer clear of him this time."

I nodded.

"So how did you die this last time? Were you an old man again?"

"Not even close. It wasn't long after you died actually. Elizabeth poisoned me."

Olive's eyebrows shot up. "She what?!"

I told her all about Walter running in the road and getting hit by that truck, and how Elizabeth blamed me. Then how I got drunk and she poisoned me.

"Wow, that's some story. I'm really sorry about your son," she replied. "How is Walter doing in this lifetime?"

Thinking of Walter, I had to press back the tears.

I squeezed the hand that was still comforting me. Olive looked down at our hands, and back up into my face. She turned and pulled me along behind her.

"Come on, we are getting all soggy out here in this drizzle. Let's go into the library and warm up."

The moment we entered the building, unease enveloped me. It's hard to describe exactly, but part of it was the feeling that everyone was looking at me. When I looked around the room though, it seemed that no one had even registered our arrival.

"Ooh, there's a table by the fireplace." She pulled me over.

Olive finally released her grip on my hand so that we could sit at the table facing each other. I didn't want to say anything to her and seem rude, but I felt a bit uncomfortable holding hands. It seemed a little more intimate than I wanted to be. I couldn't quite tell if it was just a friendly handholding, or if she was beginning to develop feelings. That would be the absolute worst thing to happen to the two of us. If some sort of relationship started, it could be devastating to both of us when it ended. And they all seem to end at some point.

As we sat in the library and talked that day, I told her how Walter didn't exist in this timeline. Elizabeth and I had not gone out long, and Walter was never conceived. Olive sat and listened to my story. She comforted me. I knew that we would always be best friends.

I couldn't help but notice the people around us. The feeling of unease that I had when we first walked in, just seemed to get worse, the longer we sat there.

"So where's Henry? You two sharing a dorm room in this life?"

I barely heard her.

"Sam!" Olive leaned across the table and was whispering animatedly at me. "Sam! Are you listening to a word I'm saying?"

"Huh?" I was startled out of whatever it was I had been doing. Spacing out, I guess. "Yeah, sorry. I guess I was just drifting there. What did you say?"

"Sam, are you all right? You seem to be having a hard time concentrating on anything I'm saying today." Her face slackened and her brow furrowed.

I reached across the table and took her hand. "Yes, I'm fine. Please don't worry about me. I just have a lot on my mind. You know?"

"Of course I know. Hell, I'm the one who just came back to life today," she replied. "Now I have to figure out everything. Who I have a relationship with, who my friends are, how I'm doing in my classes. All of it. Ugh. This is the part I hate the most."

"Yeah, me too."

"So, are you dating anyone right now?" she asked me.

I yanked my hand away from hers. By the look on her face, I could tell that was the wrong reaction to her question.

"Oh, I'm sorry." I needed to smooth things over. "Your question just surprised me, that's all."

Olive nodded without responding.

"I'm not really...well sort of...dating someone. You remember Ruby, right?"

Smooth.

Her eyes widened. "Ruby? Really? I'm surprised to hear that. Especially after all you have told me about her."

"Yeah, I know. But in this life, Elizabeth and I never really got together. I guess we dated briefly. But we never married and never had Walter. You weren't around to talk to, so I had no one," I tried to explain. "Then I ran into Ruby not long ago, and we hit it off."

"I see." Her face was flat and expressionless.

"I know, I know. I'll be careful," I tried to reassure her.

"I didn't say a word," she said to me, with that same expressionless look.

"You didn't have to."

CHAPTER 6

I spent that weekend in the dorm of one of my friends. He was fine with me crashing for a couple of nights. His roommate had gone home for the weekend, so there was a bed waiting for me. I wanted to spend as much time as I possibly could with Olive before I had to go back home.

Neither one of us dared bring up the topic of Ruby again. It was just a sore subject between us. That topic was better left alone.

Saturday morning, I woke to a commotion down in the courtyard. Our dorm room window was open and I couldn't avoid hearing whatever was going on outside.

"Ugh, what is going on out there?" my friend, Leroy, grumbled into his pillow.

Climbing out of bed, I stumbled to the window. We had both slept in longer than we planned to. The sun was high in the sky. I looked down at the gathering crowd below and gasped at the person I saw causing the commotion.

Miguel. Ruby's boyfriend.

"Oh, that's just great. Just what I need right now." I started gathering my clothes off the floor and quickly got dressed.

"What is it?" Leroy asked, not budging from his bed.

"Just some guy I know. I have a feeling he's looking for me. I better get down there before the police are called." I ran out the dorm while trying to slip on my last sneaker. I did kind of a hop skip down the hall.

"There he is."

Miguel pointed at me as I approached the crowd. All eyes turned my way. I felt the heat start in my chest and make its way to my face. I had no mirror, but knew that I had to be a deep shade of crimson by then.

"Miguel, buddy," I said to him, walking up and putting my arm around his shoulders. "Come on, let's you and me go for a walk and talk." I looked him in the eyes. "Okay?"

"You know I'm gonna kill you, right?" He grabbed my arm and flung it off of his shoulders.

"What's going on here?"

The crowd parted for the Dean of Students. He was a short, balding man with a ruddy complexion. At about 50 years old or so, he was stocky and stout looking. I remembered him as someone with a no-nonsense attitude. He was probably a great choice as someone to be in charge of the students.

I needed to head him off before there was real trouble. I wasn't even a student at the school anymore and Miguel certainly wasn't. So neither one of us belonged there. It would've taken him about two seconds to call the police once he found that out.

"Dean, Dean, everything is fine. Nothing to worry about. My friend and I here, were just putting on a show." I walked up to him and leaned in to whisper, looking left and right, for effect. "You know…for the ladies." I gave him a cheesy grin.

The man was not easy to read. No expression was registered on his face. He looked at me and then over at Miguel, then over at the crowd, and again back up at me. All with a completely blank and stern face. I feared it was not going to go well.

"You." He gestured toward Miguel. "Are you a student here?"

It was pretty obvious that Miguel was not a student there. He was older than most of the students and was not dressed like a student, nor did he carry any textbooks with him. Those were all telltale signs of being a student.

Miguel looked at me for answers. I gave him a one shoulder shrug. Miguel just turned around and walked away, with me, the crowd, and the Dean all watching him leave.

"You better stay away from her. Or else!" Miguel yelled over his left shoulder, as he kept walking.

The Dean looked at me. "If there is any more trouble from you, we are going to have a problem. Understand?"

"Understood."

The crowd had already begun to disperse. The fight was over, and the Dean was heading back to his office, so there was no longer anything to see. I decided that it would probably be a good idea for me to go back to Leroy's dorm and lay low for a while, until things died down somewhat.

I turned to head toward Leroy's dorm room. When I did, I saw Olive standing there watching me. She shook her head ever so slightly from side to side, but said nothing. She didn't need to. I knew exactly what she was thinking. She had made it no secret that she thought I should not be dating Ruby, and I was beginning to agree with her.

That night, once I heard that steady sound of snoring coming from Leroy's bunk, I got up and made my way outside. I felt that driving need to kill someone. While on my way out, I wondered if the events of the day were a catalyst for what I was about to do. The need to kill always seemed to come on after some sort of event. A pretty girl says hi to me.

I get into an argument with someone. Someone comes after me for a fight. And sometimes it is because I just arrived into the next life. I really couldn't pinpoint when it would happen. The need would just come upon me and I would have to do something about it.

Closing the dorm building door behind me, there were still quite a few students milling around. It wasn't that late so most had not gone to bed yet. Olive and I ran into each other. We walked over to the café that was still open, and had a couple of coffees while we sat and talked.

Our conversation was a bit awkward and stilted. I could see that she was struggling in an attempt to not mention Ruby. I didn't want to start that conversation either. We would just have to silently agree to disagree. After about a half hour of making small talk, we said our goodbyes and parted ways.

The campus had cleared of the students quite a bit by the time Olive and I were done. Making a show of going back to Leroy's dorm, I turned back and could no longer see Olive. I had started feeling better and thought that I would just go back up to bed, and try to get some sleep. The need to kill someone that night had almost been forgotten. Almost.

Just as I reached for the dorm building door, I heard talking. I couldn't pinpoint where it was coming from, or even hear what was being said. Dropping my arms to my side, I stood there, in the dark, listening. It was coming from the alley behind the building.

Skulking to the corner of the building and peering around, there was a young couple having an argument in the alley. They were trying to keep their voices down, but weren't doing a very good job at it.

Watching the exchange for several minutes, finally the young man told her he wanted nothing more from her and stormed off. The young woman just stood there, staring after him, until he was out of her sight. I continued watching as she walked over to the building, turned, and planted her back firmly against the dirty brick. Her hands covered her face and she began crying.

That was my cue. I quietly crept around the corner and, staying close to the building, I walked up to her. She hadn't yet noticed me there in that dark, empty alleyway.

"Hi." I wanted to get her attention.

She took in a quick breath, and put her hand over her heart. "You scared me. Where did you come from?" She stood up, away from the building and turned to face me.

"I couldn't sleep, so decided to take a walk," I explained, which wasn't entirely untrue.

"Oh, well, I should go," she replied.

"You got a smoke?" I asked her.

As she reached into her purse, I pounced. I grabbed her around the neck and twisted behind her, holding her tightly.

"Now do what I say and no one gets hurt. Understand?" That line was completely untrue. I had used it many times, on many people.

She nodded as best she could with an arm holding her by the throat.

Looking around for a secluded spot, I pulled her into the woods that started just on the other side of the alley. The young woman didn't utter a sound.

But someone else did.

"Sam!"

My body stiffened. I knew that voice. I knew it well.

"Let her go!" she yelled.

There was absolutely nothing else I could do at that moment other than let the young woman go.

I released my grip around her neck and shoved her forward. "Run. Don't turn around or I will find you." My voice was low and menacing. It was imperative that she didn't get a good look at my face.

That's when two things dawned on me. She had already seen my face when I walked up to her in the alleyway. And, Olive had yelled my name just moments before. Crap. What in the world was I going to do now?

The young woman ran. She did not turn around and look at me. However, I knew it was only a matter of a few minutes, at most, before the police and possibly a bunch of her friends showed up to deal with me.

"Olive, we need to get out of here."

Olive stood her ground. "What the hell is going on Sam? What were you doing with that girl?"

Covering the distance between Olive and me in about two seconds, I took her by the arm. "Olive, I'll explain soon. But please, we need to go, before that girl comes back with the Cavalry."

Olive jerked her arm away from me. "Fine, I'm coming, but you need to explain yourself." Her index finger was pointing right at my face for emphasis.

"Yeah, I got it," I responded. "Now let's go. Walk casually, but quickly. All right? We don't want to draw any unwanted attention our way."

A few minutes later, we had made our way across campus and to Olive's dorm room. I sneaked in, since boys were not allowed in the girls' dorm. Her roommate was off campus for the weekend, so we had all the privacy we needed.

The moment the door shut behind her, Olive spun around and faced me. I couldn't help but notice that she stayed by the door. Who could blame her for being careful and leaving herself open to an easy escape if needed.

"What is going on, Sam? And don't lie to me."

Her words were tough, but her mannerisms, not so much. She stayed with her back glued to the dorm room door. She was shivering ever so slightly. Her hand stayed wrapped around the doorknob. It was behind her, but I noticed.

"Look," I began, "it's not what it looks like." My eyes darted around the room. Making eye contact was something I was trying to avoid.

"And what did it look like?" she confronted. Her voice was trembly.

"Um…you tell me." I knew full well what it looked like, but I needed to buy some time to think about my answer. There was no denying that I had been attacking that girl. Once I told her to run and not look back, I didn't think that I could hide the truth from Olive.

"Sam, don't play games with me. You had your arm around that girl's throat and were dragging her toward the…woods."

I listened and noticed a hitch in her voice. She was disgusted with me. I could see that.

"What were you planning to do to her? Were you going to rape her?" Olive stared daggers into me.

"What? No. I would never do that." Yes, I could kill someone, but not that. Oh the irony.

"Then what? Are you the serial killer here in this town, and in Red Lake?"

I hesitated before responding.

"Sam, please. I need the truth. You can tell me anything. I am the only one on the planet who understands what you've been going through. If you can't tell me, then I don't know why we are friends."

She was guilt tripping me. And it was working.

"You are right. You are the only one I can talk to about this. About everything really." I held out my hand. "Please come sit down so we can talk."

She stood her ground. "I'd rather stand, if you don't mind."

I couldn't blame her for that. She had just witnessed me attacking someone. I was actually surprised that she even let herself be alone with me in the room.

I didn't see any point in lying by then. She knew the truth. She just needed to hear it from me. I owed her that. She had been a loyal friend, an only friend actually. I lowered my head, unable to look her in the eyes, walked over to one of the beds and sat down.

"Okay, I'll tell you everything. I just hope that you don't hate me after you have heard what I have to tell you."

"I don't think I could ever hate you, Sam."

I think she meant what she said. But that was before she heard that I was a cold blooded killer. I prepared myself for her to reject me when it was all over.

"All I ask is that you hear me out. When done, if you never want to talk to me again, I wouldn't blame you. Please though, no matter what, you can't tell anyone what I'm about to tell you today. Not ever. Can you promise me that?"

I looked up at her. There was a cold gaze fixed on me.

"Who am I going to tell? And who would believe me anyway?"

I guess that was my answer.

"Okay fine," I responded.

I spent the next hour and a half telling Olive every single gory detail of my compulsion. I explained how I would get gut wrenching cramps when the compulsion came on. I told her exactly what I did to alleviate that feeling. Then I emphasized to her how much I was revolted by the whole thing, and how much I regretted what I had done each and every single time.

As I spoke, I watched Olive for the reaction. Her expression was fixed. I don't know if that was on purpose, or she was just so shocked at what she was hearing that she couldn't respond. There was a single tear making its way down her cheek. That's what hurt me most of all. She was hurt and disappointed in her best friend.

When I was finished, she said only one thing.

"I think you need to go." She opened the dorm room door, walked out into the hall, and waited for me to leave.

I imagine that she walked into the hall, because she would be safer out there than inside the room, as I walked toward her. Either way, I complied. No words were exchanged between us. I felt my heart break as I walked out of the building that day.

CHAPTER 7

Opening her front door, Ruby was more beautiful than ever. I smiled, but there was no happiness in my eyes. Ruby could see that.

"What's the matter?"

She walked outside and we sat together on her front porch. The sky was a powder blue, peppered with fluffy clouds. The temperature was a perfect seventy degrees. Even so, I couldn't muster much enthusiasm for the day.

My best friend had just dumped me. Of course she did. She now knew my inner most, darkest, secrets. There was no way she was going to stay friends with a serial killer. I probably wouldn't either, if I was her. The thing is though, she had been friends with a serial killer for a long time. She just didn't know it. So, other than her now knowing the truth, nothing really had changed.

But it had changed. And I could tell that she was afraid of me. I wasn't angry about that. It was completely expected. I was just hurt and disappointed that my best friend was gone. Probably forever.

"Sweetheart, what's wrong?" Ruby asked me again.

I took her hand in mine. "Oh, Olive and I had a fight. I don't think she wants to be my friend anymore." God, I sounded like a ten year old girl.

Ruby squeezed my hand. "I'm sure that's not true. What did you two fight about?"

It was an innocent question, with a not so innocent answer. It was strange, now that I thought about it, but I had told Ruby all about my friendship with Olive, even before Olive woke up in this life. Olive hadn't even been aware that we were friends until this weekend. Now she hated me.

"I told Olive that I didn't like her boyfriend," I lied. But I certainly couldn't tell her the truth.

"What the hell are you doing here?"

We both looked up to see Miguel standing in front of us. Ruby released my hand. Oh great.

"Didn't I tell you that I was gonna kill you if you didn't stay away from my girl?"

Miguel's fists were clenched and I think I actually heard him growl. This was not going to be pretty.

I stood up. "Look, man, Ruby and I are just..." I turned and looked at her. What were we? Did I even know the answer to that question?

She must have seen the trepidation on my face, and stood up, getting between the two of us.

"Miguel, I'm really sorry," she began, "but I want to be with Sam."

My eyes widened. That was the last thing I expected her to say. I had been positive that she was going to kick me to the curb, not Miguel.

"The hell you do," he said through clenched teeth. "You are my girl, and this loser is not going to take you away from me."

Oh boy.

"What did you call me?" I just couldn't help myself, moving in closer.

Miguel walked toward me. Ruby put out her hands, one on the chest of each of us. "Now boys. There's no need to fight over me."

I think she was trying to lighten the mood. It wasn't working.

Shoving Ruby to the side with his left hand, Miguel came at me.

"Hey!" Ruby hollered. Neither of us paid her any attention.

Miguel was fast, that was for sure. He punched me in the face before I even had a chance to react. Fighting wasn't my forte. I responded with a right hook that missed him by a mile. When Miguel landed a deep punch to my gut, I doubled over.

Ruby jumped in front of my attacker. "Miguel, stop it!" she yelled at him.

I couldn't look either of them in the eyes. All I could think about was that the wind had been knocked out of me and I was trying to catch my breath.

Ruby put her hand on my back. "Sam, are you all right?"

Managing to straighten back up, I glared at Miguel, who had backed up just a bit. "Yeah, I'm fine."

"Miguel, you need to go," Ruby informed him.

"But you're my girl."

Miguel reached for Ruby, but she backed out of his grasp, and stood next to me. The color drained from his face.

Miguel turned his attention back to me. "I'm going, but this isn't over. You're a dead man. You hear me?"

He didn't wait for a response. Miguel walked away.

Ruby wrapped her arms around me. "Are you sure you're okay?"

I nodded. "I'm gonna kill that asshole."

"Don't say that. He's just mad because I want you, not him."

I backed up out of her embrace and looked Ruby in the eyes. "Yeah, about that. Ruby, you're a great girl, but I don't need the hassle. Miguel is not going to let up, you know that." I cringed just a bit before my next statement, afraid of her reaction. "Maybe we shouldn't see each other anymore."

Ruby's eyebrows shot up. "What the hell? I thought you wanted to be with me."

"I know. And I did want to be with you. I just don't want to have to deal with Miguel and his jealousy. Maybe if you had made a clean break from him before dating me, things would be different. But you didn't do that." Perhaps I should have left out that last part.

Ruby looked away for a moment. I expected her to get angry and to yell at me. But she was very quiet. Somehow that was worse.

"I should go." There was nothing else left for me to say.

Almost as if it were happening in slow motion, I watched as Ruby pulled her arm back and then slapped me hard across the face. My left cheek stung and my hand flew up to cover it.

"Damnit, Ruby! That hurt!"

"Good. Then I got my point across." She turned and walked up the steps. Turning briefly, she said, "You know, I should sick Miguel on you." Then Ruby slammed the door behind her.

"Well, that's done." I smiled as I turned and headed home.

CHAPTER 8

After having dinner with my parents, I decided to go out for a walk. There were so many things to think about.

It was my fault that my college roommate was in jail. He had been arrested for killing Polly. I did that.

Elizabeth and I hadn't gotten together in this lifetime, so there was no Walter. That hurt most of all. I missed my son more than words can express.

And Ruby hated me. Surprisingly, that didn't bother me at all. She wasn't the one for me. She never was. However, Miguel was a different story. He hated me, had threatened my life, and had the means to carry out that threat. That all had me worried.

About thirty minutes into my walk, I rounded a street corner, and came face to face with Miguel. The look in his eyes was enough to frighten anyone, and it certainly did the trick with me.

Miguel didn't say a word. He just stood there, staring at me with cold, steely eyes. His hands were in his pockets. That should be a sign that he was relaxed. Casual. But that wasn't what I saw. I saw a man ready to pounce, causing me to back up a bit. He matched my steps back, each with a step forward.

I put my hands up in front of me, in a surrendering motion. "Hey, Miguel, man, come on. I'm no longer interested in Ruby. You can have her."

He chewed on the inside of his cheek. "I can have her? Well, isn't that generous of you."

Miguel looked over my right shoulder, laughing at some unknown source. "Did you hear that? He said I can have her."

I spun around to see two men standing behind me. I had been completely unaware of them. That scared me most of all. Both of them were at least six feet tall, in their early twenties and looked like they spent all of their free time at the gym. I stood up as straight as I could get, needing every inch of height I had. Even so, I wasn't going to win in a fight of three against one.

Neither of the two men said a word to me. Their jobs were to just stand there looking at me menacingly. It was working. I turned back to Miguel, my eyes instinctively drifted to his hands. They were no longer in his pocket. His right hand had something in it, but I couldn't see what that was. When I looked back up at him, he smiled. He knew that I was completely aware of the predicament that I had found myself in.

Before I had the chance to react, Miguel lunged at me. I braced for impact, but he was quicker than I was. I didn't see the knife, until he pulled it back. I gasped when I saw the blood on it. Funny, but I felt no pain. He must have missed. But where did the blood come from? Looking down, I realized that he hadn't missed at all. Blood was coming from my mid section, turning my gray t-shirt into crimson, as the stain spread. I placed both of my hands over the wound.

"You stabbed me!" I yelled.

"Didn't I tell you that I was gonna kill you?" He said it so matter-of-factly. No emotion. Nothing.

I wondered if today was the day. You know, the day I would die. Again. And if it was the day that I died, would I come back? Good question. Actually, a better question was 'Did I want to come back?'

Before I had a chance to ponder that question, Miguel lunged at me again. That time, I was ready for him. I did a half spin away from him, which resulted in him stabbing at the air. Grabbing his right arm, I yanked him so that he lost his balance and stumbled forward. When he hit the ground, his knife skidded across the sidewalk and landed in the gutter, with a clank.

With no time to contemplate the knife, I pounced on top of Miguel's back. He had landed on his stomach. I grabbed a handful of his thick, coarse hair and yanked his head back. Then with all that I had, I slammed his face into the concrete. Over and over.

When I heard a shriek, I halted, mid-face slam. I turned to see Ruby running toward us. Miguel's thugs were nowhere to be seen. I guessed that they just wanted to look menacing, but had no intention of getting involved in an actual fight. It was obvious that they were all for show.

"What are you doing?!" Ruby screamed.

I promptly released my grip on Miguel's hair. Gravity took care of that one last face plant.

Ruby shoved me off of Miguel and rolled the man over, face up.

"Oh my god, I think you killed him!"

My eyes scanned the streets and houses nearby. It didn't appear that anyone else had seen us.

"Can you keep your voice down?" I whispered to her. "Where did you come from? What are you doing here?"

"I was looking for you. What happened?" she asked me, placing her fingers on Miguel's neck.

"Hey, I was just walking, minding my own business. He is the one who attacked me. He actually stabbed me. Look."

I lifted my shirt so she could see the stab wound and blood.

"That's barely more than a flesh wound. But Miguel here has no pulse. You killed him," Ruby announced.

I let my shirt fall back over my stomach. I was horrified. Though I knew this one was in self defense, I hadn't actually intended to kill him.

But worse than all of that, Ruby saw me kill Miguel.

"Did you see him stab me?" I asked her.

"No. All I saw was you slamming his head over and over into the sidewalk." She reached over and wiped the blood from her fingers onto my t-shirt. "I don't want any of his blood on me."

"It was self defense, Ruby. I swear." I threw my hands up in the air for dramatic effect.

"We need to call an ambulance," Ruby told me.

"Wait, no. We have witnesses that have seen the two of us arguing. No one will believe it was self defense," I told her.

"You are right about that," she began. "I don't even believe it was self defense. All I saw was you on top of him, slamming his face into the concrete. He was not a threat to you at all."

"Please Ruby, I wouldn't lie to you about this. He stabbed me and I had no choice but to fight back." I could hear the pleading tone in my own voice.

She just stood there glaring at me, arms folded defiantly in front of her.

Headlights turned the corner and headed straight toward us.

"Hurry, help me move him into the bushes!" I ordered.

194

Ruby didn't budge a muscle.

"Ruby! We can fight about it later, but right now we need to get him off the sidewalk before someone sees him! That car is coming. Move!" I yelled.

She moved. I took his arms and Ruby took his legs and we sort of half dragged, half carried him into the bushes that were only about three feet from us. It was enough to conceal him, temporarily at least. The car never slowed down as it passed by us.

"Can you help me get rid of the body?" I asked her, afraid of her response.

"Why should I? You don't want to date me, but you want me to help you cover this up?" She had a point.

"I just broke up with you because of Miguel. The truth is that I was afraid of him. I thought he might come after me if we continued seeing each other. And look," I turned to look at the bushes that now held Miguel's body, "he did come after me. He tried to kill me. I just got lucky, that's all."

Her face lit up. "So you want to start dating again?"

Aw, damnit. I had found myself in a tight spot. If I said yes, then she might help me. But I'd be obligated to date her again. If I answered no to her question, it was likely that she would turn and walk away, right then and there. Or at the very least, she would call an ambulance and the police. There was no right choice to be made, and I knew it.

"Of course I want to start dating again. I never really wanted to stop."

I smiled. She walked up to me and kissed me passionately. I definitely didn't miss that part.

"Okay, okay," I said to her, gently removing my lips from hers. "We need to do something about this body. Any ideas?"

"Somewhere remote, like the forest? Ooh, what about the sinkhole? No one will ever find him in there." Ruby offered, with a bit more excitement on her face than I would have expected.

"You know, that's a great idea. I haven't been there in ages. Do you remember the way?" I asked.

"Yeah, me and my friends used to go out there all the time," she told me. "Go get your car and I'll wait here," she ordered.

"I'll be right back." I took off in a run toward my parents' house.

Ten minutes later, I was back. I didn't see Ruby at first and thought that she had changed her mind. But I let out a sigh of relief when she stepped from out of the same bushes Miguel's body was in.

We wrapped the body in some plastic tarp that I had thought to grab from the garage. I also brought a wheelbarrow. Not that I had much experience moving bodies, but the thought of carrying him through the forest, was enough for me to come up with a better plan. Hence the wheelbarrow. Placing him in the trunk, we jumped into the car, and were out of there, all in under three minutes.

Deep in the forest, there was a huge sinkhole, which had formed many, many years prior. No one knows exactly when. It was just there one day. It's a bit of a hike to get to the sinkhole, so it may have been there for hundreds of years before it was discovered. Of course, once it was discovered, then everyone had to go see it. The sinkhole became a local mystery and everyone in town had hiked into the forest to see it at one time or another.

The sinkhole was quite deep, as far as anyone could tell, and was a dangerous place to be. Regardless, it was a favorite hangout for the local teenagers. Whenever someone went missing, rumors circulated that they were probably at the bottom of the sinkhole. A few times Search and Rescue teams were dispatched, but no bodies were ever recovered. It was just too dangerous to get down in there and look around. It seemed to be a vast, bottomless pit.

I parked the car off the road as best as I could. I didn't need anyone, much less the local sheriff, to drive by and see my car there late at night. I was smarter than that. Being careful to keep his body wrapped, we placed him into the wheelbarrow. I took hold of it as we entered the forest.

Ruby and I trudged through the forest, staying very close together. The forest was quite dense with trees, blocking out most of the sunlight during the day. At night, it was worse. This made it difficult to navigate our way there. And believe me when I tell you that pushing a wheelbarrow on a rocky dirt path, heavy with dead weight, was no easy task. I struggled to get it through some of the softer dirt that we encountered, and wondered if it would have been easier to just carry him.

Between the two of us, we were a bundle of nerves. Neither of us spoke much as we carefully navigated our way through. I noticed Ruby jump a few times when there was a noise. I knew it was probably just a pine cone dropping, or a critter looking for dinner, and I tried to calm her down. Her grabbing onto my arm for comfort certainly didn't help with the wheelbarrow struggle. But I didn't say anything. I was just thankful that she hadn't already called the cops.

When we reached the sinkhole, we were both terrified of getting too close, for fear of falling in. Ruby found a rock, sat down, and refused to get anywhere near the edge. I would have to do the task alone.

I got as close as I dared to, which was about five feet from the edge. I tilted the wheelbarrow and Miguel's body tumbled out. The plastic tarp unwrapped from his body as he rolled. It didn't matter though. It was all going into the hole. I knelt down on both knees and rolled him in. Then I tossed in the tarp and the wheelbarrow. I didn't want any evidence left behind. I stood there listening, but didn't hear any of it hit the bottom. I shuddered when thinking about how deep that sinkhole must have been.

I turned to Ruby. "Okay, it's done. Let's go."

It was very late, and very dark by then. Ruby took hold of my hand and held it tightly as we made our way out.

"What do we do now?" she asked me.

"About what?'

"What do you think I mean? Miguel, that's what. What are we going to tell people?" she asked.

I kept walking, keeping my eyes on the dark path in front of me. "Nothing, that's what we tell people. If it comes up… when it comes up, we don't know anything. We haven't seen or talked to Miguel in days. And nothing else. Ever. The golden rule is to not add any information that isn't asked. Got it?" I told her.

I felt her hand tighten on mine. "Yeah, keep my mouth shut. I got it."

CHAPTER 9

Staying in a relationship with Ruby was the last thing I wanted. But I had no choice. I knew deep in my soul that if I ever broke up with Ruby, she would head straight to the cops. She never outwardly brought up Miguel and what happened, but it was little things here and there that told me exactly what would happen.

She sometimes would make an offhanded comment about how terrible it would be if we ever broke up, and a lot of other little things. I was no fool, and knew exactly what she was doing.

Miguel's mother had filed a missing person's report, but I don't think that the sheriff took it too seriously. He was a known troublemaker. The sheriff made a show of asking around the neighborhood about whether anyone had seen him. But that was about it. Miguel was an adult and could leave if he wanted to. There were no news articles. There were no radio announcements. Everyone seemed to just chalk it up to Miguel leaving town.

Roughly three months into our relationship I started slowly distancing myself from Ruby. Very slowly. It needed to be gradual and I needed it to seem like Ruby's idea when we finally broke up. That was the only way I was going to get out of the predicament I was in without spending my life in prison. Even so, after all was said and done, I would still have to spend the rest of my life wondering if Ruby might tell someone.

I started making our dates further apart, and finding other things to do that did not include Ruby. I encouraged her to hang out with her friends more and go back to school. Maybe those things would take her mind off of me.

It all seemed to be working. We began drifting apart. I was happy about it, yet reluctant to leave her to her own devices at the same time. As long as we remained in a relationship together, I was pretty sure she would never say anything. But as time went on, I had no choice but to worry.

Just about the time that I thought we were very near the end of our relationship, Ruby showed up on my doorstep one day.

"Oh hi." I was a bit startled when I opened the door and found her sitting on my front step. I sat next to her and could see that she had been crying. I put my arm around her shoulder. "What's wrong?"

Ruby turned her head and buried her face into my chest. I pulled her tighter into me, letting her cry. I used my other hand to wipe the bead of sweat that had started its slow descent down my forehead. It was an unusually hot day and I could feel the stickiness of her skin on mine.

Lifting her head from my chest, she looked me directly in the eyes. "I'm…I'm…pregnant," she wailed.

My heart stopped. Or so it felt as if it had. I had to deliberately take in a breath before I passed out, either from the heat, or the news. It could have been either. Or both.

"Sam? Did you hear me?"

I reached into the pocket of my shorts and pulled out a tissue, handing it to Ruby. "Yeah, I heard you."

Dabbing at her eyes with the tissue, she sat straight up and looked me in the eyes. "Well?"

"Well what? I heard you."

In retrospect, it was the worst response I could have given. Flat out rejection would probably have been better. But a disinterested, unemotional response was unforgivable. But what could I have done? I didn't want a child with Ruby. That would tie her to me for the rest of our lives.

"Is that all you're going to say?" She stood up, facing me.

"What do you want me to say? This is brand new news to me. Can you give me a beat to process it before I have to make a lifetime commitment? Is it even my kid?" I grimaced at that last part. Even for me, it was a bit harsh.

Ruby's eyes narrowed as she looked at me and slapped me hard across the face. It wasn't the first time she had done that, but this one stung badly. I didn't react though, except for covering my left cheek with my hand. I was positive that I had a white, palm shaped handprint on my otherwise bright red face.

"How dare you! I don't sleep around!"

"I didn't say you did. But it wasn't that long ago that you were also seeing…" I hesitated. His name hadn't been spoken between us since that fateful night.

"Miguel. You can say his name. His name was Miguel," she said bluntly.

"*Is* Miguel. You need to use the present tense. If you mention him in the past tense, that makes it look like you know he isn't alive anymore," I explained. "So you need to always talk about him in the present tense." I thought for a moment. "Or better yet, don't talk about him at all. That will keep you out of trouble altogether."

"It's not Miguel's baby. I know it isn't," she told me with no hesitation at all.

I turned my head, refusing to meet her gaze. I was afraid that she would be able to read what I was thinking. It had to be written all over my face.

Ruby leaned over to where I was still sitting and put her hand on my shoulder. "I'm serious. It's your baby. There is no doubt about that."

Yes there was. There was a lot of doubt.

But how could I argue with the girl that had helped me dispose of the body of her dead lover? The man that I had killed.

Even if DNA tests could be done at that time in history, I wouldn't have insisted on getting one done. I knew what I had to do. I had to marry the mother of the baby. Whether the child was mine or not, was inconsequential. It was the right thing to do to protect my secret.

Ruby made a beautiful bride. Though it was nothing elaborate, just a courthouse wedding, with her parents and mine in attendance, it was a nice ceremony. In her condition, and it being the 1960s, a low-key affair was definitely the way to go.

"I don't know what I'm going to do. When I don't start showing soon, it's going to be really obvious."

I closed the front door quietly, so that I could hear the rest of Ruby's phone conversation. She obviously had not heard me walk in to the house.

"Yeah, I know. I've been trying, but I just haven't gotten pregnant," she said.

Unfortunately, I couldn't hear the other end of the conversation. But I didn't need to. With the small part that I had already overheard, I had all the information I needed.

Ruby wasn't pregnant. And never was.

Before I had a chance to think about what I was doing, I walked in, took the phone receiver from her hand, and hung it up. She was sitting in a kitchen chair, and was leaning back with her feet resting comfortably on the table.

Her eyes were as wide as saucers. "Sam. What are you doing home so early?" She almost fell over backward in the chair, but caught the edge of the table just in time.

"I heard your conversation, Ruby."

Standing up to face me, "No, Sam, it isn't what it sounded like."

My eyes narrowed at her. "It sounded like you are not pregnant, and you never were in the first place. Do I have that about right?"

Her shoulders slumped and she looked down at her feet. She knew that she had been caught. If I hadn't overheard her conversation, she might have been able to make up a lie about having a miscarriage. But that wouldn't fly now.

"How could you do this to me? I trusted you." I didn't yell. Though I was furious inside, I didn't let the anger show through in my voice. Only disappointment.

"I'm sorry," Ruby began. "I really did think I was pregnant. Then after we got married, I found out it was a mistake."

She reached for my arm and I pulled it away.

"You know what Ruby? I don't believe a word you say."

I turned and stormed out of the house, ignoring Ruby's pleas filling the house behind me.

CHAPTER 10

That night, I walked. And walked. And walked. I needed to get the events of the day out of my mind. Unfortunately, that was impossible. I couldn't think of anything but Ruby.

I could have killed her for what she had done.

"Hi, can I help you with those?" I asked a middle aged woman who was unloading the trunk of her car of groceries.

She turned toward me, loaded up with three large bags of groceries. "Um, sure. If you can get the rest of those, that would be really helpful. Thanks."

It never ceased to amaze me at how trusting some people were. But the 1960s was a different time.

I grabbed the rest of the grocery bags and followed her into the house, closing the front door behind me.

Ten minutes later, the deed was done. I opened the front door, just a crack, and peered out into the night. The tree lined street was quiet, save for one gray tabby crossing the road and disappearing along the side of a house. I closed the door behind me, locking the doorknob on my way out. I then crossed the grass to the driveway, and gently closed the trunk of the car. It had been left wide open, as some sort of signal to the world that something was not quite right. Luckily for me, no one seemed to have noticed.

I blamed this one on Ruby.

My parents hadn't wanted me to marry Ruby in the first place. But I didn't listen. I couldn't have the mother of my child living as an unwed mother in the 1960s. Of course, we know how that turned out. Because of that, I couldn't face my parents and go home and live with them. So back to my home with Ruby it was.

Things were never the same between us after that. It certainly wasn't due to her attempts at reconciliation. It was all on me. I barely spoke to her, avoiding her as much as I could in a small house.

A few days after the incident with the woman and her groceries, Ruby and I were sitting at the breakfast table when she handed me the front page of the newspaper. I picked it up and read the story. As I began to read the article, my heart sped up. It talked about the killings that happened in Red Lake, and that there were no suspects at the moment. It did mentioned that the latest victim was that middle-aged woman I had met. Ruby said nothing until I put the news-paper down on the table in front of me.

"Well, what do you think?" she asked me, taking a sip of her morning coffee.

"What do you mean?" I asked, feigning ignorance.

She tilted her head and narrowed her eyes at me. She wore no makeup that morning, and despite the fact that we were on the outs, I still found her beautiful.

"The story you just read. Do you think we could be in danger?" she asked.

I gave her a one shoulder shrug. "I doubt it. Just be careful, I guess."

"You don't seem all that concerned that there is a crazed killer on the loose right here in town."

The toaster popped up at that moment, and Ruby got up to butter the warm toast. I didn't say a thing until she sat back down and began eating.

"Why should I be concerned? I can handle myself. Besides, according to the article, he only kills women, so I don't think he's a threat to me." I looked into her large brown eyes. "But you should definitely be careful."

I knew that she was in no danger. Obviously. But I knew that I needed to make a show of being concerned for her safety. It must have worked, because she smiled back at me.

"You aren't the serial killer, are you?"

My entire body temperature seemed to rise by several degrees in response to her question. I looked her in the eyes, unable to tell if she was joking or not. I didn't think she was.

"Why would you ask me that?" It was all I could do to get that sentence out of my mouth without stammering. My body shook, but not enough to be noticeable.

"You know why. Miguel." Her face had no emotion showing at all. "I mean, it isn't like you've never killed anyone before."

"Ruby, you know that we vowed never to talk about that. Besides, it was a one time deal. You know that." I made sure that my words were serious sounding. I wanted to make sure that she knew I meant business.

"No, I don't know that. In fact, I did a little sleuthing and noticed that you always seem to be out when the murders happen. How can you explain that?" Ruby asked.

"I don't know if that's true or not. But if it is, it's just a coincidence. I'm sure lots of other people were out at the same time too." I couldn't look her in the eyes.

"Is that right? Just a coincidence? Maybe the sheriff needs to hear about this little coincidence of yours." Ruby crossed her arms in front of her and glared at me.

I doubled over in response to the familiar feeling of being sucker punched in the gut.

"Oh no," I said out loud.

Ruby reached over and put her hand on my back. "Sam, are you all right?"

It was all I could do to not grab her around the throat, right then and there. When the second punch hit me in the stomach, and I could barely breathe, I hit the floor. Clenching my mid section, I gasped for air. It felt as if my lungs were on fire.

"Sam!" Her voice was shrill. It made me want to rip my ears off.

At that moment, I couldn't imagine being in more pain. You know those werewolf movies where the person seems to be in agony as they make the change from person to werewolf? Well that's how it felt. My body was betraying me. I thought I was going to die of pure agony.

I needed to get to the bathroom. And fast. Otherwise I would vomit all over the kitchen floor. Neither of us wanted that.

I reached my hand up to Ruby. "Help me…get…up," I managed to say between gasps.

She reached down and took my arm. Her touch stung me as if I were on fire. But I had to endure it. I would never be able to get up on my own.

"Sam, what is happening?" I could hear the worry in her voice. "Do I need to call an ambulance?"

"N…no. I just need to get to the bathroom."

Once I was standing, I shrugged off Ruby's help and made my way to the bathroom. Just in time.

Twenty minutes later, there was pounding at the bathroom door.

"Sam! Are you okay in there? You are worrying me."

Feeling somewhat better, I answered her through the still closed door. "I'll be fine. Can you please go back into the kitchen? I'll be out shortly."

It was imperative that she be at the other end of the house, and as far away from me as possible, when I opened the door.

"Um, okay. But why? I want to make sure you are okay," Ruby responded.

"Please Ruby! Do as I ask!" My answer wasn't intended to sound harsh, but it came out that way anyhow.

"Okay, okay, I'm going!" The anger came through in her voice.

I waited a full minute before opening the bathroom door, just a crack. With one eye peering through the tiny space, no one was in view. Tentatively, I opened the door a bit more, scanning the hallway and room in front of me. Then I opened the door more, until it was wide open. No Ruby. I breathed a sigh of relief.

Slipping out the bathroom door, I quietly made a beeline out of the house. Ruby never heard me.

I squinted at the bright daylight that accosted me as I closed the front door gently behind me. Now what? I had to go to work that day, but not yet. It was much too early. I certainly couldn't hang out at my house. No, that was much too dangerous for Ruby. So, I drove to my parents' house and visited with my mother, while my father readied himself for work.

I told my mother what happened with Ruby. The lack of a baby part. Not what happened afterward.

"Well, I'm not surprised." My mother cleared the breakfast dishes from the table as she spoke.

My eyebrows shot up in response. "What is that supposed to mean?"

My mother turned toward me. "It just means that I know the type. The girls that want a husband so badly that they would lie about a pregnancy in order to trap a man into marriage. Ruby is just that sort of girl."

"Really? I thought you liked Ruby."

"I do like her. Well, I did like her, until you told me what she did to you. But that doesn't change the type of girl she is." This was a side of my mother that I was unfamiliar with. The side that gave her unvarnished opinion on things.

I was sitting at the kitchen table when my mother walked over and gave me a gentle pat on the shoulder. It was a comforting gesture and I appreciated it.

"Why didn't you say anything before?" I asked her.

"Honey, it wasn't my place to comment on your choice of a wife. You were the one who would have to live your life with her, not me. I figured that eventually you would see her for what she was, and come to your own conclusions."

I nodded. She was right. I needed to be the one to figure Ruby out on my own. I would never have let my parents voice their opinions on the woman I was about to marry. Especially when she was carrying my child. Or so I thought.

"Well, I need to get to work." I stood up. "Thanks Mom." I kissed her on the forehead and left.

CHAPTER 11

Early the next morning, I was awakened by a pounding on the front door. I rolled over and wrapped my pillow around my head in an attempt to deafen the noise. It didn't work.

Opening my eyes just a sliver, I could see horizontal streaks of light fighting their way through the blinds on my window and into my bedroom. Glancing over at the wind up alarm clock on my nightstand, it was just a bit after six a.m.

Ugh, who was at my front door so early in the morning? As I became a bit more alert, I heard voices, but couldn't make out what they were saying. My father was one of them. Twenty seconds later, there was a tentative knock at my bedroom door.

"Yeah?" I responded with no enthusiasm for visitors at all.

"Honey, you need to get up." It was my mother.

"I'm trying to sleep, Mom. I'll get up in a little while." I rolled back over and shut my eyes.

"No, Sam. You need to come to the front door. A couple of sheriff's deputies are here and want to talk to you," she explained. There was urgency in her voice.

THE MANY LIVES OF SAM WELLS

That woke me up. "Okay, I'll be right there. Let me get dressed."

One minute later, I walked to the front door. Two deputies greeted me. One was an average looking woman in her late twenties. The other was a tall black man, probably in his forties. He was the one who scowled at me.

"Hello," I greeted. "What can I do for you?"

"We would like to ask you a few questions," the woman responded.

I shrugged. "Okay."

"We received an anonymous tip that you were involved in the Red Lake serial killings that have been going on." I couldn't read the woman's face.

Ruby. I knew it was her. Who else could it have been? Anonymous my ass.

"What? Me?" I pointed at my own chest. "Why would someone say that?"

"This person also said that they saw you kill a young man, and dispose of the body," she added.

Yep, it was definitely Ruby. No doubt about that now.

I heard my mother gasp behind me.

"Deputy," my father chimed in. "Do you have any proof that my son was involved, other than one phone call?"

The woman looked up at my father. "Not at this point, no."

"So you are just going on one person's word for it? Someone who could just be angry with him and making everything up? Then you come over here accusing him, without any proof," my father added.

"We have to follow all leads, sir. No one is accusing anyone of anything at this point." She was not intimidated by my father. The fact that she had her partner standing next to her, scowling at everyone, was probably a big factor.

The deputy turned her attention back to me. "Can you

tell us where you were on the night of…" She opened her notepad and perused it.

My father put his palm up, facing the deputies. "Now just hold on here. No more questions for my son. If you have some proof, then let us know. Until then, the questions are over."

My father proceeded to abruptly close the door in the faces of the stunned deputies. That was probably a first for them.

I had never been so happy with my father in my entire life.

Unfortunately, the feeling didn't last long.

Three days later, I was arrested, and sent directly to the state prison to wait for the start of my trial. My attorney said it could be more than a year before my trial started. It didn't matter though. I wasn't going to be there that long.

One week into my stay, courtesy of the state, I was stabbed right in the middle of the mess hall. Shock was all I felt at that moment. I hadn't been there long enough to make any enemies.

"That's for killing my brother, Miguel."

It was the last thing I heard before everything went black.

PART 4

CHAPTER 1

Suddenly, my senses were assaulted. My eyes slammed shut at the bright, overhead florescent lighting. There was noise all around me. Arguing…no…screaming. When my knees buckled underneath me, my head slammed into the hard, tiled floor.

"Oh my god, Sam, are you all right?"

It was Elizabeth's voice I heard. Why was she here, in this prison with me? In the mess hall?

My mind searched for the answer. What was going on? And then it hit me. I remembered that someone had stabbed me in the neck. I had gone down before I even realized what was happening. Death must have come on quickly.

And now I was somewhere else. In a new life, I was sure. I opened my eyes and looked up at Elizabeth. The worry in her face showed through.

"Sam. Sam. Can you hear me?" Elizabeth gently tapped me on the shoulder as she spoke.

"Get out of the way!"

Someone shoved Elizabeth, who fell over in the process.

"Honey, are you all right?" It was Ruby.

Oh boy, Ruby. She called me 'Honey.' And right in front of Elizabeth too. Did that mean we were dating? Didn't she know that I hated her with every fiber of my being? She had been the one who got me arrested and sent to prison. I would probably have been there for life. Actually I was. Even though that life was only a few weeks. I did live the rest of my life there. And I died there. All thanks to Ruby.

A crowd was beginning to form around us. All I could see was a beige ceiling and those damn bright florescent lights above me.

"Where am I?" I asked.

"We are at the mall," Ruby answered. "You just collapsed. Should I call 9-1-1?"

"The mall? What are we doing here?"

I started to stand and felt several hands helping me.

"We were just doing some shopping before it was time for you to get Walter for the weekend. But then we ran into them," Ruby explained. "And your ex," I could hear the disdain in her voice, "started a fight with me."

Oh, so that was the screaming I heard just before I collapsed. It all made sense now. Wait…what did she say?

"Did you say Walter? Is he here? I want to see him." I began looking around for my son.

The crowd was thick and I pushed past them. I could hear grumblings from people as I made my way to the open mall corridor. I wasn't sure if it was from me pushing through, or their disappointment that I was fine. Nothing to see here.

I looked up at the nearest store. It was a toy store. Oh no. It was THE toy store. The very one that Walter had disappeared in more than once.

I walked back to where Elizabeth was standing. "Where's Walter?"

"He's in the toy store. What are you getting all worked up over?" she responded.

"How old is he?" I asked her.

"What? You know how old he is. Did you hit your head when you fell?" Elizabeth scrunched up her face at me when she spoke.

Grabbing her upper arms, I shook her, gently. Mostly gently. "I'm serious right now. How old is he?" It took everything I had not to scream at her.

"He's three. What's going on?" Elizabeth asked me.

"We need to find him right now. I mean it, come on." I didn't wait for anyone to follow me and took off in a sprint to the store.

"Walter!" I screamed as I ran up and down each of the toy store aisles. "Walter. Answer me!"

Nothing.

"Walter!" I ran back to the entrance to see Elizabeth and Ruby both standing there, watching me.

"Sam, where is he?" Elizabeth asked me.

"That's what I'm trying to find out," I told her. "He's not here."

"What do you mean, he's not here?" she asked me. "I saw him go in."

"And then what? You stood out here arguing…no screaming, at Ruby. No one was paying any attention to Walter. Now he's gone." My breathing was labored from all of the running.

"Are you sure?" Elizabeth asked me.

"Didn't you just see me looking for him in the store? Are you blind?" I didn't care if I hurt her feelings right then. They didn't matter. All that mattered was Walter.

Elizabeth didn't answer me. She went into the store herself and did her own search. I didn't wait for her return. I ran through the mall, searching every store. Nothing. Walter was nowhere to be found.

Just like in the past, I searched every space in the mall

where a 3 year old child could hide. It didn't matter though. I knew the search was futile. I just needed to do it anyway. In the back of my mind I thought that there was just the slightest of chances that he was hiding from us, and that he wasn't taken after all.

Forty five minutes later, Ruby found me curled up in a corner. I wasn't crying. I wasn't hysterical. I had already accepted what had happened. It certainly wasn't the first time. And might not be the last. Walter was gone. I knew that.

She sat down on the floor beside me. "Someone from the sheriff's department is here and wants to question you."

I nodded, but didn't budge.

"I'm sorry that this has happened," she told me. "I feel partly responsible, because Elizabeth and I were distracted when it happened."

My head slowly turned to face her. I stared straight into her eyes. "Distracted?" I said to her. "You and Elizabeth were distracted?" Shaking my head slightly back and forth, I leaned in so that our faces were inches apart. "You weren't distracted. You were fighting. Screaming at each other actually. And though I don't remember exactly how it started, I can almost guarantee that it was you that instigated the whole thing. So you aren't partly responsible. You are completely responsible."

Her jaw dropped as I stood up and walked away. She didn't follow me.

After giving the deputy my recollection of the events, I left the mall. Alone. I didn't speak to Elizabeth at all. There was no need.

CHAPTER 2

I knew that it was probably futile, but I spent the next two weeks searching for my son. I knocked on the door of everyone I knew, and several that I didn't know. No one knew anything.

I searched the woods, even going so far as the sinkhole. What I was going to discover there, I had no idea. There were footprints around the opening, as there always were. Many people had been there over the years. At one point, I walked as close to the edge as I could, and peered in. I couldn't see anything in the vast blackness, as expected. I sat down next to the sinkhole for a long time, probably hours, just hoping to see or hear something. Anything. But there was nothing.

The quietness of the forest was disconcerting. Eventually I realized that I was getting nowhere.

When I made my way out of the forest and reached my car, the sheriff was parked behind me. Ah, crap. Standing next to the cars, I watched as the sheriff picked up his radio and said something into it. He took his time climbing out of his car.

"Sheriff," I said, giving him a slight nod.

"Mr. Wells. I've been looking for you," he said to me.

"Well, here I am."

His eyes scanned the tree line. "What were you doing in the woods?"

"Just going for a walk." I resisted the urge to add, 'Is that all right with you?' It was none of his damn business what I was doing in the woods.

"Just going for a walk," he repeated. "I see. Do you often go for walks in the woods?"

"Sometimes. Sheriff, what can I do for you? Is this about my son?" Of course it was.

Sheriff Jay Mitchell was a wiry little man, not more than five and a half feet tall. At most. I was pretty sure he was no older than his mid-thirties, but his severely thinning hair was more suitable for a man twice his age. He wasn't quite at the combover stage just yet, but it wouldn't be long.

I wondered how he became sheriff in the first place. The man was not very popular among the citizens of Red Lake, with his quick temper and big mouth. He told people what he thought of them and didn't seem to give a damn what anyone thought.

"Yes, I'm here about your son. I'm concerned that you played some part in his disappearance." The man lowered his head and looked up at me with a glare.

I could feel the heat creeping up my neck. "You can't actually believe that I had something to do with that. I loved... love...my son more than anything." Damn, I knew better than to use the past tense. Even though I knew that it was appropriate in this case.

I'm sure that the tense I used was not lost on the sheriff.

"Hmmm, well, do you have him hidden away somewhere? You know, somewhere that his mother can't find him?" he asked me.

"I said that I don't know where he is. Even though Elizabeth and I aren't together anymore, I would never take Walter from her. I just wouldn't do that," I tried to explain.

"We have to flesh out every possibility. Most child abductions are by someone that the child knows. Very often it's a non custodial parent," he explained.

"Yes, I know that. But in this case, you are wrong. I was standing in the mall with Elizabeth and Ruby when Walter disappeared. So it's not possible that I could have taken him."

"Someone could have helped you. You cause a distraction, and they grab the boy," he told me, as if this was an actual viable plan.

I put my palm up to stop him. "No. That's not what happened at all. Besides, I live with my parents. Where would I be stashing him?"

Sheriff Mitchell looked toward the forest once again. "Somewhere in there, maybe?"

Instinctively, I turned toward where he was looking. "You've got to be kidding. You think I would hide my three year old son alone in a cave deep in the woods? That's ridiculous."

"I've seen worse," he told me.

I shrugged. "Yeah, I'm sure you have."

"The boy's mother seems to think that you had something to do with his disappearance. What do you have to say about that?" His eyebrows raised in anticipation of my answer.

"I don't know why she would think that. I've never given her any reason to think I would take my son. Or harm him in any way." At least I hoped that was the case. I, of course, had no memory of my time with Elizabeth and Walter before I woke up in the mall on that fateful day.

"Harm? No one said anything about harming him." The sheriff took a step closer to me. "Mr. Wells, did you hurt your son? Did you kill him? Is that why you were in the forest? Were you at the sinkhole perhaps?"

Ah, so that was where this line of questioning was heading. He thought I had killed Walter and thrown his little body in the sinkhole. If that was my intention, it certainly would be the perfect crime. No one would ever be able to prove it one way or another. But god, what a horrible thought. I felt a shiver climb up my spine in response.

"That's a disgusting thought, Sheriff. I love my son. Believe me when I tell you that I want to find him even more than you do. It is all I've thought about since he disappeared."

He stared at me for probably a full minute before responding. Taking a step back and turning toward his car, he spoke over his shoulder as he walked away. "Don't leave town. I'm not done with you yet."

I didn't respond. Standing my ground, I watched him pull away from the curb, until he was out of sight.

CHAPTER 3

I made the decision to go see Olive. With no way of knowing if she would talk to me or not, I knew that I was taking a big chance. Also, she might not even be aware of this life yet. Last time, I had to wait a while until she woke up.

In my last life, Olive caught me on the verge of killing a young woman. When I explained my compulsion to kill, she was disgusted by me. We haven't talked since. I had nothing to lose. She would either talk to me or she wouldn't. I was about to find out.

By the time I reached the college, it was dark. The lighting in the parking lot was quite inadequate and made even me a bit nervous to walk through the dimness. I jumped at every little noise, until I realized that it was just my nerves. I think that I was mostly jumpy thinking about having a conversation with Olive. It would break my heart if she rejected me again. I had come to count on her as being the only other person who knew about me reliving lives. Her experiences were quite different from mine in some ways, and almost exactly the same in others. We were meant to be best friends through the rest of eternity. I was sure of it.

Unfortunately, she wasn't so sure. I hoped that maybe our time apart had softened her attitude about me.

It took over an hour for me to find Olive. She was sitting alone in the back corner of the library, textbook open, pen in hand. I stood across the room for several minutes trying to work up the nerve to talk to her. Finally, I decided to just go for it. She would probably reject me. I knew that. But, maybe I would be pleasantly surprised.

I sat down in the chair directly across from her. Her eyes widened and she dropped the pen in her hand. It clanked loudly as it bounced on the table. Olive slammed her hand down over the pen to stop the noise, looking around nervously. No one had seemed to notice.

"What are you doing here?" She started the conversation. Her tone was confrontational.

"I wanted to see you. I've missed you," I told her honestly. My voice soft.

"I don't want to see you," Olive responded.

Her bluntness hurt me to the core. Her behavior was not unexpected. Though I had hoped she would be more accepting of me.

"I know. But please, can you just hear me out?" I placed my hands on the table, one on top of the other. It was an attempt to show her that I was not dangerous. Just a guy who wanted to get his friend back.

Olive looked down at my hands, and back up to me again.

"Sam, I really don't think that there is anything you could say to me that would change my mind."

"Please, Olive, I'm not a horrible person. I know it seems that way…"

"Sam." She cut me off mid-sentence. "Seems that way? Let's analyze this. I catch you red-handed dragging a poor girl off toward the woods to kill her."

My nod was very slight. I let her continue.

"Then you tell me that you have killed several people. Something deep in yourself causes this and you have no control over it. How am I doing so far?"

"Yeah, that's all correct," I replied.

"You never said that you would stop. You said you can't help it. So, I take that as confirmation that you will continue to do this time and again, through all of your lives."

I nodded once again.

"Sam, I'm going to be blunt here." She looked down at the table, as if deep in thought. When she looked back up, her eyes met mine. "I'm afraid of you. If you can't stop killing people, then I have no reason to think it won't be me at some point."

"No. I can promise with everything that I have, that it will never be you." I meant every word of it too.

"I don't think you can promise that. If this is the overwhelming compulsion that you say it is, you might not be able to stop yourself," she told me.

"Olive." I reached for her hands and she pulled them back, placing them in her lap. I deserved that. "I will kill myself before I ever lay a hand on you. That's the honest truth. I would never…could never…hurt you."

"I'm sure that you believe that," she replied softly. "But when the moment comes, you may not be able to stop yourself. I just can't take that chance. You have to understand that."

"Oh, I do understand. I completely understand. And, truthfully, I don't blame you. I would probably feel exactly the same way if I were in your shoes," I told her.

By the look on her face, I could see that she wasn't going to change her mind. Olive was lost to me. Never again would I have my best friend to help get me through the dark days of my many lives.

"Well…I guess that's that." I stood to leave.

I turned back once on my way to the front door of the library, and saw her watching me. No expression. No sadness. Just watching. It was over. We were done. The ache in my gut that day was different. It wasn't the usual. This time it was due to the enormous pain of loss that I felt. I just wanted to curl up somewhere, far away from the world.

CHAPTER 4

Before heading home from my devastating rejection by Olive, I found a pay phone and called my parents. I was sure there would be no news about the search for Walter, but figured it couldn't hurt to ask anyway. Each life was different. Maybe this time, he would come home.

"Sam!" It was my mother. "The sheriff and some deputies were here looking for you." She was almost breathless as she spoke. "They are going to arrest you for Walter's kidnapping!"

I couldn't get myself to respond.

"Sam! Did you hear me? Sam?"

"Y…yes. I'm here. Sorry. I heard you," I told her.

"You didn't have anything to do with that, did you?" she asked me quietly.

"Mom! I can't believe you asked me that. You know I would never take Walter from his mother. And I would never hurt my son. You don't actually think that I could have, do you?" Her question hurt me deeply. Though I did understand why she asked it.

"No, I guess not. I'm sorry I even asked. It's just that the sheriff seemed so sure. When will you be home?" She was changing the subject.

"Um…I'll get back to you on that."

I hung up the phone before she had a chance to respond.

There was no way that I could go home right then. And maybe not ever. However, I would go back to Red Lake. Though I was pretty sure that my son would never be found, I still had to look. This was a new life, and things may have changed. Perhaps someone had just taken him, and he would be found. There was no way to know for sure, unless I looked for him. Doing that, and staying out of sight of the authorities would not be an easy task.

I slept in my car that night, right there in the college parking lot. The darkness of the lot provided enough cover that if someone walked by, they wouldn't see me cramped up in the backseat of my car.

Very early that next morning, the first rays of sunlight hit me square in the face, which got my attention. My back and neck were stiff from the awkward, cramped position I had been in all night. I managed to crawl over and into the front seat. In case someone was in the parking lot, I didn't want them to see me climb out of the backseat. That would get me some unwanted attention.

Thankfully, no one was within sight when I stepped out of the driver's side front door. I stretched the cramps out of my body and shivered. It was chilly that early morning. I grabbed my sweatshirt and put it on.

'Now what?' I thought. I knew that I needed to look for Walter, but had no plan yet. Either way, the most obvious thing was to head for Red Lake. That's where I would be looking. So, off I went.

CHAPTER 5

I found a cheap motel outside of Red Lake to lay low in. I knew that I needed help. I couldn't find Walter alone, but I had no idea where to start. Calling Elizabeth was out of the question. Ruby was the only other person I could think of who might remember something. Of course, I know that she and Elizabeth were in a heated fight when my son went missing, but possibly Ruby noticed someone that seemed off. Even if it was just for a moment. I figured it couldn't hurt to try.

"What do you want?" It was the first thing she said to me upon hearing my voice on the other end of the phone.

"Your help. That's what I want. I'm trying to find my son. Please, can you put our differences aside and try to help me?" I pleaded.

"If I remember correctly…and I do…you yelled at me and told me that his disappearance was all my fault. Is that not how you remember it?" The sarcasm coming from her voice was almost palpable.

She wasn't going to make this easy on me. Not that I

expected her to. I was pretty hard on her at the mall on the day I lost my son.

"It got your attention, didn't it?" she added.

I paused, thinking that one over for a moment.

"What do you mean by that?" I asked her.

"Here you are, calling me for help. Before Walter was lost, you were trying to break it off with me. Don't you find all of this very interesting?" she asked me. "I do."

My heart suddenly felt like a bullet pierced right through it. "Ruuubbby?" I drawled out for effect.

"Saaaaaammmm," she replied.

"Did you have something to do with my son disappearing?" I was terrified by what her reply might be. My body shook ever so slightly as I sat down on the motel room bedspread. It was multi colored and flowery. I refused to let myself think about what might be hiding within those multi colored flower petals.

"Why would you think that?" Her reply was coy.

"What did you do with my son, Ruby?" I demanded.

"I was right there in the mall, standing next to you, when he disappeared. So it couldn't have possibly been me, now could it?"

I flew to my feet. "Then who did it?!"

"How would I know?" Her voice was teasing and light. She clearly knew something.

"Ruby! Stop playing games with me. Who helped you? Was it Miguel?"

She hesitated just long enough. "I have nothing else to say. This conversation is over." With that, the phone went dead.

Slamming the phone receiver back into its cradle, I began pacing the floor and cursing her name. Ruby. She was the one behind this. And probably Miguel. Almost definitely Miguel. I couldn't fathom it being anyone else who was willing to help her.

Besides, she didn't actually say that she didn't do it. She had danced around that little fact.

But why? Because I was rejecting her? What a stupid reason for taking someone's son. Was it that whole 'woman scorned' thing? It all seemed so unlikely to me. But there I was, positive that Ruby was behind the whole thing.

So, if it was Ruby, maybe that was a good thing. I couldn't imagine her actually hurting Walter. So, maybe they were taking care of him and just trying to hurt me. But Miguel, he's another story. If he's involved, which I was sure had to be the case, why would Miguel help her take care of my son? In fact, why would Miguel get involved at all? Especially since it seemed the reason was because she wanted me. I couldn't imagine that Miguel would go for that.

Was I wrong?

Pacing the small motel room, that's when it hit me, square between the eyes. Ruby. Was she the one who took Walter in my previous lives? Could it possibly have been her all along?

The first time I came back to life, Walter was kidnapped at the mall. His body was never found. So it seems likely that Ruby or Miguel killed him that time. Otherwise, it seems as if he would have turned up at some point. When I died years later, Walter still had never been found. I was sure he was dead. There really was no other explanation.

In my next life, I was able to thwart the kidnapping at the mall, and Walter was fine. Until he ran in front of that car and was killed. Was that some sort of cosmic joke on me?

The next time, Walter never existed.

And then there's this life. Walter was kidnapped from the mall again. Would Ruby or Miguel kill my son again? Ruby was a lot of things, but a killer? I doubted it. I'm pretty sure she just wanted to get my attention.

But Miguel? I didn't know the man well, but thought he was capable. He had attacked me before.

CHAPTER 6

I parked on the next block over from Ruby's house. The
street was lined with average looking houses that mostly all
looked the same. It was late at night and the street was
gloomy. I glanced at the clock and it was very early morning,
actually. It wouldn't be long before the sun came up. Not a
person in sight, but I needed to hurry. I kept close to the
bushes that lined the sidewalk. Being seen was the last thing
that I needed.

Ruby and a friend shared a house. I found this out from
my mother, who seemed to be a wealth of information. The
woman knew almost everything about almost everyone.

Skipping the front door, I skulked around the side of the
house. No point in knocking on the front door, she would
never let me in. The side gate hinges creaked in the stillness
of the night and I cringed, hoping that no one had heard it,
but me. I left the gate open, propping a rock against it. With
the slight breeze that night, the last thing I needed was the
gate gently rocking back and forth in the breeze, squeaking
everyone awake.

To my astonishment, the back sliding door opened right

up when I tried it. Stupid girls, I thought. Don't they know that someone could break in while they were sleeping?

I cut through the living room and headed down the hallway. Ruby was fast asleep in the first bedroom. Closing her bedroom door behind me, I crept over to her bed, not wanting to wake her before I was ready to. I watched sleep. Even with her hair pulled back into a ponytail and no makeup on, she was still beautiful, with the moonlight from the window causing her face to glow.

For a brief moment, I considered reaching down and strangling her. Thankfully, that moment passed quickly. Killing her would be stupid. If I did that, then I would never find my son. Dead or alive, I needed to know the truth. Ruby was the only one who could give me that truth.

I sat down on the bed, next to Ruby. She was a deep sleeper, something I remembered from our past. I listened to her deep breathing for another minute. Then it was time. I leaned in so that my lips were only about an inch from her right ear. She was lying on her left side with her back toward me.

"Ruby," I whispered, not wanting to startle her.

No reaction.

"Ruby," I said a little louder that time.

"Hmmm." She rolled over so that her body was facing mine. Her eyes remained closed.

"Ruby."

That got her attention. Ruby's eyes flew open and she sat bolt upright in the bed.

"Whaa...what...are you doing here?" She struggled to speak in her shock at finding me sitting on the bed next to her.

"You know why I'm here," I told her. Standing up, I walked over to the bedroom door and flipped on the light switch.

Ruby squinted and covered her eyes with her hand in response to the sudden onslaught of light.

"No, I don't." She hesitated for a moment, searching her memory. "Oh, is this about your son?"

"Of course it's about Walter," I snapped.

"You need to leave my house before I call the cops." I could see by the look on her face that she meant business.

My eyes scanned the room, landing on her nightstand. No telephone.

"Ruby, all I want is answers, and you are the one who can give them to me. Can we just talk?"

She couldn't look me in the eyes. "I don't know anything. I was preoccupied when he was taken. You know that."

"Yes, I know that." I paced the room as I spoke, keeping near the bedroom door. I didn't want her to escape when I wasn't paying attention. "I also know that you made some comments alluding to your participation in Walter's kidnapping."

"I did no such thing." Still, she couldn't look directly at me.

"Ruby, don't play games with me. You know full well that you did." I walked over and stood right in front of her, so that she had no choice but to look directly at me. "Look, all I want is to find out what happened to my son, and maybe get him back. Regardless of what happened between you and me, Walter is another issue. Can you please try to understand that?"

It took everything I had not to yell at her, not to demand that she tell me...not to strangle her. But none of those things would get my son back. I had to be calm. I had to appeal to her sense of right and wrong.

"I will forgive you for anything, if you just help me. Please." No I wouldn't.

Ruby pushed past me, toward her bedroom door.

"I don't know anything. Just leave me alone!"

Unfortunately for Ruby, I was faster than she was, and reached the door before she did. Standing in front of her, with my face hard, I dared her to try to escape that room.

With a boldness that I did not expect, Ruby grabbed the front of my t-shirt and pulled me away from the door. The action caught me off guard and I stumbled forward. The two of us went down in a heap, me landing on top of her.

It was my chance to show Ruby that I meant business, and that neither of us would ever leave that room, if I didn't get the answers that I needed. Facing her, I sat up and wrapped my left hand around her throat. I pulled my right arm back, ready to slam my fist into her face.

"Tell me what I want to know right now, or I will kill you." My face and neck felt hot as sweat dripped from me onto Ruby.

By the look in her eyes, I could tell that she knew I meant every word that I said. She wasn't going to go down easily though. Reaching up with her right hand, she clawed the left side of my face. I didn't need a mirror to know that it began bleeding.

"You bitch! I should kill you just for that!" My right hand wiped at my left cheek and my left hand involuntarily began squeezing her neck.

The pounding on the bedroom door startled both of us.

"What the hell is going on in there?"

Her roommate. Damn, I had almost forgotten about her. I let go of Ruby's throat. The screaming began immediately. The young woman didn't hesitate to burst into the room.

When she landed on my back, it threw me off balance and I fell to the side. She began pounding on me with her fists, and yelling at me.

Somehow I managed to stand up while she continued

pounding. I reared back my right arm and slammed it into her face. She went down. Hard.

"Sam! Did you kill her?" Ruby ran over to her friend and knelt down over her limp body.

"No, I didn't kill her. But she'll have a hell of a headache when she wakes."

"I'm calling the cops."

Ruby stood up and ran out the bedroom door. I didn't try to stop her. I took one more last look at the unconscious girl on the floor and walked out of the house.

Making my way back to my motel room, I decided to lay low for a bit. I had paid for it with cash and no identification. The 1960s were a simpler time. I would be hard pressed to find any motel in my time that would let me stay with no I.D.

I needed a game plan, and I needed one fast. It would not be long before every deputy in town was looking for me. They probably were already.

Within an hour of leaving Ruby's house, I was keeping my eyes on the motel parking lot and saw two deputy vehicles cruising the lot. I was unsure if they had been tipped off to my whereabouts or were just checking all of the local motels. But I kept my eyes on them either way.

I watched as a tall, thin deputy, probably in his late thirties, climbed out of his car and began knocking on doors. The deputy in the other car headed straight for the motel office and exited a minute later with the desk clerk, who was holding a set of keys.

That's when panic set in. There was no way I could walk out the front door of my motel room. Crossing the room in under three seconds, I entered the bathroom and contemplated the window. It was large enough for me to crawl out. Barely. But that was good enough. The window led to the alleyway behind the motel. Sticking my head out the window first, I looked left, then right. No one in the alley.

Squeezing through that window was no easy task, but I managed it, and made it across the alley without being seen. Stepping up onto a metal trash can, I scurried over the back alley wall, right into another alley behind a Mexican restaurant, called 'Miguel's.' Just great, I thought.

A young woman with an apron on, walked out the back door of the restaurant, carrying a trash bag, at exactly the moment my feet hit the ground. She let out a little yelp of surprise and our eyes met. I put my index finger up to my lips. She said nothing. I ran, just as the sun began to peek over the nearby lake.

CHAPTER 7

For the next few days, I laid low at a friend's house. He knew that the sheriff was looking for me. Everyone in Red Lake knew by that point. He also knew that it was very unlikely they would come looking for me at his house.

Each day, I watched Ruby's house from my friend's car, which I parked several houses down. I wanted to know what Ruby and her roommate's routines were. What time they each left for work, whether they came home for lunch, and what time each of them returned home after work.

By the third day, I was pretty certain of their schedules. Both left promptly at 7:45 a.m. Neither of them went home for lunch. The roommate arrived home each day at about 5:30 p.m., while Ruby arrived about fifteen minutes later. That gave me plenty of time to do what I needed to do.

On the fourth day, I arrived promptly at 7:35 a.m., and waited. Ten minutes later, both women were gone. I casually walked up the sidewalk and making a quick sweep up and down the street from their front yard, I determined that no one was watching me. The side gate creaked once again, but no one seemed to notice.

I found the back living room sliding door unlocked again. Apparently they didn't learn anything from the other night. All of the shades were drawn closed and the house was quite dark. Without turning on any lights, I made my way straight to Ruby's bedroom.

I turned on the light switch, but kept the shades closed. Since it was daytime, it was unlikely anyone would notice the light on from the outside.

I had no idea what it was that I was actually searching for. I just knew that I needed to see if there was any evidence of Walter's disappearance in Ruby's room. What kind of evidence she might have was in question. I started with her dresser. Rummaging around, I found nothing. I was very careful to be neat about it. It was important that she didn't come home and it be obvious someone had been there. I wanted her to feel secure enough that she would continue to leave that back sliding door unlocked. I might need to go in and take another look around at a later date.

Next, I looked under her bed and under the mattress. I found some interesting gadgets in her nightstand, but nothing related to my son.

Lastly, there was her closet to explore. It was quite the mess, to say the least. Packed with clothing that was hanging, and even more clothing just in a large heap on the floor of the closet. On the top shelf, there were several shoe boxes. I started with those.

There were more than thirty pairs of shoes in those boxes. But, once again, nothing related to Walter. I figured the clothing that was on hangers would probably be a dead end, so I skipped those and went right for the large pile of clothes on the closet floor.

It took at least a half hour to sort through those. Some seemed clean and some seemed dirty. I couldn't figure out what her system was. It was all very chaotic.

I froze when a tiny pale green t-shirt was revealed in the far back corner of the dark closet. My hands shaking, I reached in and picked up the shirt. Holding it open in front of me, the blood on it stood out. It wasn't one large stain, but several spots all over the shirt.

It was Walter's shirt. I was sure of it. Though I hadn't actually seen my son in this lifetime, due to the fact that I woke up after he went into that toy store, I did remember something. I remembered that when Elizabeth gave his description to the sheriff, she told him that Walter had been wearing a green t-shirt and tan shorts.

What did this all mean? Obviously, Ruby was involved. But how was she involved? Did she orchestrate his kidnapping? Did she find out afterward that Miguel did it? Did she try covering the crime up? And if so, why in the world would Walter's t-shirt be stuffed in the back of her closet? Had he been in her house at some point?

Now I was at a loss as to what I should do. If I called the cops, I would likely be arrested for breaking and entering. They would also probably think that I had planted the evidence. No, calling the sheriff would be a bad idea. It would get me locked up. I was sure about that.

I did make a phone call though. It was an important one. I called Elizabeth. She was Walter's mother, and regardless of our feelings about one another, she had a right to know what was going on.

"Hi. It's me. I need to see you," I said into the phone. I had used Ruby's kitchen phone to call Elizabeth.

"About what?" The tone in her voice said that she didn't want to speak to me.

"It's about Walter. I'm over at Ruby's house and I found something. Can you come over?"

"Sam, I'm busy. What did you find?"

"Please. I don't want to discuss it over the phone. But you

really need to see this. I believe Walter has been in Ruby's house."

I did my best to persuade her without divulging the bloody t-shirt over the phone. Telling her about that over the phone seemed like a really bad idea to me.

"Why do you think he's been in her house? Maybe you took him there at some point?" she asked.

"No. That's not it." My patience was running low. "Elizabeth, please. Just come over here."

"I don't want to see Ruby," she stated.

"She's at work." I gave her Ruby's address and Elizabeth agreed to meet me shortly.

An hour later, Elizabeth knocked on Ruby's front door. I stuck my head out the door, looked right, then left. Once satisfied that no one was watching us, I ushered Elizabeth inside quickly.

"It's about time," I admonished. "I'm not supposed to be here at all. Are you trying to get me arrested?"

Her eyebrows raised. "What are you talking about? Ruby doesn't know you are here?"

"No, she doesn't know I'm here. Or you. Come on." I walked toward the kitchen where I had left the shirt. Elizabeth followed.

Picking up the little green t-shirt, I turned and held it up for her to see. Elizabeth gasped, and before I had a chance to respond, she broke down sobbing.

I dropped the t-shirt in a heap on the kitchen table and turned to Elizabeth, taking her into my arms. We were no longer a couple, but we would always have a close, personal bond. We shared a son together. Whether Walter was still alive or not, he was something that would always tie the two of us together.

I held her while she cried. I understood her pain. It was something I could feel deep down inside. I had cried myself out many times over the years, and would probably do so again. And again. It was something that would never go away, no matter how many lives I led.

Several minutes later, Elizabeth's cries quieted down to a low murmur. When she pulled away from me, the shirt I had on was soaking wet. I didn't mind. I handed her a tissue and she dabbed at her eyes and nose.

"Elizabeth, we need to talk."

"I know." Her eyes found the green t-shirt that still laid crumpled on the kitchen table. "That's Walter's t-shirt. I know it is. How did it get here?"

"I don't know for sure. But I found it stuffed in the back of Ruby's bedroom closet, underneath a bunch of other clothes," I explained.

Elizabeth took a deep breath, inhaling courage. "Did Ruby kill our son?"

I could tell that was a very difficult question for her to ask. Of course it would be, for any mother or father. I didn't have any answers for her though. All we had was circum-stantial evidence. For all we knew, Miguel had taken things into his own hands without Ruby's knowledge. He could easily have planted the evidence at her place.

But Ruby not knowing anything seemed quite unlikely. Especially after the cryptic phone conversation we had. She had said something about how Walter's disappearance had gotten my attention. That made me very nervous, just thinking about the implication of her words.

"Sweetheart," it was something I had always called Eliza-beth during our sixty year marriage, "I think that it's very likely she did kill him. Or at least was involved in his killing. She probably didn't actually do it herself."

I cringed at that last sentence. That was way more information than Elizabeth needed.

"So you think he's dead?"

There was so much sorrow in her eyes. I reached over and gently brushed a tear from her cheek.

I nodded. "I have to be honest with you. Yes, I think he's dead."

She nodded back. She didn't break down that time. I think that she was beginning to accept the idea that our son was gone.

"What the hell are you two doing here?"

Startled, we both turned toward the front door. There Ruby stood, purse over her shoulder, hands on her hips.

"What did you do to our son?!" Elizabeth screamed.

Before I realized what she was doing, Elizabeth rushed toward Ruby. I sprang into action, but Elizabeth was several steps ahead of me and crossed the gap between her and Ruby before I could catch her.

The fight was on.

Before either woman could do too much damage to the other, I wrapped my arms around Elizabeth's waist and pulled her off of Ruby. I stood her up and pointed at her. I got my point across. Elizabeth didn't make another attempt at Ruby. But I did notice that she came back with a handful of dark hair. Ruby was rubbing the side of her head where that hair had just been pulled from the roots.

"Ruby, just tell us the truth. Please," I begged.

Ruby looked first at me, then at Elizabeth, then back at me. When she looked down at her feet, I knew the truth. We both did.

CHAPTER 8

"It was an accident," Ruby reported.

Elizabeth didn't need to hear anymore than that. The implications of that one sentence was enough. We all understood at that point. The mother of my child collapsed on the living room floor, sobbing. I didn't go to her. I stood my ground. It was important that I urge Ruby to continue what she had started. If I didn't, I wasn't sure that she would finish telling us what had happened to our son.

"Tell us everything," I ordered in a calm manner.

Ruby looked over at Elizabeth. "Should we do something about her first?"

"She'll be fine. We just need to know the truth. Out with it now," I told her through clenched teeth.

Ruby looked down at her feet in response.

"Ruby!" I yelled. "You better start talking."

She put her palms up facing me. "Okay, okay. I'll tell you. But I want to start by saying that I'm really sorry. It was an accident."

"You already said that. But we still don't know what

happened." I'm sure that the look on my face was enough to jolt the story out of her.

"Yeah, okay. Miguel took Walter from the toy store that day that we were fighting in the mall."

"Were you in on it?" I asked her, already knowing the answer.

She nodded without speaking.

"Why Ruby? Why would you do that?" I asked her.

"I guess I just wanted to get your attention." I was pretty sure that even she thought it was a stupid reason to kidnap someone's child.

"And you thought that I would want to stay with you if you took Walter? What were you thinking?" It was all I could do to keep calm. If I blew up then, we might never get the truth out of her.

"I just thought that if I was the one who found him wandering outside the mall, you would be grateful to me. And you wouldn't hate me so much," she tried to explain.

"I don't…didn't hate you, Ruby. I just didn't think we were right for each other," I told her. "So how did he end up here?"

"It wasn't my intention for Walter to ever leave the mall. He wasn't really kidnapped. He was just taken for a walk for a few minutes." She hesitated for a moment. "He was supposed to be found by me right away." Ruby made an x sign across her chest. "I swear it."

I nodded.

"Miguel said there were too many cops around the mall. He was afraid someone would see him with the boy. So he took off and brought him here. I looked all over for them at the mall. I didn't know anything about it until I came home," she explained.

"So why didn't you call me or the cops immediately, when you found out he was here?"

"Because I would have gotten arrested for kidnapping."

"I'm sure that's true," I told her honestly. "But that's no excuse for killing him."

"I didn't kill him!"

"Then what happened, Ruby?" I asked her, once again.

Ruby began pacing the living room floor. Somehow I managed to patiently wait for her to tell us her side of the story. After two minutes of pacing, she abruptly stopped, and turned to face me. She couldn't look Elizabeth in the eyes.

"I made him stay in my room. Miguel came over and we got into an argument, so the kid was left alone for maybe half an hour. Not long," Ruby told me.

"For a three year old to be left alone for a half hour, that's a really long time," Elizabeth said directly to Ruby. Her voice was quiet and withdrawn. She stood as she spoke.

Ruby looked over at Elizabeth, then back at me. "We didn't see what happened, but we heard the gunshot from in here."

Elizabeth gasped. I walked over to her and put my arms around her.

"It was an accident. How was I supposed to know that he would get my gun. It was in a shoebox," Ruby tried to explain.

Elizabeth pulled out of my arms and turned to face Ruby. "You left a small child alone with a loaded gun within his reach? What the hell were you thinking?"

Elizabeth didn't scream. She didn't threaten. Surprisingly it was a very calm question.

"It was hidden. I didn't think he…"

"That's your problem," Elizabeth interrupted Ruby in the middle of her sentence. "You didn't think. You conspired to kidnap my baby, then you left him here to die. Where is he now?"

That was a good question. We both looked at Ruby for

the answer. "We…um…buried him in the woods." She looked down at her feet as she spoke.

"I'm going to kill you!" Elizabeth had gotten over her initial shock. Temporarily at least. As she lunged toward Ruby, I caught her around the waist and held her back.

Ruby darted for her bedroom, locking the door behind her.

I sat Elizabeth down on the couch and stroked her hand to calm her down. It appeared to be working as she began taking deep breaths.

"What are we going to do about her, Sam?"

"I'm going to take care of her. Don't you worry about that," I told her honestly.

"We need to call the cops."

"Not yet. I'm going to go talk to her first," I told her. "Stay here."

"Ruby, come out. I want to talk to you." I knocked on her bedroom door.

No answer.

"Ruby! Stop playing games and come out here!" I yelled, pounding on the door that time.

Still no answer.

With a bad feeling creeping through me, I lifted my right leg and slammed it into the door, next to the lock. Splintered wood and part of the door jamb flew as the door swung open. Ruby was nowhere in the room. Her bedroom window was wide open.

"She's gone," I told Elizabeth when I reached the living room.

CHAPTER 9

Elizabeth was a mess, so I took her home. I got her settled into the sofa, with a blanket around her, and a cup of tea.

"Sweetheart, listen," I began, sitting down on the sofa next to her. "Don't call the sheriff just yet. I'm going to go deal with Ruby in my own way."

"What do you mean by that?" She didn't need to ask it. I was pretty sure she knew exactly what I meant.

I patted her hand. "Don't you worry about that. I'll be back in a little while to check on you. Okay?" I stood up.

Elizabeth looked up at me. "Okay."

I skipped Ruby's house, figuring that she wouldn't be stupid enough to return there. Instead, I headed directly to Miguel's place. No knocking was necessary, as far as I was concerned. Both of them turned with wide eyes toward me as I boldly walked right in. Idiots. Should have locked the front door.

I was actually surprised to find them both there. I was sure that they would be speeding out of town by that time. That was their plan, but they hadn't gotten very far yet.

Instead, I found them arguing. Ruby wanted to go. Miguel seemed to be taking his time getting out of there.

"What the hell are you doing here?" It was Miguel asking the question.

"You killed my son."

"The hell I did. I wasn't even at her house when it happened," Miguel told me.

"That's not how Ruby described it," I replied back.

We both looked at Ruby. Her face went crimson.

"He...well...he wasn't technically there at that moment. But he did take the kid." She looked over at Miguel. "It isn't like he wasn't involved."

"So you lied to me?" I asked her.

She didn't respond and looked away from me.

"You kidnapped my son. You took him to your house. You locked him in the bedroom where he found your gun. Then he got shot messing with your gun, while you did god knows what. Is all that correct?" I recounted the events.

"Yeah, I guess." Ruby shrugged.

"You guess? Is that what happened, or not?" My voice was getting louder. And angrier.

"Yes, that's what happened," Ruby replied.

"Hey. Just lay off her, all right?" Miguel chimed in.

"Are you kidding me?! You two are responsible for the death of my son, even if you didn't pull the trigger yourselves. This is all completely your fault. You get that, right?" I asked him.

"No, I don't get that. It was an accident. We only meant to..." Miguel was cut off by me.

I got right in front of his face. "You only meant to what?" Our noses were almost touching.

He backed up a step. "We only meant to scare you. Not for the kid to die."

248

"It didn't work out that way, did it?" I replied through gritted teeth.

"Hey, it's not our fault that the stupid little shit shot himself," Miguel replied.

That was it. Before I had a chance to think about it, my hands wrapped around Miguel's neck like a vice grip. His arms flailed in a feeble attempt to break my grasp. But it wasn't working. I squeezed even harder as his face turned a bright shade of red. I could feel the blood coursing through his neck in a desperate attempt to keep him alive. But with no oxygen getting to his brain, he passed out quickly. My grip held tight as we both went to the ground, me on top of him by then.

Ruby screamed. Still, I squeezed his neck. Ruby began hitting me. I ignored her. I had a one track mind at that point, and nothing was going to stop me.

When the job was done, and I was satisfied that Miguel would not be getting back up, it was Ruby's turn. However, she was no longer in the room. I could hear her in the back bedroom rummaging around. Looking for a weapon, no doubt.

When she emerged from the bedroom, I caught her unaware. She didn't see me lurking just outside the doorway. I grabbed her from behind and she screamed. Her scream was cut short when I squeezed her neck with my forearm.

I dragged her to the living room. She gasped for breath and fought me the entire length of the hallway.

Loosening my grip around her neck, I pointed to Miguel. "This is for what you did to my son."

She gasped for breath. "I didn't...I..."

Not giving her the chance to lie again, I squeezed. Her face began turning red. What I didn't see was what was in her hand.

Before I realized what she was doing, I heard the gunshot,

and felt the searing pain in my gut. Only anger controlled me then. I squeezed even harder and her body went limp. She slumped to the floor when I released her.

My t-shirt was covered in blood and it wasn't slowing down. My head felt woozy and I suddenly felt very tired. I needed to sit down. Making my way to the couch, my knees gave way just as I reached it. I felt the coffee table slam into my skull on my way down.

That was the last thing I remembered as it all went black.

PART 5

CHAPTER 1

Regaining consciousness, my hand went instinctively to the spot on my mid section where I had been shot. The pain was gone. It felt dry and clean. No blood anywhere.

My eyes flew open and landed on the ceiling where there was a poster of a bikini clad young woman looking down at me.

I knew instantly that I was back in my teenage bedroom, and was almost certainly a teenager again. Still, I looked down at my stomach to make sure there was no gunshot wound. There wasn't.

I flew out of bed and over to my dresser mirror. Young face, unruly hair, rumpled clothing. Yeah, definitely a teenager. I looked around my room. My high school diploma was pinned up on the wall. The calendar next to it told me that it was still June.

"Okay, looks like it's the summer right after graduation," I said out loud.

I was no longer surprised to find myself reliving my life. Though I hoped desperately that I was wrong, I had already resigned myself to the possibility that it might never end. I might go through this over and over, and over again, for the rest of eternity. Just fantastic.

Now it's time to figure out if I'm dating anyone, and who that person might be. So far, it had always been either Elizabeth or Ruby. Therefore, they were the likely ones. I had already been killed by both of them, so I wasn't really keen on the idea of either of them being my girlfriend in this lifetime. Maybe I would switch things up and find someone new to spend my life with.

But that would mean that Walter wouldn't exist. I already missed him so much. In my previous lives, I had barely had time to get to know him before he was killed each time. This time, I really wanted things to be different. I sat there on my bed for a long time thinking about that. What would I need to do to make sure that things were different this time? For all I knew, this would be my last life. I needed to make it count.

And Olive. I needed to see her. It was important to me that I make things right with her. I didn't know if I would ever get another chance. But hell, maybe I would get a thousand more chances. Five thousand more chances. I had no way of knowing the answer to that. And since I had no way of knowing if there would be five thousand more lives, I needed to live this life like it was my last one.

But Olive would have to wait. Dealing with Ruby and Elizabeth was first and foremost in my mind.

"It's about time you got up, sleepy head," my mother teased when I shuffled into the kitchen and plopped into a chair at the table.

"It's summer vacation," I told her.

"Oh honey, now that you've graduated, you get no more summer vacations," she laughed. "You need to get a job and then start college in the fall. That's going to be your life for the next four years."

"College?" Ugh, I had forgotten about that.

My mother turned to look at me, with a shake of her head. "Yeah, college. I hope you were joking just then. You know that you are expected to go to college. It's all we've talked about for the past year."

"Yeah, I know," I told her.

Now I just needed to figure out a sly way to get my mother to tell me who I'm dating. "Um mom. What do you think my girlfriend would like for her birthday?" I grimaced, waiting for her reply.

"Ruby? I don't know. She likes flashy stuff. I do know that much," Mom said without turning from the stove where she was frying some bacon.

Ruby. So she was the one. Just great. At least Elizabeth I could deal with. But Ruby? She was a loose canon, and I didn't need that in my life. I would have to figure out how to break that off.

"Okay thanks. I'll figure something out. That bacon smells great," I told her.

"It's almost done. Then I'll fry you up some eggs." She began humming as the bacon popped and sizzled in the pan.

I knew that I needed to go see Ruby. There was no getting out of that. I also knew that I hated that woman with every fiber of my being. From my point of view, I had just found out hours ago that she had been responsible for my son dying. She had left him locked in her bedroom, where he found her loaded gun, and had accidentally shot himself. He was three years old. Three. I would never...could never... forgive her for that.

Ruby and Miguel had been instrumental in kidnapping, and killing Walter, in more than one life. Even if the Ruby in this particular life had not done anything wrong yet, she was still Ruby. And, I had to make sure that she could never get her hands on my son.

I didn't want to kill her. I never intended to kill her. I just wanted to be done with her. I wanted to never see her again, as long as I lived. As much as she might have deserved it in my last life, I couldn't kill someone for something they really hadn't done in this life.

Walter didn't exist. Not yet anyway. So she clearly hadn't hurt him yet. I needed to make sure things stayed that way.

After breakfast, I headed straight for Ruby's house. Her mother answered the door. I sat down on the front porch, while her mother retrieved Ruby.

About a minute later, the front door squeaked and I turned toward the sound. I do have to say that even though I hated every bit of her, Ruby was always gorgeous. Her long, dark hair swayed in the slight breeze. She wore short white shorts and a lime green blouse. The colors complimented her beautifully.

"Hi Sam." Ruby sat down next to me on the porch and leaned in for a kiss. I dodged her attempt and she frowned. "What's going on?"

I was positive that no one ever in Ruby's life had dodged an attempt from her for a kiss.

"Ruby, look," I began. "I have to go get a job, and then I'm starting college in the fall. That's going to take up a lot of my time. Besides, it's hours away from here. I don't think we will have time to see each other. Not much anyway."

Ruby smiled and I realized that I hadn't quite gotten my point across.

"It's fine. I will come see you some weekends, and you come here on others. Then we'll see each other on holidays. It'll be a lot more than you think." Apparently she had it all worked out.

"No. I don't think you understand," I tried to explain. "I expect to have a lot of homework to do. I doubt I'll be able to drive home. And if you drive up there, I won't have time to hang out."

Ruby frowned that time. "What are you trying to say?"

I looked down at my fidgeting hands. "I'm trying to say that maybe we should see other people. You will be happier with someone nearby that you can be with a lot. And…" I was cut off.

"And what? You will be happier with a college girl? I'm not good enough for you now?" Her voice was rising.

"No, that's not it. I just meant…" She cut me off again.

"Yeah, I know what you meant. You are trying to break it off with me." She stood up then and glared at me. "Fine. If you don't want to be with me, there are plenty of other boys who do! In fact, there's this boy, Miguel, who has been asking me out. I always said no, because of you. But maybe I'll say yes next time." She stormed into her house and slammed the door behind her.

"You and Miguel deserve each other," I said quietly. She didn't hear me.

Well, that's done. I walked home.

CHAPTER 2

For the next few days, I laid low, staying mostly in my bedroom at my parents' house. Before I approached Elizabeth, I wanted to make sure that I knew exactly what I was getting myself into.

I found out through some mutual friends that Elizabeth had a boyfriend. Just my luck. But I wasn't about to let that deter me. Apparently, we had dated for a short time in high school, but I was the one that broke it off. This wasn't going to be easy.

It had finally hit me that Elizabeth was the one who I wanted to be with. The one who I wanted to marry, have a child or three with, and grow old together. During our first lifetime together, even though we were married for sixty years, I really never gave us a chance.

Elizabeth was a sweet, easy going person. And she loved me back then. I was the type that never appreciated what I had, until it was gone.

In my subsequent lives, I thought that I wanted someone more exciting. Someone like Ruby. That whole thing turned out to just be one nightmare after another. And once I found out she was the one responsible for Walter disappearing and ultimately dying, I would never want to be with Ruby again. Even though this Ruby is not that same Ruby, it didn't matter. I would never trust her.

Of course, Elizabeth did poison me to death in a previous life, but I couldn't hold that against her. She was a grief stricken mother who thought I was to blame for her son's death. Since I was the one who was supposed to be supervising Walter when he ran in front of that car, I guess it was my fault. I couldn't fault Elizabeth for hating me. I hated me.

My current problem was to figure out how to get Elizabeth to get rid of the boyfriend and date me instead. The first thing that I needed to do was some reconnaissance.

I watched her house. Yeah, I know, kind of stalkery. It was harmless though, so I didn't worry about that part. It was harmless to Elizabeth anyway.

For the first two days of my stakeout, I must have missed her. I only spent some sporadic hours there, not wanting to draw any attention my way. On the third day…success. I skulked down in the front seat of my car and watched her climb into her mother's car and drive down the road. Just before she turned a corner, out of sight, I followed.

She drove to a familiar sight. The local Red Lake burger place. It was a staple in town, and would be there for many more decades to come. I remembered taking my own grandchildren, Ivy and Parker, there for a few outings myself. Of course, that wouldn't happen for many many more years, if at all. There was no guarantee that I would get Elizabeth back, or have Walter. If there was no Walter, there would be no Ivy and Parker.

From my spot in the parking lot, I watched Elizabeth walk in and kiss a young man just inside the front door. The two of them walked to a booth and sat down, next to each other. I contemplated what to do then. Walk in and ask her out in front of her boyfriend? No. Bad idea. I might get my ass kicked for that one. Go in and act like it's a chance meeting and chat with them? Maybe. Either way, I needed to do something.

Without a definite plan in place, I went inside anyway and sat at the booth closest to the front door. I sat where I could watch them. After ordering, I tried to not look at them too much, otherwise it would become obvious. I wished I had brought a book in with me. Anything to occupy me while I waited for my food.

It turned out that I didn't have to do anything at all. Elizabeth got up and headed right for me. I panicked, not knowing what to say.

She stopped at my booth. "Hi Sam. How are you?"

"Oh, hey." Smooth.

"I saw you come in, but you seemed like you wanted to be left alone, so I didn't say anything," she told me.

"Why don't you sit down?" I gestured to the seat opposite me.

Elizabeth quickly glanced at the seat, and then back at her date, who was watching us. "Oh, I shouldn't. I don't want my boyfriend to get mad. I'm supposed to be heading to the ladies room."

So did that mean she made up needing to go to the ladies room, so she could stop and talk to me briefly? Or did that mean she actually needed to go to the ladies room and was forced to interact with me because she had to walk right past me on the way?

"I see. Can I ask you something?"

She nodded.

"Would you like to go out with me?" It was super bold of me to do that with her boyfriend only a few booths away, but he couldn't hear us. I didn't know if I would get another chance.

Her eyebrows shot up. "Sam, why do you want to go out with me? You are the one who broke things off between us before."

"Yeah, I know. I was young and stupid back then. I'm more mature now." I gave her a cheesy smile.

"That was only a few months ago." She smiled back.

I gave her a one shouldered shrug. "A lot can happen in a few months." Didn't I know it.

Elizabeth glanced back at her date, who was frowning at us. "Well, I should go. Come by my house tomorrow morning around eleven. Okay?"

"Yeah okay," I quickly responded, before she changed her mind.

With that, she continued her trek to the ladies room. I was eating my meal when she emerged and barely glanced her way. I didn't want to make any trouble for her and her boyfriend. Wait...yes I did.

Promptly at 11 a.m. the next morning, I rang Elizabeth's doorbell. She answered in a pretty yellow summer dress with white flowers adorning it. Her smile made the beautiful day even more so. I think I was in love from that very moment.

We were virtually strangers in this life, yet we had lived together for decades. I hadn't appreciated her in the past, but that was about to change. I would do whatever it took to get Elizabeth back in my life. And surprisingly, this wasn't even about Walter. It was about Elizabeth and me. I realized at that moment that I had missed her terribly and hadn't even known it.

Her light brown hair was up in a ponytail and when she smiled at me, I couldn't help but smile back. I held out my hand and she placed her soft hand in mine. Guiding her out the door and down her front steps, we stopped and faced each other on the sidewalk in front of her house.

"Would you like to go for a walk?" I asked her, staring into her beautiful, deep eyes.

"That would be nice."

We walked hand-in-hand that day. I apologized to her for my previous behavior in high school and told her how much I had missed her and hoped she would give me another chance. She said she would. She said that her current boyfriend was not the one for her and that she had been thrilled when they had run into me the night before.

It was almost like old times. Better than old times actually. Elizabeth called the boyfriend that very day and broke it off with him. After that, we were inseparable. And though the circumstances were not ideal, as we were unmarried, she became pregnant. I was beyond thrilled to have my Walter back.

As they say, all good things must come to an end. It was still a small town, and Ruby got wind of our relationship and our child on the way. About two weeks after I learned the good news, Ruby stopped me on my way to work one day.

"So, I heard about the baby," she told me, catching up to me on the sidewalk.

I glanced at her and didn't slow my pace. "What do you want, Ruby?"

"What? Can't we talk? Aren't we still friends?" She stuck out her lower lip in a bratty kind of pouty way.

"I really don't think that's a good idea. I have a girl now. She wouldn't be too happy for you and I to remain friends. I don't think you would like it if the roles were reversed. Would you?" I asked.

"It wouldn't bother me. I would trust you," she told me, struggling to keep up with my long strides.

"Sure you would. Well if there's nothing else, I need to get to work."

"Sam, wait. Can't you just stop for a minute? I want to talk." She grabbed my arm and stopped on the sidewalk, pulling me to a stop alongside her.

Turning to look her right in the eyes, I could see the pain in her face. My shoulders slumped. I really didn't want to hurt her. I didn't want to hurt anyone. Not emotionally. Not physically. But I needed to make sure that Ruby got the point. She needed to know that we were over permanently.

"What do you want to talk about?" I asked her with as even a tone as I could muster.

"Why do you like her and not me? I know I'm prettier than she is." She was serious. And she was right.

I nodded. "Yes Ruby, you are prettier than Elizabeth. But that's not what this is about. I love her. Please understand that. She is the one who I want to be with." I put my hand on her shoulder in a comforting manner. "Don't get me wrong. You are a nice girl. But, you aren't Elizabeth." I cringed a little after those last words escaped my lips. They were harsh, which wasn't my intention.

Ruby hung her head low. I watched as a single teardrop hit the sidewalk between us. I didn't know what to say. What could I possibly say to make her feel better?

I wrapped my arms around her and pulled her to me. I wanted to comfort her. I wanted her to feel better. It hurt me to be the cause of her pain. I struggled with the fact that this Ruby was not the same person who was responsible for my son's death in my last lifetime.

But Ruby didn't want to be comforted. She squirmed out of my arms. She took a swing at me, and missed. I guess it made her feel better to lash out. It didn't make me feel any better though.

Saying nothing, Ruby turned and walked away. I stood

my ground, watching her go. A breeze swept through her, making her hair dance around her head. She didn't seem to notice and kept moving. She disappeared around a corner, and that was that.

God, I hoped that I wouldn't have to do that dozens of more times in dozens of more lives. How many times can I possibly break a girl's heart before it takes its toll on me?

CHAPTER 3

The following week, Elizabeth and I went to the courthouse and got married. It certainly wasn't an elaborate wedding, and thankfully, Elizabeth didn't seem to care. We were deliriously happy.

I spent each day waiting for my life to end, and a new one to begin. This one was just too perfect.

Right after school started in the fall, I made my way to see Olive. I didn't know if she would talk to me, but I had to try.

I had made the decision not to attend college this time around. Been there, done that. My parents were horrified when I made the announcement, but it wasn't their decision to make. I had a wife, and a child on the way. I needed to provide for them, not let them live with Elizabeth's parents this time. I would not be persuaded otherwise. At least my mother respected my decision.

"Hello Olive."

She turned toward my voice. Olive had been standing in a small group of students, having an animated conversation. They all turned to look at me, the conversation ceasing immediately. I felt heat slowly climb from my collarbone to my cheeks.

Our eyes met. Was there recognition? Did she have any idea who I was? I couldn't tell. Her face did not give away her thoughts or emotions. I was terrified that she had no idea who I was. And if that was the case, it could be months, or even years, before she jumped into this body. I dreaded the thought of the wait for her to return.

Three seconds later, she turned back to her friends, without acknowledging me verbally. Leaning in, she whispered something to them that I could not hear. Each of them in turn, looked my way again, nodding toward Olive.

Then her little group dispersed. Olive stood and watched them all walk away, until they were far enough not to hear us. Only then did she turn back toward me.

"Do you know who I am?" I asked her, before she had a chance to speak.

"Yes, I know who you are, Sam."

"Do you still hate me?" It was a valid question.

"I never hated you, Sam."

"I have a couple of lifetimes to show that you did," I told her.

Olive smiled. "Yeah, I guess you do."

"Can we try to be friends again?" I asked. "I'm doing my best not to be that person that you remember."

She stood for a moment, contemplating me. "You know, I want you to be the person that I remember. I loved that guy. He was my best friend. It's the other part that I'm worried about."

I nodded. "I know. I can tell you honestly that I have not hurt a single person in this lifetime. And I have no intention of ever doing so."

"I believe that you mean what you say. I just don't know if

265

you can actually make that happen." She was being honest. I could respect that.

At that moment, a pretty blonde walked past us, right behind Olive. I recognized her immediately. It was Polly Sanderson. Henry's girl. She was also the girl I killed more than once in past lives. My eyes followed Polly, and I was completely drawn out of the conversation with Olive. My body shivered and my gut ached.

Oh no. It was that familiar feeling, and it was all I could do not to follow her. But I wouldn't let myself do that. I planted my feet firmly on the ground and refused to let them move, no matter what my body did to me in response.

Olive turned to see what I was looking at. Or rather, who I was looking at. When she realized that it was Polly, Olive turned back and looked at me with an incredulous look on her face.

"Are you kidding me? That is the same girl that you killed before. What is going on right now, Sam? You haven't changed a bit, have you?"

I tore my eyes away from Polly's back, and looked at Olive.

"No, Olive, it's not what you think."

"It's not? I saw how you looked at her. I saw you squirm, almost like you were in physical pain. Isn't that what happens when you feel the need to kill someone? Are you going to deny that?"

She looked at me hard. I looked away. She was right. Of course she was. I couldn't deny it. But I could try to explain it.

"Olive, yes, I felt that urge come on. I can't help that. It's just a biological part of me, I guess. You can't blame me for something that I have no control over. But what I can control, usually, is how I react to it. At least I can try. I owe that much to you. And to Henry. And most of all, to Polly. I won't hurt her. I swear it."

Olive did not respond. I was sure that she just didn't know what to say in response. That she didn't believe me? She probably didn't. There was something besides suspicion that I saw in her face also. I think it was concern. Or possibly understanding. I couldn't be sure. Either way, I think she was softening to me. I think she did believe that I wanted nothing more than to not have the urge to kill.

"Listen, Olive. I will kill myself before I hurt Polly ever again. I don't want to be that guy anymore. Actually, I never wanted to be him. But this time, I will make that happen."

She nodded. "I know. I believe you."

"Hi sweetheart."

Both Olive and I looked up at the sound of Henry's voice. He reached Polly and they embraced. It was very sweet, really. The scene made me smile. This time, in this life, Henry and Polly could be together. Of course, Henry had no idea who I was, since I wasn't his college roommate. I missed him, but that was okay. He could live a happy life without me.

Olive turned and I could see that she was trying to read the expression on my face.

"You're happy, aren't you?" she asked me. "About those two." She tilted her head toward the loving couple.

I nodded. "I am. In my past lives, they could never be together, not for long anyway, because of me. This time, they might get that happily ever after they so much deserve."

Olive smiled at me. I took her hand and we walked together to one of the tables outside the cafeteria. It was a warm, fall day. The sunshine on our skin was heavenly.

We spent the next two hours talking about everything. I told her about my marriage to Elizabeth, and our upcoming child. She was happy for us. Olive also was dating someone. It seemed that the planets had lined up properly this time.

Or had they?

CHAPTER 4

Walter was born on a blustery spring day. Elizabeth was a trooper, and I couldn't have been more proud of her. Our son entered the world screaming his head off, making me the happiest man on the planet.

It was the 1960s, which was a time when fathers paced the waiting room. They didn't go in until everything was done, cleaned up, and perfect. It was as if the whole sordid ordeal was a simple procedure.

I wasn't one of those fathers. I insisted from the beginning that I be there for the birth of our son. The first time he was born, I was the one pacing the waiting room. This time, I wanted to be there. It might be the last time I got the chance.

Elizabeth was a bit taken aback by my request. It just wasn't done.

"Honey, don't you think that I want to see my son come into the world?" I had told her during that conversation.

"It's not going to be pretty, you know. I don't know if I want you to see me like that."

"Don't worry. Nothing will make me ever stop loving you." And I meant every word of it.

She agreed.

Both families came to see the new addition. After about an hour, the vigilant nurse noticed that Elizabeth was tiring.

"Everyone out now. This young lady needs her rest." She pointed at me. "You can stay. I like you."

I smiled at the nurse. She seemed to think that she had all the power in the room. Maybe she did.

"What do you think of the name Walter?" Elizabeth asked me once we were alone.

Elizabeth's hair was a mess, sticking up all over the place, and some of her makeup was running down her face. She was still the most beautiful woman in the world to me. She had given me my son and I would always love her dearly for that.

"I love it. Can I hold him?" I reached for the little bundle.

"Of course. Now hold his head like this." She demonstrated. He squirmed in my arms.

I let her think she was teaching me something completely new. In reality, I had been a father for over 80 years, give or take a few.

A few days later we took Walter home. We were deliriously happy for a few weeks.

Until we weren't.

I decided to give Elizabeth a much needed break and took Walter for a stroll around the neighborhood.

"Well, well, well, what do we have here?"

Ruby was standing in front of me on the sidewalk. I hadn't even noticed her. My pulse quickened at the sight of her. Not because I was excited to see her. Just the opposite, actually. Dread clutched at my soul. There was just something about her that made me want to turn and run.

"What do you want, Ruby?" I wasn't beating around the bush. I had no intention of making small talk.

"I'm out for a walk, just like you are."

Ruby walked up and stood right in front of the carriage. When she looked down into it, I instinctively reached down inside the carriage and pulled the blanket up higher, as if to shield my son from the devil standing in front of him.

"You don't even live in this neighborhood. So, why are you really here?"

She looked down at her feet and I knew with certainty that I was the reason she was there. It was no coincidence. Not that I thought it was, even for a second.

"I just wanted to see you. I miss you."

I believed that much.

"You know I'm married now. And we have a son. Obviously."

We both looked down at Walter. He let out a gurgle and I laughed. Ruby's expression did not change.

"Is this what you really want? A family and a picket fence? I remember you being more daring and spontaneous. Settling down doesn't seem like you at all," she told me.

"Ruby, we only dated for a short time, and to be honest, we barely know each other." I knew her well enough. I had seen all of her crazy over my many lifetimes. "I don't want to be harsh, but you just need to move on."

"Don't tell me to move on!" Her scream filled the air all around us.

I patted the air. "Ruby, please calm down. You are going to draw attention."

"I don't care what people think. You had no right to break up with me, just to be with her. I don't know why you want to be with her anyway. She has nothing on me."

I didn't even know how to respond. If I explained that I loved my wife, Ruby would probably flip out. If I said nothing, I might get the same reaction. Either way, I was screwed.

"Ruby, look…"

"Don't 'Ruby look' me. I should be the one you are

271

married to. I should be the one having your children. Why her, and not me?"

Her face drooped when she asked the question, and I could see that she was hurting. As much as I hated her for the sins she committed in my past lives, I tried to tell myself that this wasn't the same person. Maybe she deserved some compassion.

None of that really mattered though. I was with Elizabeth, and I wanted to stay that way. I wanted Ruby out of my life permanently.

"It's nothing personal, really. We just are not meant to be. Besides, it doesn't matter anymore. I'm with Elizabeth, and I'm going to stay that way."

I didn't wait for a response. I took hold of the carriage, turned us around, and headed for home with my son. I looked back to see Ruby still standing there where I left her. From a distance, it kind of looked like she was crying, but I couldn't tell for sure. A minute later, when I turned again, she was gone.

The sound of glass breaking jolted me awake. Elizabeth was still snoring softly next to me. Not wanting to wake her up, because she got so little sleep anyway, I carefully crawled out of bed to investigate. I lifted my robe off the hook on the bathroom door, grabbed the baseball bat that I always kept next to the bed, and quietly opened our bedroom door, just a crack.

I stuck my eye up to the crack, to make sure no one was standing just outside, ready to pounce. The hallway was dark. I watched for a full minute. Nothing. No movement, no sound.

I pulled the bedroom door fully open. Perhaps I had

imagined the sound of breaking glass. I had to have been dreaming. I decided to check the doors and windows anyway. A quick stop in Walter's bedroom, which was right next to ours, would give me a feeling of peace.

There was a dim nightlight in the outlet just inside Walter's bedroom door. Not wanting to wake my son, I crossed his room and peered into his crib. What I saw made my blood run cold.

Nothing. No one. Walter was not in his crib. He was much too young to have climbed out himself, and Elizabeth was sleeping soundly in our bed.

I flipped on the bedroom light, just to make sure that I was seeing what I thought I was seeing. It was quite dark in the room and perhaps my eyes were playing tricks on me. Back to the crib, nothing had changed.

I bolted out of the room, down the hallway, and toward the front of the house. I fully expected to see the front door wide open. But I never even got that far. Through the glow of the moon peeking in between the slats of the window blinds, I could see the outline of a woman sitting on the couch in the living room, holding our son. I couldn't see her face, but there was no doubt in my mind who it was.

I flipped on the light switch and the room came to life.

"Ruby, what the hell are you doing here?"

She barely glanced up at me, and back to the baby.

"Ruby!"

"Sam, the baby is asleep. I'm sure that you don't want to wake him."

I walked over to the couch and reached for my son. "Give him to me."

Her arms tightened around the bundle inside the blanket.

"Ruby, I'm serious. Hand him over right now, or I'm calling the cops."

"No. In fact, if you don't go stand over there," she tilted

her head toward the hallway leading into the living room, "then I'll kill him."

I didn't think that there was any way that she could possibly hurt my son while I stood right in front of them, but I didn't want to take any chances. I moved over to the other side of the living room.

"What do you want, Ruby?"

"I want you to take me seriously," she told me, refusing to make eye contact with me.

"Meaning what, exactly? That's a pretty vague statement."

"Sam, what's going on in here?"

I turned to see Elizabeth walking up behind me, shuffling, with her robe hanging open. She stopped dead in her tracks at the sight of Ruby sitting on our sofa, holding our son.

"Sam?" Elizabeth pushed the hair away from her eyes and I could see the pained expression on her face.

"Come here." I took her hand and gently guided her to stand next to me. I didn't dare turn my back on Ruby. "It's all right. Ruby here was just visiting and was just about to hand Walter back to me, so he can go back to bed." I turned to Ruby. "Isn't that right, Ruby?"

"Your baby is pretty cute, you know." Ruby was ignoring me.

Elizabeth looked up at me with questioning eyes. I had no idea what to say. If I told the truth, that Ruby was a psycho and holding us hostage in our own living room, I didn't know if Elizabeth could handle that.

"It's okay. I've got this all under control," I whispered. With a quick glance, I could see that Ruby was paying us no attention. At least that's what it looked like.

"It doesn't look like you've got it under control," she whispered back. "Why is she really here and why does she have my baby?" She didn't take her eyes off of Walter and Ruby.

"Apparently, she wants me back," I admitted.

Elizabeth gave me a glare that caused shivers to run down my spine.

"I don't want her back. That girl is crazy," I whispered.

Glancing back to Ruby, it appeared that she hadn't heard our exchange.

"Stop whispering over there!" Ruby yelled.

That startled Walter. He began screaming.

"Give me my baby," Elizabeth called from across the room. She began to make a move toward Ruby. I stopped her with just a touch of her arm.

"I think he's hungry." Ruby looked up at us. "Go get some formula and I'll feed him," she ordered.

"I can feed my own baby," Elizabeth retorted, with almost a snarl.

"Go get the formula!" Ruby screamed. Walter then did his best to rival her.

I gave Elizabeth a head tilt toward the kitchen. She complied. I kept a close eye on Ruby while Elizabeth went about preparing the formula. About two minutes later, Elizabeth emerged from the kitchen with the warm bottle of formula, and handed it to Ruby.

"Go back over there and stand next to him," Ruby ordered.

The word 'him' sounded like it caught in her throat. I thought it weird that if she hated me so much, why was she in my living room, trying to get me back? If that's what she was doing.

"What are we going to do?" Elizabeth stood next to me and whispered. "We should call the sheriff. Don't you think?"

CHAPTER 5

Elizabeth turned to head back down the hall, toward our bedroom, where there was a phone extension she could use, without Ruby overhearing her.

"Where are you going?" she asked Elizabeth calmly.

Elizabeth stopped and turned around. "I'm just going to go use the bathroom. Okay?"

"No, not okay. Just stay right there. I don't want either of you out of my sight. Got it?"

We both nodded.

My gut lurched and I grabbed it in response. Oh god, not now.

"Are you all right?" Elizabeth's brows furrowed. I could read the worry on her face.

"I…yeah…I'll be okay. Just a stomach ache, I guess," I tried to explain.

"Do you want me to get you something for that?" my wife asked.

"No." Another wave hit me. I turned toward Ruby. It was all I could do not to walk over and break her neck for what she was doing to us.

I had to resist though. I just had to.

My legs gave way beneath me and I hit the ground with a thud. Elizabeth dropped to her knees beside me.

"What is he doing?" Ruby called. "Don't be playing any games with me."

"No one is playing a game. He's in serious pain!" Elizabeth shot back. "I need to help him."

"He'll live," Ruby said.

"Yeah, but you might not," I whispered. Elizabeth's eyes grew wide, but she said nothing.

The next ten minutes were like agony to me. It felt like someone was repeatedly gut punching me. I even vomited all over the floor, while Ruby was sure to let us know how disgusted she was about that. She made no move to help though. Elizabeth did her best to comfort me, but Ruby refused to let her leave the room. And Elizabeth wasn't about to leave while Ruby was holding our son hostage.

When it was all over, I sat up, drenched in sweat. Elizabeth smoothed my sweaty hair back with her fingers. I smiled in response.

"Can I get some water?" I asked my wife.

She looked up at Ruby. "Go. Get some water. But don't try anything," she ordered.

"I won't."

Elizabeth returned less than one minute later with a glass of water, a clean dish towel, and some paper towels. I downed the water in just a few swallows. Elizabeth wiped my face and neck with the dish towel. It was a bit damp and felt cool against my hot skin. Then she proceeded to clean up the vomit.

"Are you okay now? What was that?" Elizabeth asked me.

"Um, I don't know. Maybe just something I ate," I lied.

"Maybe. Now that you are feeling better, we need to figure something else out. We have to do something about her," Elizabeth whispered to me, sliding just her eyes Ruby's way.

I looked up at Ruby and she was ignoring the both of us.

"What is it that you want, Ruby? We can't all stay here in the living room indefinitely. At some point people need to eat, and sleep, and even go to the bathroom," I explained. "So, I'm going to ask you again, what is it that you want from us?"

"Oh, I don't want anything at all from you. I'm not an idiot and I know that you will never come back to me, as long as she is around." Ruby shot daggers at Elizabeth with only her eyes.

"Elizabeth is not going anywhere. She is my wife. Please understand that. You and I had some great times, but we just weren't right for each other. You have to see that."

I did my best to appeal to her sense of humanity. She had even said that she knew we couldn't get back together as long as Elizabeth was around. I was trying to play on that and hoped that it might work.

"We can still be friends. I would love that. What do you think? Can we be friends, Ruby?" I asked.

"You don't want to be my friend. So, if I can't have you, then I can still have a part of you," Ruby told me.

"What is that supposed to mean?" Elizabeth chimed in.

"You shut up!" Ruby screamed.

Walter let out a yell, in response.

"Oh sweetheart," Ruby said soothingly to my child. "It's okay. I'm here. Nothing to worry about."

I turned to see Elizabeth flinch when Ruby did that. I reached over and gently rubbed her back, hoping it would ease her tension.

"Ruby, why would you want to hurt an innocent baby?" I asked her, knowing full well what she was capable of.

"I would never hurt him. Not unless you made me do it, that is," Ruby answered.

"Ruby, what are you talking about?" I asked her.

"I would make a better mother for this boy than she is."

Elizabeth's eyes grew wide. "Excuse me?"

Not responding to my wife, Ruby continued. "What do you think of the name, Ethan? I've always liked that name."

"Are you out of your damn mind?" Elizabeth yelled. "He is my child!"

With that, Elizabeth closed the gap between us and Ruby in a matter of a second or two. She reached for Walter, while Ruby pulled him in closer to her chest, cradling him tightly.

"You better back off," Ruby told her with authority in her voice.

"Give him to me!" Elizabeth reached for him again.

The two women struggled. I ran over to help. I got in next to Ruby on the couch and grabbed her throat with one hand. I squeezed. She couldn't struggle over the baby if she couldn't breathe.

She released Walter and Elizabeth took him from her. Still, I squeezed.

"Sam, let her go!" Elizabeth demanded. "I'll call the sheriff and he can arrest her for kidnapping."

Ruby's face was turning a horrible violet color. Still, I squeezed.

"Sam!" Elizabeth screamed.

I let go. Ruby immediately went into a coughing fit. We watched while the lavender color faded and her face slowly regained its normal pale coloring.

Choking out her words, Ruby was finally able to speak. "Why the hell…did you…do that?" She rubbed her throat as she spoke.

"You were threatening to take our baby. That's why," I told her in no uncertain terms.

"Oh, you think that was a threat?" she retorted.

"Wasn't it?" I asked her.

"No. Not at all. It was a promise."

Her eyes were cold, causing me to shiver slightly. Yes, I had killed many many people over my several lives, and people didn't tend to scare me. But looking into Ruby's face that day, I have to admit that fear grabbed onto me. I had no doubt whatsoever, that she would make good on her promise.

"I'm calling the sheriff." Elizabeth headed for the kitchen with Walter cradled lovingly in her arms.

Before I realized what was happening, Ruby bolted from the couch and ran for the kitchen. I jumped up, hot on her trail. With no regard for the child that Elizabeth was carrying, Ruby jumped on her back.

Startled, Elizabeth almost dropped Walter, but I grabbed him just in time. Elizabeth stumbled, hitting her forehead on the kitchen counter.

I couldn't help my wife with a baby in my arms. I ran to Walter's room and put him carefully into the crib. I didn't have time to do anything else but run to the aid of Elizabeth.

When I reached the kitchen, the women were in a full out battle. There was a lot of screaming going on, and a lot of blood. I didn't think that anyone had been seriously wounded, just that head gash of Elizabeth's, and perhaps a bloody nose. Or two.

My wife had her back to me, and was in a better position for me to intervene. I wrapped my arms around her waist and pulled her away from Ruby. As I backed up, Elizabeth's legs shot up into the air, and both bashed Ruby hard. Ruby slammed into the kitchen counter, back first. I heard her scream as Elizabeth and I hit the ground, stunned.

Before the two of us could regain our senses. Ruby bolted past us and down the hall, toward Walter's room. We both jumped up as quickly as we could and chased her. Surprisingly, she ran right past Walter's room, flung the back door open, and out into the backyard. We gave chase.

Probably because I reached her first, Ruby attacked me. Why I was surprised, was a good question, but I stumbled when Ruby slammed into me. As her fists were flying, it was all I could do to keep her from seriously hurting me. My nose was broken. That was for sure.

"Ruby, stop!" I yelled.

But she didn't let up, even a tiny bit.

"I'm going to kill you for what you did to me!" she screamed.

"For what I did to you?" I managed to say, while trying to block her scratching at me.

Just as I managed to grab her wrists to stop the onslaught, I heard a sharp, metallic sound. Ruby's eyes grew wide as she slumped to the ground. I let her go as she fell.

That's when I saw the shovel buried in her skull. I looked up to see Elizabeth also watching Ruby hit the ground. When she burst out sobbing, I went to her. I wrapped my arms around my wife.

"I…I…killed her," Elizabeth choked out.

I cradled her head against my chest. "It's all right, baby. You had no other choice. She would have killed us both, given the chance. We both know that."

Elizabeth nodded. "I want to go check on Walter. Can you call the sheriff?" She pulled out of my arms.

"Yes, go check on him. I'll deal with her." We both looked down at the body on the ground. Ruby would never hurt anyone again.

I watched Elizabeth head into the house. Now what? Should I call the sheriff? I had a bad feeling that by doing so, I would be opening a can of worms that I didn't want to open.

What if she had spread her venom already around town?

She could easily have made up lies about me that I would have no way of defending without her here to corroborate whatever I say. Besides, would anyone believe that it was self-defense? Or would they believe that we lured her over to our house to kill her? That did seem a bit crazy, but I never knew what people might believe.

A few minutes later, Elizabeth emerged without the baby. "Everything is fine. Walter is sleeping soundly. Though I don't know how. We made quite a ruckus. Is the sheriff on his way?"

"Um, no. I didn't call him," I answered.

"What? Why not?" Her eyes cut toward the body on the ground.

"I don't think we should call the sheriff. What if he considers this murder?" I asked.

"Why would he think that? She attacked us in our own home. She took our child and threatened to harm him or take him from us. The sheriff will believe us," Elizabeth tried to explain.

"I'm not so sure about that. If I were the sheriff, I would take one look at this scene and think that it was quite unlikely that Ruby would come here on her own, and attack the two of us. I mean look at her." We both looked at her. "She is the one with the shovel in her skull. One, or both of us, could end up in prison. Then Walter would have no one. Do you want that?"

Elizabeth shook her head in response.

"I think calling the sheriff is a bad idea," I added.

She nodded. "Yeah, those are some good points. But what do you propose we do with her? We can't just dig a hole in our backyard. Where do we take her?"

I knew the perfect place.

CHAPTER 6

"I don't know, Sam. Do you really think this is a good idea?" Elizabeth grabbed the back of my shirt.

"Elizabeth, please let go. It's hard enough to carry this dead weight. Having to pull you along, is making it more difficult." I tried not to sound harsh, but it was true.

"How much further to the sinkhole? It's dark and creepy out here at night." She let go of me.

"I don't know. A mile maybe. Just stay close behind me."

"Okay," she replied. I could hear the fear in her voice.

I didn't think there was any chance of her wandering off.

I did have to agree with her about it being creepy. The trek through the forest to the sinkhole was a long one. At night, it seemed as if you could hear every single little noise. It also seemed as if every forest creature was out and about. Though we were making enough noise on our own, crunching through the dense forest, we could still hear critters making their way around us.

"I gotta stop for a minute and catch my breath," I told her, stopping abruptly and dropping the body on the ground in front of me. It landed with a thud.

A growl made us both snap our heads to the right, toward the sound.

"Sam, what was that?" Elizabeth grabbed my shirt and pulled me toward her.

"A wolf maybe, I don't know. But I don't want to stick around to find out."

I bent over and heaved Ruby's body up and over my shoulder, continuing our journey.

"Come on, let's hurry up."

I thought about my last journey through the forest. Ruby was my cohort that time and we were taking Miguel's body to the sinkhole. We used a wheelbarrow, but it wasn't any help really. Pushing that thing over the soft dirt was torture. Surprisingly, carrying a body was a bit easier.

An hour later, we finally arrived at the sinkhole. I dropped the body next to the edge. I don't really know why I hesitated to push her in. I hated this woman with every bit of me. She had messed with me in several lifetimes. She had kidnapped my son on more than one occasion, causing me terrible heartache and pain. There certainly was no love loss between us.

So why was I hesitating? There was no reason to. She had earned the right to spend eternity at the bottom of the sinkhole, never to be heard from again. It would serve her right for anyone that knew her to have no idea what had ever become of her.

"What are you waiting for?" Elizabeth's voice brought me back to the moment. "Push her in."

I obliged, kneeling down and rolling her over the edge. Standing up, I put my arm around my wife's waist. We stood there listening to the dirt and rocks falling in along with her. There never was a thump at the end when her body hit the bottom. No one knew how deep the sinkhole was. It might have been twenty feet, it might have been a hundred feet.

Maybe even a river at the very bottom to carry her away. Either way, she was gone and we were both happy about that fact.

"Come on, let's get back over to your parents' house and get Walter," I told her. "I want us all to be together tonight."

Elizabeth and I walked in silence most of the way back to the car. No words were necessary. We knew what each other was feeling. At least Ruby would never be a problem again. As long as I didn't wake up dating her again. Oh god. The horror of that thought almost made me lose my dinner. Again.

With no moon, the dim forest was almost impassable. Luckily, I had thought to bring a flashlight with me. It barely penetrated the thickness of the night.

"Now what are we going to do?" Elizabeth whispered as we were nearing the end of our journey out of the dark forest.

"Why are you whispering?" I asked her, half whispering myself.

"Because it's dark and creepy in here. I feel like I should whisper," she whispered again. "Besides, what if someone is out here. I don't want them hearing our conversation about you know who."

I understood where she was coming from, because even I was a bit freaked out by the dark forest. I felt shivers as we made our way through the dense brush. We could both hear every crunch underneath our feet. And occasionally, we could hear crunching noises somewhere behind the trees. Neither of us dared investigate. Each time there was a crunch or a snap, our pace quickened.

"Honey, if there is someone out here in the forest, in the middle of the night, I can guarantee that he already saw us dragging a dead body to the sinkhole and dumping it in. So, yeah, it's too late to worry about that now."

I wrapped my arm around her shoulder and kissed the top of her head. She nodded, smiled, and we continued on our way, at almost a jog. We both let out a sigh of relief once we were safely encased inside our car.

"You never did answer my question about what we are going to do now," Elizabeth reminded me on our drive home.

"About what? Ruby?"

"No. The vacuum cleaner." She frowned at me. "Yes, of course, Ruby. Why are you being so thick?"

"Sorry," I replied with a frown. "I've just got a lot on my mind I guess. Really, there's nothing left to do. We just lie low and get on with our lives."

"So what if someone comes around looking for her?" Elizabeth asked me.

"Why would anyone come to us looking for her? I haven't dated her in a while. There's no reason they would. And if they do, then we will just say that we haven't seen her. No one can prove otherwise," I explained.

"Yeah, I guess," Elizabeth responded.

"Hey, why don't we make a pact to never mention her again? What do you say? You in?" I asked.

"Definitely. I have no reason to ever speak that name," Elizabeth agreed.

CHAPTER 7

Pounding on the front door woke both of us up early one morning. It also got to Walter. He began to screech.

"Who is here at…" Elizabeth looked over at the bedside clock, "six thirty in the morning?"

"I have no idea. I'll go see who it is. You can tend to the baby," I told her.

Grabbing my robe, I shuffled to the front door. I ran my fingers through my short, morning hair. It didn't help. My eyes widened when I saw the sheriff standing on my front porch.

"Good morning, Sheriff. What can I do for you?" I did my best to keep the irritation of being awakened so early in the morning, out of my voice.

"Hello, Sam. I apologize for showing up here so early, and obviously waking you, but I need to talk to you. Do you have a few minutes?"

Sheriff Jay Mitchell, was not a large man, and completely the opposite of what someone would expect in someone in that position. He was thin and a good six inches shorter than I was. Though he was only 10 or 15 years older than me, he had very little hair left on his head. The half assed combover did him no favors.

"Sure, come in."

I stood aside and opened the door wider. Mitchell walked in and stood in the living room. His eyes darted around the room, clearly taking a mental inventory. Subtlety was not his strong suit. Elizabeth walked in the room, carrying Walter.

"Good morning." Sheriff Mitchell tipped his head toward my wife.

"Sheriff, hello. Is something wrong?" she asked him.

"Perhaps. I came about your girlfriend, Ruby," he told us.

Elizabeth and I looked at each other for just a second, and back to the sheriff.

"Ex-girlfriend. I'm happily married now, as you can see." I gestured toward Elizabeth.

Mitchell looked over at her, holding the baby.

"I see. Well, Ruby's mother has reported her missing. She hasn't seen her in about a week. When was the last time either of you saw her?" He looked back and forth between the two of us.

I shrugged. "I don't know. Why are you asking us? Ruby is not in our lives."

"Because Ruby's mother said that Ruby told her she was coming over here to see you. This would have been right about the time she disappeared," Sheriff Mitchell explained.

"Well, I did run into her down the road when I was taking my son out for a walk one day." I didn't see any point in lying. This was a small town. It was quite likely that someone saw us talking. If I lied now, it could make things worse.

The sheriff didn't seem surprised by my admission. "And what did the two of you talk about during this chance encounter?" The snarkiness in his voice was not lost on me.

I could easily lie to answer that question. I was positive

that no one heard us, so he had no one to corroborate my story with.

"Nothing really. I think she was just out on a walk. She wanted to see the baby, so I stopped and we chatted. Small talk. That's all," I told him, with a dismissive wave of my hand.

"I see," he replied. "Has she been here to this house since the day out on your walk?" His eyes scanned the room again.

Was it possible that someone saw Ruby break into my house the other night? Yes, technically it was possible. But I doubt anyone saw her in the middle of the night. Especially since no one mentioned it to me, or called the sheriff when they saw someone breaking in.

The conundrum I had at that point was whether to tell the truth, that Ruby came into our house and held us hostage, or to lie and say that we hadn't seen her since that day on the sidewalk. There were pros and cons to both. In the end, I decided to tell him that our chance encounter the week before outside, was just that, and the last time that I had seen her. I didn't want to get into all the details about her being in our house, what happened, and where she went after that.

"I haven't seen her since," I lied, keeping eye contact with Mitchell. Looking away, was a telltale sign of lying.

After several seconds, he finally broke eye contact with me and turned to Elizabeth. "And you, Mrs. Wells, have you seen Ruby in the last week?"

Elizabeth looked directly at me before answering. This caused the sheriff to shoot a glance my way. It seemed as if he was evaluating me. My demeanor. My stance. The look on my face. I stood rigid, not letting him read me at all. At least I hoped that was the outcome.

He turned back to Elizabeth. "Mrs. Wells?"

"Oh, sorry. No, I haven't seen her." She shook her head slightly while she spoke.

Walter then decided to chime in with his signature high pitched squeal. All three of us turned his way.

"Well, if there's nothing else, I really need to get this little guy fed." It was more of a rhetorical question than a request. Elizabeth didn't hesitate and walked out of the room toward the kitchen immediately.

"Is there anything else I can help you with, Sheriff?" I asked him.

"Do you mind if I take a look around?"

He wasn't looking at me as he spoke, but glancing down the hallway. I felt my palms turn sweaty and wiped them on my pajama bottoms without thinking. The sheriff looked down at my hands and back up into my face.

"You know, Sheriff, it's very early in the morning. We would like to get on with taking care of our son and I have to get ready for work. So, this is really not a good time. You understand, right?"

I started walking toward the front door, hoping that Mitchell would follow suit. He did. Opening the door, I stood back to let him walk out. He turned toward me as he stepped on the front porch.

"Thank you for your time. If you remember anything else, please contact my office." His words were lighthearted, but the look on his face was not.

"I will. Thank you for stopping by," I responded, with the most cordial voice I could muster, as I closed the front door before he could say another word.

Elizabeth ran in from the kitchen, the moment the door latched. "Oh my god, oh my god!" she squealed. "What are we going to do now?" She was cradling Walter in one arm and holding his bottle with the other.

"About what?" I asked her.

She playfully punched me in the arm. "Don't be coy with me, Sam Wells. You know perfectly well what I mean." She frowned at me.

I pointed toward the front door. "Oh, you mean that? No, I wouldn't worry about him. He's just searching for a missing person, and talking with everyone. Believe me, if he suspected us of anything, we would be on our way to the sheriff's office right about now."

She lowered her head. "Yeah, I guess you're right."

"So, just act natural. Being weird and suspicious acting will get us in trouble. Got it?" I asked her.

"Yeah, okay. The baby's just about done here. I'm going to go put him back down in his crib. We all woke up pretty early."

I nodded and she went about her task.

CHAPTER 8

Over the course of the next few weeks, the sheriff and his deputies spent some time searching for Ruby, but didn't really try all that hard. I heard through the grapevine that he told Ruby's mother that Ruby was an adult and had the right to leave if she wanted to. Since there were no leads on where she went, he would be putting her search aside, unless something else showed up.

Because we had vowed never to speak Ruby's name again, we never did.

A few years later, I was starting to get the sense that this might be my last life. Walter was growing into a strong, healthy, happy young man and it made my heart full. Elizabeth and I were wonderful together. Sure, we had our moments, as all married couples do, but she was the love of my life. I had never realized that, really, during our first marriage. But this time, things were different.

This time it was all on me. I made the effort to make our marriage work. And it seemed to do the trick.

Another thing that I found interesting, was that I never did have the urge to kill anyone again. I don't know if that had something to do with me really living my last life, or if it had something to do with me being happy with my marriage and my son and my entire life in general. But whatever it was, I was just fine with that.

I never did talk to Olive again. She had moved on with her life, and I had moved on with mine. I wish things had been different, but there was nothing I could do about that now.

Many years later, I attended the wedding of Walter and his new bride, Ellen. Not too long after that, they gave me my wonderful and sorely missed grandchildren, Ivy and Parker.

It seemed as if everything was falling into place.

I'm now 83 years old, four years older than I made it to in my first life. That's when I finally realized that I didn't need any more lives. Things had worked out well and I was perfectly fine with this being the last one.

The next book in this series is The Many Lives of Jack Wells. He is Ivy's son and is convicted of a crime he didn't commit.

After his execution, 42 year old Jack wakes up as a 19 year old, and he remembers everything from his past life. The only thing he doesn't know is who killed those boys. The murders have yet to be committed. Can Jack save the boys in time, and his own life in the process?

A NOTE FROM THE AUTHOR

I hope you enjoyed reading The Many Lives of Sam Wells.

If you liked this book, please leave a review. Your opinion

matters to me, and makes me work harder to bring you entertaining stories!

You can find the review page by going to my website below and clicking on the book.

If you enjoyed this book and would like information on new releases, sign up for my newsletter here:

www.MichelleFiles.com

Oh, and don't forget that there are two more books in this series:

The Many Lives of Jack Wells - Book 3
The Many Lives of Georgie Wells - Book 4

Enjoy!
Michelle

Printed in Great Britain
by Amazon